SPACE RACE

BOOK 1

SHOOT FOR THE MOON

Copyright © 2019 Chrome Valley Books and Case by Case Publishing

Space Race: Shoot for the Moon

Written by Charles R Case and Andrew Mackay

Edited by Ashley Rose Miller

CHROMEVALLEYBOOKS.COM

ISBN: 9781796615289
Copyright © 2019 Chrome Valley Books and Case by Case Publishing

Chapters

Chapter 1 1

Chapter 2 9

Chapter 3 25

Chapter 4 49

Chapter 5 65

Chapter 6 77

Chapter 7 91

Chapter 8 101

Chapter 9 113

Chapter 10 123

Chapter 11 137

Chapter 12 147

Chapter 13 153

Chapter 14 167

Chapter 15 183

Chapter 16 203

Chapter 17 215

Chapter 18 229

Chapter 19 245

Chapter 20 267

Author Notes – Charles R Case *279*

Author Notes – Andrew Mackay *283*

Acknowledgments *295*

Chapter 1

Low Earth Orbit
14:03 EST

What was it?

God alone knows.

What little we know was this - it was five meters long, and two meters at the widest point of its ovoid shape. We know it had taken a long journey through space. Unlike anything we'd ever seen before, it would transpire. The light from the sun bounced off its smooth and unblemished black surface.

The object rebooted.

Passive scans collected data from around the globe. Small flickering lights came to life around the object's circumference. Its orientation changed at once, pointing a ten centimeter opening at its rear at the planet below.

Time passed as the object lined up with the first of many targets.

Its first target was Japan.

The metropolis lined up at the fire trajectory. A ten centimeter thick javelin fired at incredible speeds toward the unsuspecting city.

As the missile raced towards Tokyo, the object reoriented to the next target.

United Kingdom. Fire - recalibrate.

Canada. Fire - recalibrate.

Moscow. Fire - recalibrate.

The Middle East and United States, too. Each had their own missile fired at them as they rolled into view around Earth's horizon.

Its payload spent, the object turned around. In a show of incredible engineering, it shot through Earth's gravity headed for the great big ball of cheese we call the moon.

Bunker in Unknown Location: USA
14:37 EST

Private Hacker scanned his display unit.

"It's gone, Sir."

Colonel Dumas leaned over the nervous Hacker's shoulder, "Where did it go?"

"The last we saw it was on a trajectory to intercept the moon, Sir."

"And the missiles?" he asked, pulling the chewed half-cigar from his mouth.

"Still on target, Sir. It seems they have timed their respective arrivals to coincide with one another."

"ETA?"

"Ten minutes. Maybe less, Sir."

"Get NORAD on the line. We need to shoot these things down."

"Yes, Sir."

The Colonel produced a grim smile as he put the soggy end of his cigar back in his mouth, "No commie bastard is taking out any state on my watch."

"There's a missile headed for Russia, Sir."

The Colonel frowned at the screen, "So I see. What's your point?"

"Uh, just it's a communist country, Sir?"

"And?"

The Private gulped, "Well, why would the commies be firing—"

"—Commie *bastards*, Private."

"—Why would the commie *bastards* be firing on their own, Sir?"

Colonel Dumas, back on firm mental ground after the clarification, smiled again. It seemed his subordinate needed a fast lesson on history.

"Because commies are *stupid*, Private."

The Private looked to his Sargent standing against the wall, and saw the slightest of head shakes directed at him. *Don't argue with him*, the shake seemed to suggest.

Private Hacker picked up his phone to call in the air strike on the Commie bastard's missiles.

"Yes. *Sir.*"

Upper Atmosphere - Earth
14:45 EST

Most countries launched two or three counterstrike missiles to intercept the incoming bogies. An understandable - and inevitable - precautionary measure.

The USA launched thirty seven.

The Russians launched twice as many.

The United Kingdom didn't fire any at theirs, however. Instead, they set about trying to communicate and embarrassing it into submission.

Fat lot of good *that* did.

The intercepting missiles closed the gap quickly. Their on-board targeting computers adjusted their flights to ensure a perfect strike.

Final trajectories calculated. Afterburners ignited. The missiles raced towards the doomed hostile objects at incredible speeds.

At the last possible moment, the incoming javelins shifted and dodged the impact, much to the interceptor missile's great surprise. The maneuver happened so fast that the interceptors had no time to adjust.

They missed their respective targets completely.

The interceptors - unable to catch their prey and

refusing to fall back to Earth - detonated. The upper atmosphere blazed with impotent fire. Each incoming javelin made it through unscathed.

All but one.

The Canadian aerospace defense platform Esper Halo, (EH for short) had missed their target along with every other country. NORAD, in their over exuberance, had fired so many missiles that subsequently detonated, producing a blast so powerful that it caught the javelin headed for Toronto by complete accident.

Canada had been spared.

In the confusion of the blast, the incoming javelin was lost to the observers in their bunker, presumed destroyed in the explosion.

The hit javelin took a few minutes to reboot its flight computer after the impact. When the flight computer finally reinitialized, it found itself nearly 800 km off target. With no recourse, it initialized emergency landing protocols and applied its reverse thrust. The javelin slowed considerably but was unable to cancel its forward momentum before slamming into the ground.

The emergency landing disabled the computer.

It cross-referenced the topography of the surrounding landscape with the scans it had taken while incoming. It was only able to narrow its location to <*West Virginia; Appalachian Mountains*> before impact. The retrieval message it was supposed to forward to its mother ship in case of faulty landing died with the computer.

That message never made it out.

New York City
14:55 EST

Citizens across the globe cowered in their homes as the unidentified objects streaked towards their cities. It was not until the time of impact came and went that officials cottoned on to the purpose of the javelins.

4

They were not intended to destroy.

Eventually, people filled out into the streets to see what had happened. In the center of every targeted city, citizens and officials alike found that the javelin centers had formed into large diamonds hovering just above the ground. Needle-thin at the north and south end, and with a fat diamond-shaped middle.

Like a giant diamond on a skewer.

People gathered around the strange and physics defying objects like feral apes around large black monoliths.

In New York City the javelin had landed in Central Park. While central to the city, it was not as full of people as one would hope, despite the warm spring day. And so it was that the first American to encounter the alien object was a homeless man by the name of Stabby Pete. His interaction with the alien object was only thirty seconds long, but it would change the course of history.

Stabby Pete (or *Yo, Piss Off!* to his friends) jerked awake when the javelin's sonic boom rattled his bones. He had been sleeping in a bush not far from the landing site. When he rubbed the sleep from his eyes he saw the silvery object floating to the surface of earth. Not fully comprehending what he saw, Stabby stumbled out into the open and towards the slowly rotating object. He leaned in close and stared at his warped reflection in the smooth, silvery surface. It stared back at him.

He unzipped his pants, took out his *whatdoyoucallit*, and took a leak on the javelin.

"Ahhh, that's better."

The last few drops of urine trailed down his pants leg. He turned and stumbled back into his bush where he promptly fell asleep again.

Thirty seconds later, the clearing filled with police and civilians. They all came to see the thing from the sky.

So enraptured with the javelin's floating form, no one noticed the yellowish brown liquid collecting into a puddle at its base. Though, a few of them remarked that it smelled quite "organic" for being from space.

At exactly 15:00 EST each diamond pulsed brightly, sending observers stumbling back in panicked fright. Seconds later, another pulse occurred, followed by a prolonged tone. The javelins appeared to test the emergency broadcasting system.

A holographic sign appeared above each javelin, displaying weird text in their respective nation's language. Each read the same thing. An over the top game show host voice boomed from the diamonds, making everyone within earshot jump.

Then, the diamonds began to speak.

Hello!

Welcome to the Race.

After careful consideration, you have been selected to participate in this wondrous event for pride, bragging rights, and fabulous prizes!

Please prepare your racer, and select your crew! Only the best of the best will make it in this grueling completion of physical endurance and mental capacity.

In this container is the approved allotment of Moronium for one racer. Please note that if you are caught using more than the approved allotment, you will be disqualified.

The goal? The Moon!

The Prizes? Fabulous!

The time? Now!

In a quieter and quicker tone the voice added, Please race responsibly. **This message brought to you by *SHLOOM* - The Official Beverage of Mur'kroznitck.**

The voice went silent, and a timer appeared in the hologram reading 72 hours. Time to Race Start was written above the timer as it began to tick down by the second.

Everyone looked at each another in confusion.

It wasn't long before each country's "Men in Black" showed up and took control of the situation.

Chapter 2

The time had finally come.

Bucky was about to fulfill his life's dream.

He had been working on this one moment ever since his left ball moved out into a sack of its own.

Not long after, his voice stopped cracking every time he tried to talk to a girl.

Why did they call him Bucky? He wasn't bucktoothed, but whenever he spoke it sounded like he was.

Bucky Yeager - your typical Republican-lovin', rifle association card-carrying southerner without a care in the world.

A smile spread across the bottom half of his face as he reclined on his stained mattress and watched the show unfurl in front of him.

His cousin, Bobby Jo, untied the tails of her flannel shirt from around her thin waist. Her constant gum chewing drew attention to her bountiful red lips, which caused a bit of commotion inside Bucky's pants.

Bobby Jo's blond pigtails bobbed as her arms moved. Bucky admired the white fringe of her daisy dukes against her intensely tanned thighs, and licked his lips in anticipation.

"Are you sure, Bucky?" she asked, in her southern,

9

girlie drawl. "You ain't just makin' this up, are ya?"

Bucky pressed his fist to his heart, "Hand to God, Bobby Jo. I wouldn't lie to you. I saw it on the internets."

The statement seemed to mollify her. *A bit.*

She continued to work at the knot in her shirt, "Cause Momma always said, 'Don't you break no laws, Bobby Jo.'"

"I know she did."

"And I don't wanna break no laws, Bucky."

"Ya mamma's a retard, girl."

"Ah know that," Bobby Jo said. "But I don't want to disappoint Momma none, neither."

Bucky watched Bobby Jo's hands work with rapt attention. "Ain't no laws gettin' broken today."

"No?"

"Naw."

In his mind he added an addendum: *unless I get real lucky (!)*

Bobby Jo finished with the knot and unfastened the three buttons holding back her ample breasts. Beads of sweat appeared on Bucky's forehead in anticipation.

Bobby Jo frowned, "I just don't know that cousins should be gettin' jiggy—"

SMASH.

The window in the small bedroom exploded.

Bobby Jo hit the deck tits-first and squealed.

"The hell was that?"

Bucky rolled off the bed as the blast shoved him forwards. He hit the floor in a daze. A ringing sensation rifled through his ears. He opened his mouth to shout, but couldn't hear anything but the continuous tinnitus screech in his brain.

He pulled himself up over the edge of the bed, and saw Bobby Jo yelling at him. He couldn't make out her words over the ringing in his head.

"What?" he shouted.

And she shook her head, mouthing something.

He shouted again and stumbled to his feet. "Whatizzit? I can't hear you."

Bobby Jo stumbled to her bare feet as well, "I can't hear you," she shouted, making Bucky wince as his hearing suddenly returned.

"What was that?" Bobby Jo asked, wiggling a finger in her ear canal.

"Probably Skeez's trailer."

Bucky joined her in trying to massage his own ear drum with his nicotine-stained index finger.

"He's been making a few bucks on the side cooking meth. Bet that sucker finally blew himself to high heaven."

"Goddamn asshole," Bobby Jo said. "Who does he think he is? Walter White? He's crazy."

"Yeah. Nuttier than squirrel turd."

Bobby Jo lifted her finger at the shattered window and the road behind it.

"Skeez's trailer is a mile down yonder. If that wasn't his lab blowin' up, it must've been somethin' else."

"Sounded real loud, Bucky."

Bucky sighed, it looked like he was going to have to wait to get insde Bobby Jo's daisy dukes till later. *Goddammit Skeez!*

"Ugh. Let's go check on that retard's dumb ass," he said, stomping down the hall of his small cabin.

Every window in the place had shattered upon impact of whatever had exploded. The whole place now presented a perilous walkway of sharp bits of glass.

"Uh, Bucky?" Bobby Jo hollered from behind him.

"Yeah?"

"Can you get my shoes for me? There's an awful lot of glass up in here."

Her toes flexed, the red polish on her nails gleaming in the light.

"Uh. *Sure.*"

Bucky crunched his boots across the fragments of glass and retrieved her red platform heels. He brushed them down and handed them to her.

"Here."

"Much obliged."

Bobby Jo leaned on his shoulder and slipped one shoe on at a time. The sight made Bucky's pants tight, but he managed to suppress his urges. He was going to beat the tar out of Skeez.

Bobby Jo stomped her feet on the ground, "Cool. Are we ready to rock and/or roll?"

"Sure am. Let's go."

Bucky opened the ill-fitting door of the cabin and stepped out into the afternoon light. He shaded his eyes and his breath caught in his throat.

The clearing in front of the cabin was a mess. Fresh dirt and mud had been flung everywhere. The ground blasted apart with incredible force. Clods of the stuff stuck to the walls of the cabin. His old Chevy truck looked like a group of mud monsters had filmed a Bukakke porn film with the truck as their eager starlet.

Clumps of dirt and mud slid down the rusted red finish. In the center of the clearing, a crater spat a plume of white steam into the sky.

"What in hellfire is *that*, Bucky?" Bobby Jo said, peering over his shoulder.

Bucky was too shocked to answer.

The honking of a vehicle coming down the lane caught their attention.

The roar of a turbo diesel engine between honks suggested it was probably Skeez coming to see what all the ruckus was about.

A huge Ford 4x4 came roaring around the bend and slid to a stop beside Bucky's Chevy. The jacked-up, extra-fat tires kicked the sloppy mud over the smaller truck.

"God damn it, Skeez," Bucky shouted as the man slid out of his Ford. "Why you got to disrespect my Chevy like that?"

Skeez - Bucky's best friend - never wore a shirt despite

his underwhelming and gaunt physique. His mutton chops came down to connect with a thin mustache, leaving his weak chin exposed. He did, however, have an unlimited supply of green camo cargo pants. Its pockets usually held a few spare cans of Rollneck Kojak beer.

Skeez snapped his head to the side, flinging the tail end of a long, turd-brown mullet behind him.

"*Sheeeeit*. What the hell you do, boy?" Skeez said, ignoring Bucky's remark about his truck.

He caught sight of Bobby Jo standing behind Bucky and stopped to strike a pose he thought made him look manly.

"Hey there, Bobby Jo. Is this dumb ass of a cousin still tryin' to get inside your panties?"

"I ain't answerin' that dumb question."

"You should forget about him and come over to my place. I have a pool you know."

Bucky flipped Skeez the bird.

"That ain't no pool, you dumbass," he spat.

"Sorry Bukkake, man."

"And stop calling me that, you lamebrain," Bucky snapped. "It weren't funny the first time."

"Sorry."

"And y'ain't got no pool, neither," Bucky continued, making damn sure his integrity and sexual prowess bettered his friend's. "It's a hole in the ground you dug out with a shovel."

Skeez snorted at Bobby Jo and tried to turn the telling-off into a joke, "Yeah, but—"

"—Goddamn frogs are livin' in it. And I looked it up. It's completely legal to procreate with your cousin, provided you're cool with any learnin' disabilities, "Which I am."

"Y'are?"

"Amen, buddy," Bucky said. "We gotta rack up 'em disabilities to bolster the welfare payments."

"*That's* what he told you?" Skeez asked Bobby Jo, his

face frozen in mock disbelief.

She nodded, "For real. He saw it on the interwebs."

"Oh," Skeez spat with disappointment, "Well it *must* be true then."

Bucky produced a triumphant smirk as he marched towards the new crater in his front yard. The other two followed right behind him. He crested the mound around the crater and raised an eyebrow at the sight within.

The crater measured twenty feet from side to side.

The edges had been blown smooth to reveal ten feet down into the dark, Appalachian soil. The bottom of the crater was slowly filling with muddy brown ground water. Sticking straight out of the small puddle was a five foot long shaft that ended in a point, as if a needle had pushed itself up from the ground.

Curious, still, was its diamond-shaped middle.

Bucky elbowed Skeez, "Looks like I've got a pool, too, now."

Bobby held onto Bucky's shoulder to find balance in her platform shoes on the soft mound of soil.

"What is that?"

"I dunno."

Skeez jumped over the edge to get a closer look. Bucky helped Bobby Jo down and approached the strange needle-like object. They all stared at their reflections in the smooth, silver finish.

"Did you finally order that dildo from Amerzon?" Skeez said, making Bobby Jo giggle.

"Fuck you."

Skeez winked at Bobby Jo.

"Fuck me? Hell naw, not if you're plannin' on using this new dildo of yours. It might be perfect size for your loose ass, but I keep mine tight."

Bobby Jo frowned, "Eww, gross. I don't want to know what you do with your ass."

Skeez's eyes went wide, "I, uh—thats not what I meant."

"Heh," Bucky smirked. "Skeez likes butt stuff."

"Fuck y'all," came Skeez's inevitable response as he retrieved a lukewarm can of Rollneck Kojak beer from his cargo pants.

"You drinkin' already?" Bucky asked.

"This is just my mornin' beer," he said as he cracked it open and tipped the contents into his mouth.

Bucky walked around the object, trying to determine just what in the ever-lovin' hell had fallen into his yard.

Bobby Jo averted her attention to strange object and wrapped one of her pigtails around her finger.

"Could be some military weapon? Like a missile or something?"

"If it was a missile it would have blown our cocks off and taken out half the state," Bucky thought aloud. "No, no. I think it's, like, a satellite or something."

Skeez took a loud sip of foamy beer and let out a guttural burp of death, inches away from full-blown projectile vomit.

"Man, that dildo thing is so obviously an alien probe."

"Yeah?" Bucky asked.

"Uh-huh," Skeez said with a steely determination. "You know my uncle, right?"

"Luther?"

"Yeah, that's his name. He told me about them one time. You know he's been, like, what do you call it? Abductificated."

"*Abductificated?*"

"Yeah, a bunch of times. Up in the ship and *examinated—*"

"—That's *abducted*, you dummy," Bucky quipped. "The fuck you talking about?"

Skeez snorted and spat a wad of phlegm dangerously close to the thing in the ground.

"Shoved all manner of nonsense up his ass."

"Fuckin' taken up and got anally prolapsed by aliens, is it? Taken to *the jug*, more like, Skeez. Shit."

"M'uncle's a goddamn genius."

"Your uncle's a no-good drunk. Not exactly a reliable witness."

"Hell naw, straight up," Skeez protested. "He may be a drunk, but he ain't no liar."

"Yeah," Bucky spat. "He probably just wandered into one of them gay orgies at the rest stop down on the highway."

"Don't you talk about my uncle."

"Ain't talkin', man. Just stating facts is all."

"Take it back, man."

"No."

"Fuckin' take that back," Skeez shouted in a state of delirium. "Uncle Luther is a war hero."

"Trippin' out your head on shrooms and dancing to the lights of the cop car that pulled you over don't make you no war hero, dickhead."

Bobby Jo shrugged, "Just because he was a war hero doesn't mean he *ain't* no drunk who *don't* like bum games. I hear your family likes to keep it tight."

"Yeah," Skeez said. "We're tighter than a nun's pisshole."

"Gross. Must want to keep it tight for a reason."

"Speaking of tight, you guys sure are assholes on occasion." Skeez said, taking another long sip of beer. "Talkin' smack about my uncle Luther like that."

"Better than being assholes *all the time*, huh?" Bobby Jo chortled.

Bucky jumped back as the object flashed. It produced a low-pitched tone that reminded him of the public access station when it went off the air. A sign in blue lights appeared above the object, but it immediately began to flicker as if it were glitching out. The words were a jumble of different characters and symbols, like a corrupted email Bucky once got from a Nigerian Prince. A voice boomed from the object, but it was obviously in a foreign language. Only a handful of words were recognizable.

Hola!

Ongi etorri race!

Po pečlivém zvážení roghnaíodh tú chun páirt a ghlacadh san ócáid iontach ionas go bródúil, 吹牛的权利, BIG ACTION FUN!! 牛的 Bean Fried Rice!

Você tem três semanas to select your racer, and select your crew!Alleen het beste van het beste zal het in dit slopende maken завершение физической выносливости и умственных способностей.

In this container is the approved allotment of Moronium forun corredor. Tenga en cuenta que si usted está atrapado using more than the approved allotment cewch eich gwahardd.

The goal? The Moon!

Τα βραβεία; Υπέροχο!

The time? Now!

In a quieter and quicker tone the voice added, Please race responsibly. **This message brought to you by** *SHLOOM* **- The Official Beverage of Mur'kroznitck.**

A timer appeared in the flickering hologram counting down to the start of the race. This part was at least all in English and mostly legible, despite its incessant flickering.

The booming game show host voice died down.

The three of them looked at each another with slack jaws of disbelief. They had never heard so many languages in all their lives. Bobby Jo was sure she had had a visit from an angel speaking in tongues till she saw that the boys were equally as shocked. She knew it wasn't an angel, because any angel with more than two brain cells would never *choose* to speak to Skeez.

"Did that thing say somethin' about a race?" Skeez asked.

He fished a crooked cigarette from a half-crushed pack inside one of his many cargo pant pockets. His fingers shook slightly. It took him a few attempts to finally get the flame up and running.

"Ah, fuggit. C'mon, c'mon."

Success. The tobacco sizzled to life at the end of the paper.

Skeez inhaled deeply and blew out a blueish cloud of smoke. From the smell, Bucky could tell that it was actually a joint, and if he were honest, he couldn't blame Skeez.

Bucky adjusted his trucker hat as he looked up at the half moon glowing in the morning sky.

"Yeah, it did. But I didn't catch much else. Just that it seems like the goal is the fuckin' *moon*."

"This timer is for three days," Bobby Jo said, leaning in and laying a hand on the silvery surface, "Is that when the race starts?"

As soon and her fingers touched the surface of the silver rod it gave a hiss.

A line appeared close to the top.

"Yikes."

Bobby Jo jumped back and tripped as the top quarter popped off and fell to the ground in a squelchy splat.

"Well bless your heart," Bobby Jo squeaked as she fell onto her butt.

Bucky leaned forward and peered into the opening.

The object was actually a container filled with a glowing blue substance.

"Huh?"

He dipped his middle finger into the substance up to the first knuckle. A tingling erupted around his slightly dirty digit. It reminded him of a mild electrical shock like when he would lick 9v batteries in his formative years. The sensation was shocking on multiple levels.

A glob of the jelly-like substance flung away as he shook his hand. The goo arched through the air. The majority of it slapped across Bobby Jo's left tit.

She shrieked as it splatted on her flannel and soaked into the fabric. Her eyes grew as the tingling fluid came in contact with her skin. In a move faster than Bucky had ever seen from his cousin, she had her flannel shirt untied, unbuttoned, and flying through the air as she tossed it away.

"Gross."

Bucky and Skeez stopped watching the shirt as soon as it was off the shapely woman, and instead were slack-jawed staring at the white push-up bra that barely pressed Bobby Jo's melons into submission. It took them a few seconds to realize the shirt never hit the ground. Bobby Jo didn't even try to cover herself.

Something more important than her shirt loomed before them.

It took all the willpower Bucky had to look away from the mountains of Bobby Jo's promised land. Her complete and utter lack of modesty finally kicked some part of his brain into rational thought.

He glanced over at where she had thrown the shirt, but couldn't find it. He looked back at Bobby Jo, to see her looking up in the sky, and he turned to follow her gaze.

He stumbled back when he saw her flannel shirt rising like a party balloon into the afternoon sky.

"What the fuck?" he said, readjusting his trucker hat out of nervousness.

Skeez regarded his joint skeptically, "This is some gourmet shit. You guys need to hit this."

Bucky craned his neck back watching the red and black flannel rise ever higher and higher.

"It ain't the weed, Skeez."

They kept their heads as far back as they could till the shirt was too far up to see at all.

Then, they stared a little longer.

Bucky lowered his head and settled his eyes on his cousin's breasts, satisfying the caveman part of his brain.

Bobby Jo reddened under Bucky's intense scrutiny, but it was Skeez's greasy smirk that made her cross her arms to hide her ample bosom.

"We need to call Satchel." Bucky said, still staring, but

obviously in another world in his mind.

Skeez rolled his eyes and took another puff on his smoke, "That asshole's such a dick."

"The other way round you mean?" Bobby Jo spat.

"What, that dick's such an asshole?"

"No," she said. "*You're* the dick. Your brother's okay."

"Doesn't that make him the asshole?"

Bobby Jo raised an eyebrow, "He's your brother. Thr'ain't no assholes in your family. Just one dick, and that's you."

Bucky tried in vain to process the conversation.

"Uh, I'm confused?"

"Whatever, y'all," Skeez snatched another look at her rack and spoke before his brain engaged, "Tits."

"Skeez?" Bucky asked. "Tits?"

"Huh?"

"Why did you say tits?"

"I, uh, I never said tits?" Skeez frowned and thought he'd lost his mind. "Did I?"

"Yeah, you did."

Bobby Jo turned her chest away from Skeez and folded her arms.

"Stop rapin' me with your methy eyes," she growled and folded her arms tighter. The move only made her boobs fold out even more, much to Skeez's delight.

To suppress his desire to pounce on her, Skeez took another sip of beer and swallowed, "Yeah."

Bobby Jo struggled to her feet, trying to keep Skeez's eyes from getting too much, but still needing to use her arms to get to her feet. She ignored Skeez as best she could and turned to Bucky.

"Why do we need to call Satchel?"

"Because he's rich." he revealed, as if it weren't totally obvious. "As much as I hate to admit it, Skeez is right. Satchel's lower than a snake in a wheel rut. Who cares if he won the lottery? If I was gonna use one word to describe Satchel, it would be *morally bankrupt*."

"Nah, Bucky. He ain't bankrupt. He's rich."

"That ain't what I said, dickhead," Bucky said. "I said *morally* bankrupt."

"Huh?"

Bucky gave up trying to aid his friend's comprehension, "Forget it."

Ping!

The two brain cells in Skeez's head finally arranged to meet for a dinner date to see how they'd get along.

"Oh! I get it now," he said. "Morals. Like when you do good and bad stuff?"

"Yeah, exactly."

"So, a bit like *not* trying to fuck y'own cousin?"

Bucky and Bobby Jo looked away from each other, embarrassed.

"Ha. *Gotcha*," Skeez chuckled and clapped his hands together, preparing himself for receipt of the Nobel Prize for Intelligence. "Besides, why do we need money?"

Bucky smiled, finally breaking out of his own thoughts, and looking at Bobby Jo and Skeez in turn, "Because building a spaceship is going to cost a lot."

Skeez tipped the remainder of his beer down his throat, crushed the can between his fingers, and tossed it into the crater.

BUURRRPPP.

Bobby Jo felt like puking, "Ugh, you suck."

"A spaceship?" Skeez asked. "What the fuck are you talking about?"

After more consideration, he climbed out of the crater and pointed at the cabin.

"Ya'll heard *the thing*," Bucky said. "It's a race. With fabulous prizes. I don't know about you, but I want me some fabulous prizes."

"Hell's yeah," Skeez said.

"God knows I could use some good luck. Come on, it's nearly ten in the AM. He's probably just getting home from the breakfast buffet at the strip club."

Bobby Jo climbed out of the crater, "Ugh. That strip club is brimming with chlamydia."

"Hey," Skeez protested. "The strip club ain't got no STDs. My momma's worked there for years. The chicken wings are actually pretty good."

"Yeah, and them chicken wings are the only things that are meant to have wrinkles on 'em," Bucky offered.

Chapter 3

Chrome Valley, Northwest London, United Kingdom

Chrome Valley - ugh, you couldn't imagine a worse shit hole if you tried.

Go on, try it.

Got a picture forming, yet?

Good, now imagine it's ten times worse and covered in horse feces, and you're only 0.11928% closer to how much of a cesspit the valley actually was.

Chrome Valley's west side had seen much better days - and months, and years. Decades, even. The result of a generation's-worth of neglect on behalf of the government.

And don't get us started on the influx of Chinese investors buying up all the property.

All aspects of society in these here parts had fallen into the doldrums.

Decrepit buildings loomed in front of the distant freeway.

Recycling extended way past plastic bottles to what looked like bits of dead dogs and mattresses littering the sidewalks.

The smell of wet tarmac and death hung in the air, awaiting the nostrils of those who dared venture outside.

Of course, anyone who braved a visit to the food bank or nearby shopping mall might get mugged, raped, or murdered.

The very unlucky ones would experience all three, usually in that order.

An elderly man carrying a plastic bag full of *something* crossed the pothole-ridden road, giving little less than a rat's ass about the prospect of being hit by any of the cars whizzing in each direction on the main arterial road.

Car horns blared at him as they shot past - not so much advising for him to move for his own safety, rather, reducing the odds of damage to their hood.

Unfortunately for the elderly man, today wasn't the day he'd get killed and put out of his misery. For this first time since leaving his apartment in the Freeway Five Estate, he lifted his head and expected to find further signs of disrepair and another reason to run into the traffic and end it all.

A sharp pain rifled through his arm, having connected with someone else's shoulder.

"Oops, I'm sorry," the elderly man said, even though the encounter wasn't his fault. If anything, the knock on his arm seemed to have been malicious.

"Fuck you, you old-timer."

The unforgiving, London-drenched response came from the lips of an eighteen year-old lad dressed in a hoodie, "Fuckin' look where you're going, yeah?"

The man grumbled to himself - something about how he'd dare not speak to his elders like that when he was that young - and shook his head.

The boy stopped in his tracks and snorted as he eyed-up the elderly man waddling his way down the path.

"Yo, old man?" he barked.

"Huh?"

"What's in the bag?"

The man turned around and hoped he wouldn't get stabbed by the youth.

He lifted his carrier bag up to his waist, "Oh, this? It's nothing."

The man squinted at the young man and seemed to recognize him. "Hey, I know you."

"What?"

"You go to Chrome Junction Academy, don't you?"

The young man reached into his coat pocket and pulled out a 2.5 inch blade.

"Fuck junction, and fuck you. Gimme the bag?"

"But, but—"

"—Gimme the fuckin' thing, yeah," he threatened as the light bounced off the blade and onto the man's face. "Or I'll open you up."

The bag flew out of the elderly man's hand and into the clutches of his assailant. The lad looked inside the bag and groaned.

"Ugh. Fuck's in here?"

"P-Please," the elderly man begged. "It's all I have left—"

The handles of the bag yawned open and released dozens of empty tins onto the floor. They bounced off the tarmac and rolled around the man's feet.

"Fuck's this?" the lad asked. "Why you carrying tins?"

"I, er—"

"—Allow that shit. Fuck it, gimme your wallet."

"What?"

The lad lifted the end of his blade at the man's neck, "Gimme your wallet, you deaf twat."

"I d-don't have a wallet."

The youth's eyes scanned the elderly man. The sensory information blasted through to his brain to be met with confirmation that the elderly man was likely broke.

And he probably didn't have a wallet, either. How very disappointing.

"Ghost, man."

The elderly man looked at his assailant in confusion. He didn't know what the term *ghost* meant. The boy felt the need to adjust his language.

"I said fuck off."

The lad's victim did as instructed, and carefully *fucked off* as fast as his withered old legs could carry him.

The Caucasian-challenged teenager had a name - Danny Hook.

A scar ran down his right cheek, taking the attention away from his beautiful green eyes and cherubic face.

His pulchritudinous visage didn't match his manners, that much was clear. He stood out like a swollen, syphilitic penis in front of the freeway.

A boy of his age should surely be in class at this time of day. Not Danny Hook, though. He had other matters to attend to.

He folded his pocket blade into the handle and placed it in his pocket. Out came his cell phone and, with a swift dexterity only available to teenagers, managed to both unlock and dial his intended caller in one go with this thumb.

Danny placed the phone to his ear and kept a keen eye out on the cars parked by Waddling Gate cemetery.

"Yo, Barry, man," he huffed as he picked up the pace, "Fuckin' pick up."

Danny raced forward and arrived at a red Ford Mondeo parked a few meters from the black, iron gates at the cemetery.

Ring, ring. Ring, ring.

"Come on, come on," Danny said as he tucked his phone under his chin and pulled his knife back out.

A quick glance in either direction was all he needed to perform. No one around to see him perform the action he was about to perform.

Finally, his call was answered.

"'Sup, D?" came a voice form the other end of the line. "You got that thing, yet?"

"Yeah, mate. I got one."

Danny smiled at his reflection in the Ford window and bent his elbow.

"Meet me at the Kaleidoscope, yeah?" the voice said.

"Safe, man. Five minutes, yeah?"

"Cool."

Danny dropped the phone into his pocket, bent his elbow, and pushed it forward.

SMASSSHHH.

The driver's side window exploded, coughing fragments of glass onto the seat as the car alarm sounded off.

WHAARRKK—WHAARRKKK.

"Fuck's sake, shut up," Danny spat as he reached through the door and unlocked the car.

The side of his hand brushed the spent glass into the foot well, to be replaced by his behind as he sat in the car. He looked around the dashboard, wheel, and levers, deciding that he was in a position to get this party started.

"Where's the fuckin'—"

He needn't have asked. His boot did the talking, crunching through the under carriage, and breaking the flimsy plastic, exposing the starter wires.

He grabbed the two ends and pressed them together, kicking the engine into a frenzied roar. He floored the gas pedal and pulled the car door shut.

VROOOM. VROOOM.

"Yeah, man," he squealed as the engine cut the alarm off in one fell swoop.

He threw the stick shift into first gear, enabling the wheels to kick up a flurry of dust, released the handbrake and bolted off down the road.

No one had seen him.

Danny drove onto the freeway. A sign for the industrial section of the valley whizzed past the car.

The freeway was unusually empty, providing a pass for this opportunistic boy racer.

Danny stepped on the gas and kept an eye on the speed counter.

75… 80… 85 mph.

"Come on. Let's go, man," he yelled, intending to overtake a couple of cars in front of him. "Let's go. Let's go."

VROOOOM.

The Mondeo sped up and threatened to rear-end the car in front. Danny blared the horn and lifted his middle finger up at the windscreen.

"Move."

The car in front veered to the left and allowed Danny to pass by.

"That's right, dickhead," Danny yelled. "Fuck outta my way."

A clear and open path invited Danny to speed up even more.

90 mph… 95 mph…

"Let's see if this piece of shit can do one-twenty."

The scenery seemed to blur as the car bolted forward. The fifth gear and engine groaned as the car sped up even faster.

Danny's enjoyment at his need for speed was interrupted by a stupid whistling sound coming from his pants pocket.

"Ugh, what now?"

He reached into it with his right hand and pulled out his cell phone. He glanced at the screen, keeping one eye on the road ahead.

Someone by the name of Stupid Bitch was calling.

"Ugh, allow that man," he said as he swiped the screen up. "All right, mum?"

"Oi, you little turd. Where are you?"

"I, uh—" he said, swerving the vehicle into the middle lane and undertaking a truck, "Mum, not now. I'm a bit busy, yeah?"

"Don't *not now* me, you little prick," the woman's voice flew through the device, "What's that noise? Where are you?"

"I'm at school, innit."

BLAARRREEEE.

The horn from a car blasted through the windowless driver's side, accompanying the rush of wind.

"Sounds like you're on a train or sumthin'," his mum yelled. "What you doing?"

"Mum, I gotta go—"

"—If you're at school, then why did Mr. Foster call em up sayin' you wasn't a school?"

"Mum, not now—"

"—You best be at school, or I'll kick the shit outta you when you get back home, ya hear me?"

Danny focused on the rear view mirror. His face lit up with intermittent pangs of blue light.

"Oh shit."

"You what?" his mum asked.

Danny focused on the truck he'd past and saw a police car peel out from behind.

"Sorry mum, gotta go—"

"—What the fu—"

Danny cut the call off and flung his phone to the dashboard.

"Shit, shit, *shit.*"

The police car bolted forward and ran up behind him.

Danny had one of two choices available. He could pull over and risk serious trouble, or… *speed up.*

SLAMMMM.

His foot hit the gas, pressing the full weight of his body to the floor. The Mondeo struggled past the 100 mph mark as it flung forward, throwing Danny's shoulders against the seat.

The police car sped up and trailed into the fast lane a few meters behind the Mondeo.

"Fuck's sake," Danny said, averting his gaze to the forthcoming junction to the industrial estate. "Get ready for some *torque.*"

He clutched the steering wheel in both hands as he sped past a black van in the slow lane.

The police vehicle entered the middle lane and fired its sirens at Danny, "Driver, pull over."

"Nar, man. I don't think so."

Danny slammed on the breaks just before the turn-off, screeching to a halt on the fast lane.

The police car rocketed into the distance, completely unprepared for their suspect's next move.

Danny spun the wheel to the right and glanced into the rear view mirror. The humongous truck careened towards him.

In roughly five seconds from now the back of the Mondeo would concertina into his body and kill him.

"Fuck."

He hit the gas and blasted toward the junction, narrowly avoiding a passing car.

NEEAAWWWW.

The truck clipped the back of the Mondeo as it barreled along the fast line, sending Danny spinning around on the spot like a coin

"Whoa."

SCREEEEECH.

With no time to catch his breath, Danny floored the pedal and shot off the freeway and down the junction exit.

The Kaleidoscope Shopping Mall, Chrome Valley, United Kingdom

A thoroughly battered Ford Mondeo crawled along the road with its tail pipe scraping across the tarmac. It rolled to a stop outside the mall entrance, a few meters behind a stone fountain.

Danny caught his breath and peered through the passenger window.

"Where is he?" he muttered and hit the car horn.

The car horn blasted a miserly rendition of *Land of Hope*

and Glory, catching the young children's attention as they splashed around in the fountain.

A teenage girl pushed through the double doors to the shopping mall and entered the concourse. She clapped eyes on Danny in the driver's side and chewed her gum with anticipation.

"He's here, man."

"Yo, Chelsea," Danny hollered through the window, "Fuckin' get in, man. We need to go."

"Yeah, I know," she shouted back as she waved her hand at two teenagers making their way out of the mall. "Baz, Stevie. He's here."

Baz and Stevie, two lanky eighteen year-olds, barged their way past the crowd of shoppers and joined Chelsea.

"Where?" Baz asked.

"Over here, come on," she said as she skipped past the fountain and swiped a woman's handbag from the bench. "Nice. This'll come in handy."

Baz and Stevie sniggered to themselves as they watched Chelsea pull the handbag over her shoulder. A swift move of thievery in broad daylight - so brazen that no one noticed.

"She's got some balls, yeah?" Stevie said as he eyed up Chelsea's behind.

BEEP — BEEP.

"Come on, you bunch of faggots," Danny yelled as he roared the engine. "Get in."

"Nice car, babe," Chelsea said with a salacious grin, revealing her train-track teeth.

Danny eyed the handbag and nodded, "Nice bag."

"Yeah, it's all right, innit."

She opened the passenger door and climbed into the front. The handbag rolled off her shoulder for immediate inspection.

"Let's lookie here and see what we got."

Stevie and Baz opened the back passenger doors and rifled in.

"Hey, Danny," the former said.

Danny looked forward and slammed his foot on the pedal.

The Ford Mondeo rode along the dual carriageway. Danny had no particular destination to reach. He was happy enough to have secured a ride for today's shenanigans.

Chelsea rifled through the handbag. A tube of lipstick and a packet of tissues were the first items to hit the dashboard - of no interest to her whatsoever.

"Ah, allow this shit, man," Chelsea grumbled through her three-hour-old chewing gum, "Trust me to swipe some social security scum mum's bag. No fuckin' paper in here. Just tampons and stuff."

"Where'd you get the ride?" Stevie asked Danny.

"Dunno, found it outside the cemetery," he said. "So, where we going? You hungry?"

"Yeah, man," Stevie said.

"Let's hit Burger Face drive thru," Baz added. "I'm Hank fuckin' *Marvin*, mate."

"Cool. Yeah, I'm a bit *peckish*, myself."

Danny couldn't help but check Chelsea's thighs out. He knew that if she caught him staring at her legs, he could just shrug it off and pretend he was interested in the handbag.

Chelsea's right hand lifted a pink purse out from the bag. A stupid, glittery cat face adorned the side with "Symphony" written in sans serif text underneath it.

"Ugh," Chelsea complained, "Seriously? Look at that, man. Tasteless."

"Whatever," Danny said. "How much is in it?"

Chelsea pinched the purse open and took out three twenty pound notes, "Forty quid."

"Forty quid?" Danny chuckled. "There's three of 'em. That's *sixty* quid, you dopey mare."

"I dunno, I'm no good at maths," she complained as

she clocked the windowless driver's side. "Maths is for gays, anyway."

She flung the purse past Danny's face and out of the window.

"Hey, be careful."

"What's up?" Chelsea giggled as she folded the money into her bra, "You don't like me touching you?"

Stevie and Baz sniggered from behind.

"Danny's a batty man," Baz said.

"I ain't no batty man, you prick," Danny protested. "She nearly clipped me on the chin."

— Five Minutes Later —

The Ford Mondeo rolled to a stop at the order box in the Burger Face drive thru.

Danny looked up at the stupendously happy face made of plastic. It glared down at him with its daft blue eyes.

"Welcome to Burger Face," the voice beamed through the plastic speaker protruding through its mouth, "Can I take your burger?"

"Uh. Yeah," Danny hollered at the metal mesh microphone-type thing on the front of the box. "Gimme four Artery Specials and a large *stent* fries," Danny said.

"What else do you want?" the high-as-a-kite speaker asked.

"Four blueberry milkshakes, an all."

"Four blueberry," the voice lowered, indicating the owner might fall asleep right there and then. "Does that complete your burger?"

Danny screwed his face, wondering why the voice hadn't finished its last sentence with the word 'order'.

"Uh. Yeah? That's it."

"Good. Come down to the next thing, whatever. The window."

"Cool."

Danny looked at Chelsea's bra as he drove the car to

35

the second pay window, "Yo. Gimme the money."

"Okay, okay," she said as she covered her chest with her forearm.

A plastic window opened up and slid alongside the smashed driver's side. A goofy-looking youth with acne looked at Danny. The chap could barely keep his eyelids up.

"Gimme your money."

"How much is it?"

"Duuh," the attendant blinked at the screen. "Nineteen-fifty."

"Safe."

Danny snapped his fingers at Chelsea's chest, much to the amusement of the two boys in the back of the vehicle, "C'mon. Open up your tits and gimme the cash—"

"Yeah, yeah, I'm doing it."

She wasn't acting fast enough, and so Danny reached over and slid his hand in her left bra cup.

"Hey."

"Gimme the money."

Danny yanked three notes away from Chelsea's right boob and passed one of them to the attendant.

"There, take it."

CH-CHING!

The cash register flew out and punched the attendant in the balls.

"Ooof."

The swift hit to the groin was followed by a flurry of silver coins in his face, which he caught, clumsily.

"Your change."

"Thanks."

***

NOM-NOM-NOM.

Danny, Chelsea, Baz, and Stevie sat in the Ford Mondeo, chomping on their undercooked burgers.

The main parking area adorned the front of the Burger Face building.

Danny parked next to the garbage bins at the side of the building a few meters from the staff entrance. A white outline of a stick man in a wheelchair crept under the front tires. A convenience that meant the food could be consumed quickly.

"Oi, Danny, man" Stevie said with a mouthful of food, "Out of order parking it here, innit? It's a disabled spot."

"Nar, man."

"Why?"

"Parking is a bit like trying to get laid, yeah?"

"Is it?"

"Yeah, man," Danny swallowed. "You try to fuck the best ones, but every now and again you have to stick it in a disabled one."

Stevie and Barry burst out laughing, much to Chelsea's consternation. She bopped Danny on the shoulder.

"Hey, man, that ain't funny."

"Yeah, neither are *handicappeds*."

"Ugh," Danny swallowed his mouthful of cow, "This tastes like shit."

"Way better than KMC," Stevie said with a mouthful of lettuce.

Two Burger Face employees in aprons carefully slid out through the side entrance. One of them produced a dirty roll-up and lit the end.

Denny's attention broke when he heard a sucking noise melting into his left ear.

SLOOOOO.

It hadn't gone unnoticed that Chelsea's chest heaved out as she vacuumed the contents of her drink via the straw. The wrinkles on both sets of lips left a trails of blood-like marks across the plastic. Of course, it wasn't blood, but the red mixture streaking down the white front afforded Danny a confusing vision.

"Uh, where you wanna go next?" Danny asked everyone in the car as he tossed the greasy wrapper through his window.

Baz burped, taking himself by surprise, "Ugh, I was nearly sick in my mouth just there."

"I'm tryna' fuckin' eat, bruv," Danny barked, unable to look at his burger.

"Sorry, yeah?" Baz wiped his lips as he snorted down a ball of snot, "You wanna go check out that new bowling alley they have now?"

"Yeah, safe. Just stop burpin', yeah? You're putting me off my burger, mate."

Danny turned to the two employees sharing a crafty marijuana joint. The smaller of the two coughed and spluttered and passed the roll-up to his buddy.

Sniff-sniff.

Danny's nostrils twitched, "Look at 'em, man. They've got a blunt on the go."

He placed his right hand on the driver door handle and went to open it, when the smaller employee peered behind the building and jumped back in astonishment.

"Whoa."

Stevie and Chelsea's eyes widened. The man had seen something, and they'd seen him see it.

"What's got that fucker so rattled?"

The employee grabbed his friend's shoulder and squealed.

"That's some good shit they're smoking," Danny mouthed. "I'mma take their shit off 'em. Wait here."

WHUMP.

Danny pushed the driver's door shut and approached the two employees.

"Yo," he hollered none-too-loudly, "Pass us the blunt, yeah?"

"My God," the smaller employee blinked hard at a strange object by the garbage cans, "You seen that shit?

That's *amazing*."

"Gimme the blunt, man."

Danny snatched the lit roll-up from the employee's shaking hands.

"Must be some wicked good shit, yeah?"

"No, no," the employee said. "Look at that. Over there."

"Eh?"

Danny lowered his arm and walked to the back of the building.

The rats jump away from the garbage cans and scurried around in a stupor. A strange radioactive sound permeated the waste ground, shifting the discarded burger wrappers, French fry boxes, used condoms, and spent syringes across the soaked mud.

"What in the name of *fuck* is *that?*" Danny said out loud.

"I d-dunno, maaaaan," the employee said. "I don't like it, it—"

Danny dropped the joint to the floor. Whatever was inside it, or whatever it was laced with, had clearly gotten to all three of them.

"Fuck, back up."

Danny took a step back and blinked once more.

A giant diamond, seemingly made out of water, hovered three feet above the floor.

"I-I m-must be fucked in the h-head," the larger employee said. "What is that?"

A blue, neon sign flashed above its structure.

Hola, man!

Ongi etorri race!

Po pečlivém zvážení roghnaíodh tú chun páirt a ghlacadh san ócáid iontach ionas go bródúil, 吹牛的权利, BIG ACTION FUN!! 牛的 Bean Fried Rice, Buddy!

Você tem três semanas to select your racer, and select your crew!Alleen het beste van het beste zal het

in dit slopende maken завершение физической выносливости и умственных способностей.

Danny shook his head and tried to rid himself of the bizarre sight.

"You what?"

Yo, check dis. In this container is the approved allotment of Moronium forun corredor. Tenga en cuenta que si usted está atrapado using more than the approved allotment cewch eich gwahardd.

The goal? The fuckin' *moon*, you know.

Τα βραβεία; Υπέροχο!

The time? Whenever!

"Okay, that's some fucked-up next man's bull shit. I'm pretty sure that thing is *bare* high."

This sum wicked good shit, yeah?

The diamond in the javelin revolved at a ridiculously slow pace, almost as if it was high. It slowed to a stop and spotted the hood of the Mondeo.

Fuck, bruv. I've been here, like two days and ain't seen a car. Till now.

Danny shook the fatigue from his head and squinted at the object's perfectly smooth shell.

"The fuckin' thing's talkin' at me, mate."

Nice car. That'll do very nicely.

Danny tried to pass the joint back to the smaller of the two employees, but his feet dragged across the mud, headed for the peculiarly-shaped object.

"Ah, ah, h-help me."

The tone of the announcement quietened, **Please race responsibly, yeah? This message brought to you by *SHLOOM* - The Official Beverage of Mur'kroznitck.**

SCHPLATTT!

A torrent of blue goo vomited from the diamond and drenched the employee from head to toe.

"Yaarrghhhh."

"My God," his colleague gasped. "Help him. He's been slimed."

Danny hid behind the employee as the smaller man lifted into the air in front of the diamond.

Their eyes followed his body lifting up by his groin higher and higher into the air until, eventually, he disappeared into the clouds.

"I think we better get out of here."

"Yeah, okay," Danny said. "If anyone asks I was never here, yeah?"

"Ugh, okay."

No! I want that fuckin' ride, bruv.

SCREEEEEEEEEEECH.

The unmistakable sound of tires scraping through mud and tarmac erupted behind Danny.

He turned around to find himself greeted by the Ford Mondeo and his three scared friends inside it, wondering if they should vacate or not.

"Danny," Chelsea squealed. "The car. It's moving by itself."

"Oh, fuck."

Danny jumped out of the way as the front bumper magnetized itself towards the diamond.

"Chelsea, stay inside. Don't get out," Danny said.

Stevie and Baz pressed their palms to the glass windows and squealed for dear life.

"Agh, agh, we're gonna die."

Chelsea leaned forward and pointed at the diamond, "What's *that?*"

"We dunno," Danny said as he stepped back to the building. "Uh, just, you know, stay in the car and it won't be able to touch you."

"*What* won't be able to touch us?" she screamed blue murder.

"That *thing*."

Danny pointed at the diamond as it spun around. The smaller of the employees wailed for his life as his body lifted into the air.

"Jesus H. Shit."

Chelsea squealed and pulled herself across to the driver's seat and looked around the controls, "Danny?"

"What? No, don't do that—"

VROOOOOOM.

The car's locked tires daggered through the mud, magnetizing towards the diamond.

"How do you drive this thing?"

"Fuck this," Stevie said. "I'm outta here."

The chubby boy booted the door open and rolled onto the ground, covering his arms with mud.

A torrent of blue goop coughed out from the top of the diamond and covered Stevie's chest.

"Yaagghhh."

Baz was about to hop out of his side of the car, but stopped when he saw what had happened to Stevie.

"Oh, shiiiii—"

"—Yuurgghh."

Danny ran over to Stevie and tried to help him up. He was too late. The blue goop hardened and wrapped around the boy's chest and catapulted him into the air like a stone.

WHOOOSH.

Danny cowered and lifted his head to the sky as his friend's screaming voice disappeared beyond the clouds.

"Whoa."

SCREEEEECH.

The car's bumper rammed into the diamond, forcing Chelsea and Stevie forward.

RAMMMM.

"What's g-going on?" Chelsea squealed. "I can't m-move."

Danny thought on his feet. It looked as if the car was about to get crushed by the diamond.

He bolted back to the driver's door and yanked it open.

"Chelsea, move."

Danny sat into the seat and yanked, handbrake off, and shifted the stick into reverse.

ROOOAARRRR.

The vehicle's engine growled, pulling away from the diamond.

Congratulations, Bro. You have been selected to participate in our intergalactic experiment. Dude, this is some good shit.

"What the fuck?" Danny screamed as he throttled the gas, producing a bizarre tug-of-war between his stolen car and the diamond.

Please note: Resistance is futile. Thank you for your cooperation, yeah?

"Bollocks to this."

Danny threw the stick into first gear and slammed his foot on the accelerator.

"Danny, what are you doing?" Chelsea said.

"I'mma fuck this bad boy up proper."

The car shunted forward and smashed into the diamond. Its shell liquefied and spread over the hood and chassis, surrounding the windows in a peculiar amalgam of crystal-infused blue goop.

"Wahhhhh," Chelsea screamed as the ground and scenery seemed to shrink through the window. "What's happening?"

"How the arse should I know? Just hold on tight," he said as he turned over his shoulder, "Baz, man, you okay?"

Baz had fainted. His mouth gurgled with ketchup and mayonnaise down his front.

"Aww, shit."

Danny turned front and saw the horizon lift into view.

The car hovered into the air.

The diamond had absorbed itself into the car.

"We're flying, man."

Chelsea began to hyperventilate, "Damn, that weed must've been fuckin' lit, mate."

The sound of an object plummeting through the air occurred above the car as it lifted more than a hundred feet into the air.

"Nah, this is some next sci-fi shit," Danny said. "Grab

hole of the handle, Chelsea. We're dead if this fucker drops—"

NEEAAWWW — SMASSSHHHH.

A dead body crashed onto the hood. The metal cracked upwards, producing several sharp shards splaying in all directions.

The body of an over-sized human being had produced it. Its bloodied face looked remarkably like Stevie's.

"H-Heeellppp m-meeee," Stevie said as he reached his right hand to the windscreen.

"Fuuuuuuuck that," Danny gasped.

Stevie's face had turned blue. The skin around his eyes welted into a scaly lizard-like creature.

"H-Hellpp m-meeee—"

"—Yaarggghhh," Danny squealed. "Get the fuck off of my car."

WHUD-WHUMP. WHUD-WHUMP.

Danny pushed the windscreen wipers on in an attempt to push Stevie's blue-colored talons away.

Danny pushed the steering wheel forward. The action enabled the car to tilt down like a helicopter.

"Whoa."

Stevie grabbed the lip of the hood for dear life as his legs swung out and bounced across the front bumper.

"H-Help—m-meee—"

YANK.

Danny turned the wheel and pulled it back. The car banked to the left and ducked its behind, throwing the screaming Stevie legs up and over his head and crashing onto the roof.

Meanwhile, a mother and her young daughter, watched the event taking place one hundred feet above the Burger Face parking lot.

"Mum?"

"Yes, honey?"

"Why is the car flying?"

"I dunno, honey," the mother said with astonishment. "That's some fucked up shit going up there."

The kid blinked and considered her mother's assessment.

"Mum?"

The woman couldn't tear her eyes away from the scene. Scores of civilians came racing over to watch the extraordinary event taking place beyond the clouds.

"What is it now?"

"What does *fucked up shit* mean?"

The mother pointed at the poor young boy hanging off the flying car as it swerved around and tried to steady itself.

"Look up there. That's a good example."

Back in the sky, Danny decided to set the wipers to full speed and throttle the gas.

WHOOOSH.

The unconscious Baz flew forward as the car reversed in the sky. His face slammed against the back of Danny's seat.

"Stevie, man" Danny gasped through the windscreen. "What happened to you?"

"Danny, get us out of here" Chelsea screamed and thumped him on the shoulder. "You're gonna get us killed."

SPRRIISSSHHH-SWITCH-SSHHHHH.

The car's internal audio bank sprang to life and produced an holy voice.

The visual display unit showed the frequency - DR: 118 - along with an audio wave form.

Congratulations, my friends.

"Gahhh," Danny squealed. "The thing. It's come to life."

"Make it stop," Chelsea cried.

VROOOOOOM.

Danny flung the steering wheel forward and hit the gas,

pushing the car 70 mph forward in less than three second.

The Mondeo rocketed across the sky.

Please race responsibly, yeah? This message brought to you by *SHLOOM* - The Official Beverage of Mur'kroznitck. An' 'ting. I feel like I already said that, but whatever. Allow me, man.

Stevie couldn't keep his grip on the hood.

One by one, his fingers broke away and rolled down the metal, leaving a trail of blue goo streaking across the chassis.

"P-Please—"

"—Sorry, man," Danny whispered as he squinted at his friend's face. "This is too fucked up."

WHUP.

Stevie's pinkie lifted away.

His body rolled off the front and tumbled through the air.

The Ford Mondeo exploded in a shower of orange sparks and blasted into the horizon, leaving a trail of blue liquid hanging in the air.

The only thing left to witness was Stevie's body plummeting back to Earth.

Which it did.

Hundreds of onlookers crowded the road and sidewalks. Each of their heads lowered, slowly, as their eyes followed Stevie's trajectory towards a building hundreds of feet below.

A police car screeched to a halt and produced dozens of traffic officers, who quickly held out their hands and attempted to placate the frenzied scene.

"Okay, move back, people. Move back."

The girl's mother considered covering her eyes, but the spectacle unfolding before them proved impossible to look away from.

"Mum?"

"Uggghhh. The fuck is it now, you irritating little brat?"

"Why is that man falling?"

"How the fuck should I know—"

Stevie screamed his last as his chunky manboobs smashed through the building below, killing him instantly.

CRUNCH — SCHPLATT.

Everyone's eyes - including those of the police officers - traced the boy's fall through the roof and arrived at the sign at the front of the store.

HEY PRESTO FIREWORKS.

"Oh dear," everyone said in unison.

The first policeman turned to the crowd and shooed them away.

"Okay, everyone. Please disperse."

WHIZZZ-BANG-KABOOOM.

A thousand fireworks vomited into the clear blue sky. The shittiest of shit firework shows, by all accounts.

"Get back," the policeman screamed. "Nothing to see here."

Chapter 4

Satchel squinted the late afternoon sun away as he peered down at the upturned diamond on a stick stuck in of Bucky's front yard.

He gave the cigarette between his chapped lips a long drag before flicking the stub into the small pool at the object's base. The cigarette butt sizzled away as he, Bucky, Bobby Jo, and Skeez contemplated their new destiny.

Satchel pulled a fresh menthol from his shirt pocket and lit it, "Well... *shit*."

"So. What you think?"

"*What I think*?" Satchel asked as if it was the most stupid question in the galaxy, "I think y'all been at Skeez's stash."

"But we ain't."

"If you say so. You say we need to use that blue stuff to make a spaceship?"

"It took Bobby Jo's shirt right into space. We all saw it." Bucky said.

Satchel scanned Bobby Jo from head to toe and back again, pausing briefly for a stop at her not-inconsiderable cleavage.

"Fuck y'all lookin' at?" she said, covering her chest with her forearms.

Bucky's old tee shirt wore a little *too* large on her. In her

49

view, tight-fitting clothes made her seem somewhat more intelligent. She felt a little self-conscious in the baggy shirt. The fact that the text on the front read "Female Body Inspector" made matters all the worse.

And that was just her top half.

Her tiny shorts were hidden under the long shirt. It looked like she wasn't wearing any pants at all.

Bobby Jo cringed at Satchel's leering, but nodded at Bucky's words.

Satchel's reputation as a complete and utter scumbag was well-earned. He had won the state lotto a few months back and netted $14m. New-found fame and fortune hadn't changed him into the suave man of the world he thought it did. It only exacerbated his *scumminess*. His slick-backed hair got greasier. His jewelry became gaudier, and the truck was awarded a pair of huge truck nuts hanging from their hitch.

Money well spent - *not.*

"Lemme get this straight," Satchel spat through his cigarette. "Y'all want my help, right?"

"Uh. *Yes?*" Bucky tried.

"Okay. Why should I help y'all?"

"Fabulous prizes. That's why," Bucky said, more excited than he had been in years. "Whatever's out there musta known that my pa was a jack-man for the late Mr. Earnhardt himself."

Skeez rolled his eyes, "Pfft. Here we go."

"Everyone knows the '86 and '87 first place seasons were because of my pa's advice." Bucky said, defensively, clocking Satchel's refusal to believe him.

"What advice?"

"Mr. Earnhardt was thinking about changing his number. But my pa convinced him that the number three was lucky and that the next year would be his."

"So?"

"So? You know what happened after?"

"Naw."

Bucky punched the air, "*Boom*. We all know that the *Holy number three* took number one both seasons. All because my pa happened to be his jack-man."

Skeez frowned, "Didn't your pa get fired for doing coke or some shit?"

Bucky fanned his hands out enough for Skeez to shit and *shut the hell up*.

"Nah," Bucky shook his head. "Enough of that—"

"—For real, he got busted hosing up chalk—"

"—Fuckin' shut up," Bucky whispered. "He never touched the stuff. He got fired for *stealing tires*. Not doing coke. It don't change the fact that he was instrumental in the great man's life, God rest his soul."

Bucky kissed his index and middle finger of his right hand and lifted them towards heaven. A gesture immediately mirrored by the other three.

"God rest his soul," they mumbled in unison. "Lucky number three. God sent."

A moment of reverence befell the area, unaided by the stupid diamond thing buzzing a few feet away from them.

Satchel flicked his spent cigarette at the object, only for it to rebound off its shiny surface and splash into the water below.

"Fuckin' weird thing."

"Amen to *that*," Skeez said. "I guess it don't like smoke, none."

Satchel ignored the man's remark and folded his arms.

"Bucky?"

"Yeah?"

"It don't make no sense," Satchel spat and pointed at the javelin. "You ain't no jack-man. Why would whoever sent this Toblerone-looking motherfucker down here want you to participate in some race?"

Bucky threw up his hands, "Obviously because they know that you don't keep your best dog in the kennel."

"Woof woof," Bobby Jo added, only to be shot a look of disdain by the two men.

"Bobby Jo?" Bucky asked.

"Yeah, cuz?"

"Shut the hell up, okay? We're trying to conduct business here, and y'ain't helping none."

"Fine."

Bobby Jo revealed her teeth and held her middle finger up at him. She coiled her gum around her finger, keeping the bird well and truly *flipped*.

Bucky frowned at her digit and launched into serious-mode.

"Look, Satchel. This is what I've been waiting for. What I was born for. My whole life. My destiny. *Finally*, something to make my pa proud of me. He taught me everything he knew about being a jack-man before he moved on."

"*Jack off*, more like," Bobby Jo muttered.

"I didn't know your pa was dead?" Satchel said. "That's messed up. I apologize."

Bucky cocked his head to the side, "He ain't dead."

Satchel had trouble digesting the information, "But you said he moved on?"

"Yeah. Down to Jacksonville. Like, five years ago, but that ain't the point, man."

Bucky slid into the crater and stood beside the goo filled pole. He surveyed the fantastic mess and took a deep breath. Only one thing was clear in a sea of confusion - *his belief*.

He pointed at the diamond and produced a shit-eating grin.

"This here is our ticket out. We have a chance to prove that us rednecks are the best racers in the world. Everyone else won't even try to race us in a stock car. They know they ain't got a pedophile's hope of gettin' laid in an old folk's home of beatin' us."

"Huh?" Satchel asked. "That doesn't make any sense."

"What doesn't?" Bucky asked, uneasy about the interruption of his soliloquy.

"Yeah, I don't think the analogy works, Bucky," Bobby Jo offered.

"Never mind."

Bucky thought Satchel had lost his mind. The fact that he was stinking rich quickly helped him get over the disappointment pretty damn quickly, though.

He looked up at the sky and held his braces with pride.

"This, man. *This* is how we take our racing pedigree to the next level. Think about it. *Fuckin' space.* Who's with me?" he shouted and rammed his right fist into the air.

Skeez, Bobby Jo, and Satchel didn't immediately display any notion of camaraderie.

"You what?" Skeez asked, quite likely that he hadn't been listening.

"It's cock-smokin', over-the-moon-ridin', father-rapin' SPACE. Now, who's with me?"

"Well, I wanna go to space," Bobby Jo yelled with excitement. "Can I come?"

"Dunno," Bucky mused. "I hear you don't usually have trouble in that department."

"Naw, you dickhead. Not like *that*. I mean can I ride with you?"

"Heh," Bucky grinned, and was about to make another jovial quip, only to be cock-blocked by Bobby Jo's interruption. "I hear you can ride—"

"—I mean in space, ass face."

"Uh. Yeah. Sure you can."

"Oh," Skeez snapped his fingers, connecting the dots. "I get it. It's a space race vehicle type of thing?"

"Ya-huh."

Skeez glanced over at Bobby Jo hopping up and down next to him.

"Fuck yeah. Count my beautiful skinny ass in, too."

Less than jubilant, Satchel fished for another menthol within his shirt pocket. "Forgive me if I don't ejaculate all over your fine property with excitement, Bucky, but I still don't know what you need me for?"

Bucky rolled his eyes and chuckled, "Ha. Y'ain't figured it out yet?"

Satchel flipped the lid down on his lighter and dropped it into his pocket. He took a long draw and spoke with the cigarette paper still stuck to his lips.

"Nope."

"*Money*, my good man," Bucky said. "We need money. You won the lotto, right?"

"Sure did, and the money's all fuckin'—"

"—So y'all got the money," Bucky said. "How ya fancy being a bona fide, paid-up sponsor for our entry into the race?"

Satchel considered the proposition as he sucked the burning paper down to his fingers.

Skeez pulled a lukewarm beer from his cargo pants and cracked it open.

"Man, I can't believe this. This is great news," he said as the froth spunked around the ring pull and bubbled over his spindly fingers, "This causes for celebration."

Bobby Jo coiled her left pigtail around her index finger and chewed her gum.

Skeez offered her a fresh beer from another pocket. She took it and cracked it open, clinked cans with Skeez, and took a sip.

Bucky eyed Satchel and grinned, "Well?"

"Well what?"

"You gonna give us the money to make this happen?"

The ground water in the crater seeped into his shoe. He hated squishy socks and wanted to get it over with before his shoes were waterlogged.

Satchel inhaled, causing the other three to do the same in anticipation.

"No," Satchel said.

He flicked his cigarette butt out towards the woods at the edge of the clearing.

"No?" Bucky shrieked in disbelief. "Whaddya mean *no*?"

"I mean, uh, *no*."

Skeez scrunched his face and thought aloud. "Huh? Is that a *no* like no? Or a *no means no and yes mean anal* kinda *no?*"

"Imbecile," Satchel snapped. "Do I look like I went to college?"

"Uh, no?"

"Damn right," Satchel shook his head and sighed. "It means no. No, as in, *I can't even afford a hand job from the strippers* kinda *no*."

Bucky found himself at a loss, "So, that's a no, right?"

"Yep."

"Yep, no?" Bucky confirmed. "Or, yep, yeah?"

"No."

"Which one?"

"Oh, *fuck this*," Satchel shouted. "It's a *no*."

"No. Why?"

"Because I ain't got no money left. Okay? *Happy, now*?"

The news came as a complete shock to Bucky.

"The fuck? How y'all got no money left?"

"I just don't. Stop askin' me questions. This ain't Jeopardy or sum' shit."

"It *ain't*?" Bucky roared with sarcasm. "You're right, it ain't jeopardy. But *you* spunk your money away and leave us without sponsorship is really gon' fuck my shit up and put it in jeopardy."

Satchel's face turned beet red. He couldn't look anyone in the eyes. He'd intended to keep the fact he'd lost his money a secret - forever.

"How y'all spend fifteen million bucks so damn fast?" Skeez asked, flabbergasted.

"Fourteen. and it's none of your bum fondlin' business how I lost it, ya hear? But I have an idea."

"I hear ya, I hear ya," Skeez booted one of his brother's spent cigarette ends across the ground. "S'all right, though, coz I done talkin' to *poor dudes*, anyhow."

Satchel ignored him and turned to Bucky, invading his

personal space.

"Ugh," Bobby Jo said as the tips of each men's nose touched. "You two gon' make out?"

"Wassup, Satchel?" Bucky asked. "You said you had an idea?"

Satchel double-took and realized he was *far too close* to Bucky's face. He took a step back and cleared his throat in a way that suggested he definitely wasn't gay.

"Yeah, I do. I put all my money into buying the strip club."

"What? That ol' shit hole?"

"Yeah."

"The fuck you do that for?"

Satchel shrugged, "Figured why give the girls all my money when I could just buy 'em outright."

Bobby Jo raised a finger, demanding to be heard, "Uh. I don't think that's how it works."

"No one cares what you think," Satchel quipped.

"You sexist."

"Don't bring that *hash tag-me-too* shit round these here parts or I'll tan your hide."

"Aww, *shit*."

Satchel continued with Bucky, "Lookit. I need to get the word out that the place is under new ownership."

"I figure there's eyes watching whatever's about to go down, man. All eyes on sponsorship."

Satchel nodded and felt a sluice of regret juice its way to his heart.

"Yeah, I know. Like you said, I could be a sponsor. I wanna help you win and do yo' pa proud, Bucky."

The news socked our intrepid protagonist right in the heart. He nearly burst into tears like a little bitch.

"Aww, gee. Thanks, man."

"Yeah," Satchel continued. "I could re-brand the club to a space theme. Be known as the first club owner to sponsor some space race or whatever."

Bucky adjusted his hat. "But how y'all gon' sponsor us

with no money? That's kinda the sponsor's job, right? To provide the money in return for us providing your good name on the side of our vee-hick-ull?"

"I ain't talkin' about no cash, Yeager," Satchel said.

"What? You gonna pay me in blow jobs instead?"

"Naw, Bucky. I don't do that no more, I don't care what you heard—"

"—I ain't heard nuthin', man. My lips are sealed."

"Hur-hur," Skeez interrupted the conversation having heard everything, "They weren't exactly sealed before he won the lotto."

Satchel closed his eyes and clenched his fist, "Skeez?"

"Uh-huh?"

"You speak again and I'mma put my knuckles down your throat, grab hold of your sphincter and pull you inside out. Ya hear?"

"Sorry, Bucky. I never mean nuthin' by it."

Satchel hooked his thumbs through his belt loops and rocked his hips forward in a 'power pose'.

Bobby Jo nearly gagged at Satchel's unfortunate display.

"Okay, so here's what's up," Satchel said. "I ain't got no money. But I *do* have the perfect vehicle for the spaceship. Fuck, it already looks like a space ship."

— Later That Day —

Satchel, Bobb Jo, Skeez, and Bucky, traipsed along the strip club's gravel path and laid eyes on the vehicle.

"She's a *beaut*, ain't she?"

Satchel grinned as his three buddies stood before his supposed 'perfect spaceship': a brand-new, 30 foot aluminum Streamliner camper trailer. The windows still had cling film on them from delivery. Bucky had to admit it was a beautiful trailer, but that was the problem - it was merely a trailer.

No motor. No driver's seat. Two things Bucky

considered to be essential in a race car these days.

"Let me get this straight. You won the lottery and spent all the money on a strip club and a pair of rubber testicles for your truck—"

"Hehe, yeah," Satchel grinned, satisfied with his decision.

"And this here fancy-ass camper?"

Skeez shook his head and failed to suppress his misgivings as he analyzed the silver camper.

"Yeah, and why would you buy a camper when you live in a trailer? Ain't that a little redundant?"

"It's not redundant."

"No?"

"Nah, man," Satchel said. "This has wheels, look. You know my trailer home is a permanent structure now that the axles have rusted through."

"Yup."

Satchel got all defensive, "I was thinking about taking a tour of the west. Then I thought, why not do it in style? Plus, I was fucked up on Rollneck when I ordered it."

"How fucked up?" Bucky asked.

"Three crate's worth."

"*DAAAAAAAYYYAAAAAMMMMNN,*" Skeez, Bucky, and Bobby Jo blurted in harmony.

"Yeah-huh," Satchel chuckled with pride. "I mean, I coulda sent the product back, but I don't think they accept piss."

Bucky shook his head and tried not to laugh, "I'm surprised your bladder didn't fall out your cock hole."

"Who says it never?"

Bucky walked along the side of the camper in something of a disappointed stupor.

"Whatever. How are we supposed to drive this? A racer needs a drive train."

"A drive train?" Satchel asked.

"Yeah. At the very least."

"How's a drive train going to help you in space?"

Satchel said. "That's what the blue goo is for, if what you said is true."

Satchel had a point. He supposed they could just build a cockpit. Plus a camper like this was already self-contained for long journeys. It wasn't exactly sexy for a race car, but then again it was pretty *sexy* for a camper.

"All right. This could actually work."

Satchel flicked his cigarette to the ground and threw a fresh one between his lips.

"*Could work*? Fuck, man. A trailer is practically a spaceship already."

"Is it?"

"Yeah, you never seen that movie Spaceballs?"

Bucky's brain worked overtime and produced an answer.

"No."

"Ah, whatever. It don't matter none," Satchel continued. "We just need to figure out how to slather that goo on her undercarriage to get her legs up in the air. She'll glide like a wet stripper on a greased pole."

Skeez nudged Satchel on the arm and giggled at Bobby Jo's face of disgust.

"Are we still talking about a spaceship?"

"Go fuck your Momma," Bobby Jo spat and placed her hands on her hips in defiance.

"Less it, the pair of you," Bucky huffed and turned to Satchel. "Okay, seems Satchel has us a ship. We provided the crew, and the goo."

Skeez nudged Bobby Jo and licked his lips, "I'll provide you with my goo if you like?"

Bobby Jo felt a glob of vomit bleed into her mouth, "Oh, please go away."

Bucky held out his hands, "Sounds mighty good from our end. Y'all skinny ass in, Skeez?"

"Yeehaw, motherfucker," Satchel added, much to Bucky's confusion.

"Is that a *yes*?"

"Yeah-huh."

"Good," Bucky snorted and turned to Satchel to complete their business. "So, Satch. What do you want out of this exchange?"

The man grinned, his cigarette stained teeth flashing in the early evening moon.

"Simple."

"Is it?"

"Yeah. I wanna be able to paint an advertisement on the ship."

"For the strip club?" Bucky asked.

"No," Satchel spat with sarcasm. "For yo' Momma's pantyhose."

"Huh?"

"*Yes*, the fuckin' strip club," Satchel huffed and placed his hand on Bucky's shoulder, all friendly like, "Look, don't get your panties in a twist, *Bukkake*."

Bucky grabbed Satchel's wrist and flung it away, "Don't never call me that."

"Call you what?"

"Bukkake. I'm sick o' hearing that shit, and it weren't funny the fiftieth time."

Bobby Jo and Skeez sniggered to themselves. Bucky turned to them and snapped his fingers.

"Fuck y'all laughin' at?"

"Sorry, Bucky," they said, trying not to laugh.

"I'm sorry, *Bucky*," Satchel said. "Those darn Porn Cabin videos again. Fuckin' up my head space."

"Whatever, just don't say it again."

"I won't," Satchel continued. "And don't worry none about the advert. It'll be all tasteful and shit."

"Uh-huh, *yeah*," Bucky quipped with a modicum of disbelief, "I'm sure it'll be all tasteful. *And shit.*"

Satchel took an inordinately long drag from the last of his smoke and flicked the spent butt in a suggestive manner. It accidentally bounced off the side of the vehicle and nearly landed on the propane tanks attached to the front.

"Whoa," everyone shrieked. "Damn it. Be careful."

"Sorry, I meant to miss it," Satchel said. "Besides, don't worry. The advert will be good."

Skeez returned to his feet and brushed down his shoulders, "I feel like if he has to say 'don't worry' we should be worried."

Satchel shrugged and sparked up another menthol.

"Of course, I can just call the whole thing off. No sponsorship. No camper. Fuck y'all good, and take that trip out west on m'own after all."

Bucky held out his hands to calm everyone down. "Wait, wait. It doesn't really matter if there's an advert on the side. We won't be able to see it. Ain't no one in space that'll see it, either."

"No?" Bobby Jo said. "How you figure that?"

"Because there ain't no-goddamn-body *in space*, dickhead," Bucky said. "Unless we get pulled over by space cops or aliens or some shit."

Bobby Jo's brain revolved in her skull, processing the information at a rate of two cells per hour.

"Huh."

Bucky didn't have time to allow his cousin to connected the dots, "Plus, the more I think about it, the more I like the idea of using the camper. It has real promise."

Satchel held out a hand, "Hells yeah Let's seal this deal."

Bucky and Satchel shook hands. The pair were on each other's wavelength, at least for now.

"Take the trailer back to your place when I'm done airbrushing," Satchel said. "Sometime tomorrow."

"Okay."

Satchel took a deep pull on his smoke, "Now I just need to think of the perfect name for the re-branded strip club."

The thought of what that might be sent chills down

everyone's spines.

Chapter 5

Stereotype Industries Inc, Harajuku, Japan.

Kenzo rolled his shoulders and muttered to himself in his native tongue.

Angelic choral music whirled around the boardroom providing a serene soundtrack to accompany the painting of a star-filled skyline on all four walls.

A ten foot screen behind him displayed a revolving space ship, with arrows blasting in all directions.

Something about speed, velocity, heat shields, and a whole host of stuff written in Japanese.

The investors sitting in the seats marveled at the image, thoroughly impressed. They took out their tablets and began making notes, not wanting to miss any valuable details.

Kenzo opened his eyes and took in the sea of the delegates sitting before him, eager for his explanation.

"Laydeez anna gennhuull-menn," Kenzo started in his thick Japanese accent, "We-uh ar-ha show to you, this, our newestest spacesest ship."

Kenzo pressed a button on his presentation clicker and enlarged the ship.

"It is we called it, ah, *Tempura-Four*."

A collective sound of *oooohs* filled the room.

"We like very a lot Tempura-Four go in space," Kenzo continued, his ability to communicate in English weighing on him like a sack of bricks, "It go very far to Saturn. Many, big, powerful rockets."

A big, powerful rocket at the back end of the ship lit up on the screen, and then on each delegates tablet.

Kenzo launched into a sound-effect tirade.

"Waaahhh, bang, bang," he gesticulated. "Big bang. Bang. Nuclear rockets, they go—whoosh. Bang bang. Now with Brown Hole *incruded*."

The delegates smiled and clapped politely. Some could be seen mouthing 'brown hole' to one another in confusion.

"For this, price. We charge, uh," Kenzo said as he consulted his tablet to no obvious avail, "Four-ah hunn-red and nine million dollar."

A white man in his sixties raised his hand, "Excuse me. Mr. Kenzo?"

"Yes. Me, Mr Kenzo-san."

"Uh, okay?" the man winced. "Can you please explain how Tempura-Four is an improvement over previous exploratory vessels?"

Kenzo squinted at the man in confusion.

"I plead your pardon?"

"Oh, for heaven's sake."

The man took out a black device, held it to his throat, and proceeded to speak very slowly.

"How... is... Tempura-Four... improved?"

As his voice escaped his lips, the device produced the same sentence in Japanese.

"宇宙のレ-Tempura-Four—スのため?"

"Ah," Kenzo nodded and threw a subtle wink at his colleagues waiting at the stage wings.

After they took a polite bow, Kenzo returned to the questioner, "This, Tempura-Four. Name... after steamed vegetable in batter."

"No, no," the man said. "That's not what I asked. I wanted to know—"

"—Very tasty," Kenzo smiled. "Is good questions."

The man lowered the device and shook it, "Hopeless. Absolutely hopeless."

Kenzo took a bow, "We very hopeless. Yes."

Just as the questioner lost the will to live, a stick-thin Japanese woman ran onto the stage in haste. She tugged at Kenzo's arm, forcing her name badge to shake across her left boob - *Laskar*.

"すべてです。そ!'"

Kenzo's eyes widened, "はあ?! diamond—な陰茎?"

"の," Laskar said, encouraging Kenzo to leave the stage and run off with her. She turned to the confused delegates and attempted to apologize.

"てください," Kenzo whispered and looked at his lab technicians staring at him from the side of the stage.

Laskar stepped forward and pressed her palms together.

"Uh, genitals and ladyboys," she opened in her slightly-better-than-her-boss's-English. "I am most sorry about this unfortunate transpiration of events. There is no cause for circumcision at this time."

A concerned voice came from the back of the crowd, "What's going on?"

"Please remain seated," Laskar advised.

Kenzo stormed off the stage with excitement. He barked over his shoulder at Laskar as she followed behind him.

A thoroughly confused audience sat back in their chairs wondering just what in Satan's testicle's name was going on.

"宇宙の—colossal thyroid— レースの," Kenzo snapped at Laskar.

"No, Sir."

It took about half an hour to reach Stereotype's laboratory. Technically, it resembled a self-contained city.

Dozens of spaceships and assorted generic sci-fi paraphernalia lined the walls.

Things like ray guns, big stupid machines, and more spaceships - all of them clinical white in color, and threatening in demeanor.

And very, *very* futuristic. And impressive.

Kenzo sprinted with his team through the laboratory and met with a bespectacled, genius-looking scientist in a wheelchair named Krutch.

"Krutch—私の陰茎?" Kenzo demanded.

Krutch moved his head forward and hit a button on his electronic armrest.

"Come, sir," the armrest said in its robotic English accent. "Outside. It is most unusual."

"私の陰茎を—the fuck—の陰?"

"It is probably better that you see with your own eyeballs."

Krutch wheeled back along the shiny floor and spun around one hundred and eighty degrees.

Laskar walked alongside him as they made their way to the glass window. A beautiful horizon of Bonzai trees and green grass lay behind it, offering a veritable utopia of futuristic wonder.

"What you did find?" Laskar asked.

"It is not we what finded," Krutch's wheelchair said. "It finded *us*."

Kenzo, Laskar, and Krutch, moved through the sliding glass door and into the bio-dome proper.

Tempura-Four hung to the left in its scaffolding.

"ために巨—*blairwitchsymbol*—?"

"Huh?" Krutch asked as he watched Kenzo begin to freak out, "Blair Witch Symbol?"

"大," Kenzo replied.

"Oh," the chair said as Krutch dribbled down his chest, "Look. Over there."

Kenzo turned his head to see a beautiful, transparent diamond gyrating around a silver javelin several feet above the ground near the Pond of Tranquility.

"見せたい!"

Kenzo couldn't believe his eyes.

With great care, he took a few steps forward and smiled at the bizarre entity before him.

"Amazement," he muttered. "Lookie it, so byootiful."

"Big happy fun," Krutch advised.

A neon sign sprang to life at the top of the diamond.

Hello!

"Hello?" Kenzo repeated, "Is Yankee jo—"

Welcome to the Race.

After careful consideration, you have been selected to participate in this wondrous event for pride, bragging rights, and fabulous prizes!

Please select your racer, and your crew! Only the best of the best will make it in this grueling completion of physical endurance and mental capacity.

Kenzo, Laskar, and Krutch simply stared, aghast, at the bizarre event and waited for its next move. They weren't sure if it would attack or screw them to death.

Perhaps both?

Dozens of Japanese scientists raced over to watch what was happening.

"What is going on here?" asked one of them.

"We do not possess knowledge at this time," Laskar said. "Please remain standing and refrain from walking near the foreign alien object."

Kenzo's jaw dropped as the top of the diamond folded open like a hippo's yawn. A flood of clear blue goo bubbled out from within and formed a strange, horizontal line - headed straight for Tempura Four.

"チーズが好きです," Kenzo marveled. "それはああはい、宇宙のレースのためにすべてです‼"

"Yes. I agree," Laskar said.

The bulbous, thick end of the goo streaked through the

air and splashed across the side of the spaceship, just in time for...

WHOOOOSH.

The airlock hatch opened, releasing a man in a spacesuit complete with a glass domed helmet. The name tag sewn onto the breast of the suit said Geoffrey - the commander of the Tempura-Four program.

"Hey, guys," Geoffrey said in his thick Australian accent, unaware of the cataclysmic event unfolding from the other end of the dome. "What's going on—oh, *Christ mate.*"

He clapped eyes on the blue goo fountaining towards his spacecraft.

"Jeezus-a-Krisst," Kenzo, Laskar, and Krutch - and the dozens of scientists - gasped at the same time.

GLUMP.

The blue goo enveloped the entire vessel as Geoffrey leapt from the airlock and ran towards them.

"Bonza! What the hell is it?"

"We do not know at this present moment in time," Laskar said. "It is best you remove yourself from the proximity of this new thing."

"B-But that's *my* spaceship," Geoffrey complained. "We're due to launch the day after tomorrow."

"たは私のた," Kenzo said.

Geoffrey squinted at his boss, failing to understand the instruction.

Despite his half-Australian, half-Japanese ancestry, Geoffrey had grown up in the West and understood little of the Japanese language.

"What did he say?"

"He said be quiet and let the alien entity perform its duty," Laskar said.

GLUB — GLUB — GLUB.

Before long, the blue goo covered the entire vessel.

Fascinated by the actions of the goo, Krutch wheeled his stationary body forward in its chair.

"No. Krutch, where do you think you are traveling to?" Laskar hollered after him.

In this container is the approved allotment of Moronium for one racer. Please note that if you are caught using more than the approved allotment, you will be disqualified.

Krutch's wheelchair stopped dead as Tempura-Four rumbled. Sections of the blue goo hardened out into a pair of missiles and slotted onto the wings of the vessel.

"Wow," Krutch's voice box said. "That's some *serious* firepower."

Biddip-beep.

A blast of white light shot out from the front arms of his chair and scanned across the vessel.

"Pure nuclear."

Geoffrey stepped over to Krutch and folded his arms, "*What* is pure nuclear?"

"Missiles," Krutch said.

Both men looked down to see some of the blue goo had soaked into the frame of his wheels.

"Ah, sir—"

A confident voice blew out from the diamond, forcing everyone to give it their attention.

The goal? The Moon!
The Prizes? Fabulous!
The time? Now!

A neon-looking holographic countdown appeared above the line of goo spilling out of the javelin.

"Huh?" Laskar said.

SPRITCH-SPRIZZZ.

Krutch's wheelchair danced around like an epileptic ballet dancer, shuffling its metal in time to the Japanese music.

WHUP-BOP-BUP.

"に書かれた!!" Krutch complained as his two left wheels slammed to the ground.

"Somebody save him," Laskar said.

Kenzo held her back, evidently afraid of what could happen if she went anywhere near the disco-jumping mound of metal throttling the disabled man inside it.

"書—Playstation9—に書かれた," Kenzo confided.

"But, Sir, he is—"

Krutch's tires spun around as the chair lifted into the air. Of course, the man it contained didn't put up much resistance - although that wasn't by choice.

It didn't stop him screaming via his voice box.

"Help me," it said. "Help me, et cetera."

Geoffrey stood back and waved everyone away, "Everyone, get back. Don't touch that blue stuff!"

The scientists acted accordingly. They shuffled back, but kept their eyes on the poor man in his wheelchair floating towards the glass dome.

"Uh, Krutch? Mate?" Geoffrey asked, hoping the man hadn't been killed. "Are you okay?"

SPLUTCH—SLURRPP.

The blue goo folded around the metal arms and seeped into the voice controller.

COUGH — COUGH — SPLUTTER.

The alien entity spoke via the box, its voice sounding like a mix between Stephen Hawking and a movie trailer.

Ladies—and g-gentlemen, this is Mur'kroznitck. Please may I have your attention.

"Yes?" Geoffrey said, braving his way forward.

Remove your helmet.

"Okay."

Geoffrey unfastened the rubber around his neck and lifted the glass bowl away from his head.

What is your name?

"Geoffrey. Geoffrey Perkins."

Doesn't sound very Japanese to me. Geoffrey.

"No, my parents," he said, quickly changing tact. "It's a long story. Who are you?"

I am your Mur'kroznitck sponsor.

"Right," Geoffrey said. "I don't know what that

means."

I am your Mur'kroznitck sponsor.

"Yeah, I heard you the first time," Geoffrey pointed to Krutch as the side of his face pressed against the dome glass one hundred feet in the air. "Could you, uh, please let my friend down?"

Certainly.

CLIP — WHOOOSH

The blue goo disappeared and released Krutch - and his wheelchair - into free-fall.

"Shit, no—"

Geoffrey ran toward Krutch's falling path.

"Ah. I appear to be falling," Krutch's voice box said as the chair and its occupier rocketed towards the ground, aiming straight for the Pond of Tranquility.

Mur'kroznitck officials see you are fast, Geoffrey Perkins. But are you fast *enough*?

Ignoring that remark, Geoffrey barged everyone out of the way and raced to the pond.

It was too late.

Krutch splashed wheels-first into the water and bobbed up and down like a buoy, soaked in water.

Kenzo and Laskar raced over to the pond, but didn't dare enter.

"Hey, Krutch," Geoffrey shouted, "Are you okay—"

FIZZZ — SPARK.

Electricity and water proved, as ever, to be a less-than-welcome mix. The wheelchair exploded.

Its wheels shot out in opposite directions as the skin on Krutch's face bubbled and melted down his flesh-laden skull.

A distinct waft of barbecuing human and metal drifted into the air as Krutch continued to cook.

"Please be advised," his voice box squirmed. "I appear to be melting. Assistance required."

KRA-BA-BOOOOOOM.

Krutch exploded, sending everyone onto their asses.

The dome above their heads cracked out like a spider's web and rained down sharp pieces of glass that crashed around those on the floor.

"Waahhhhhh," Geoffrey screamed and rolled around on the floor, covering his eyes.

Dozens of dead fish bobbled up to the surface of the water as everyone witnessed Krutch's wheelchair submerge.

The poor guy's ass was well and truly kicked.

The diamond beamed and rolled to a stop.

Kenzo brushed the glass off his trousers and jumped to his feet with anger.

"なたは成功し‼" he screamed with sincerity. The man was *mega* pissed off. "た翻訳者になるために優れた??‼"

Mur'kroznitck officials do not understand Chinese. The voice now seemed to emanate for the diamond.

"マンド—fucking chinese, you plick—が必要です。翻訳者," Kenzo shouted, evilly.

The diamond just stood there, silent. It seemed to blink at the man, as if to say "are you quite finished?"

"Why you look at my face like that?" Kenzo asked. "God damned father fucker."

Laskar ran over and tried to calm him down, "Please, Mr. Kenzo, sir—"

"—翻訳者べて," he said.

Whatever Laskar had said seemed to calm him down. Witnessing his lead scientist's messy death had put the damper on the situation. The other scientists were none-too-happy about the prospect of war that had visited them.

"者べ翻訳," Kenzo confided in her.

He managed to calm down and see sense as he held her arms.

"Please, Mr. Kenzo?"

He nodded and turned to the diamond.

"What it is that you wanted?"

The diamond began to flow towards Tempura-Four as the silver javelin melted and flowed along with the blue goo. Soon all the alien liquid was soaked into the spaceship and the diamond was embedded in its hull. And after a second or two, even that was absorbed.

All it left behind was the countdown timer resting against Tempura-Four's hull.

Please race responsibly. This message brought to you by *SHLOOM* - The Official Beverage of Mur'kroznitck, the voice bellowed from within the ship."

Chapter 6

Private Hacker read the update on his tablet.

"The object is arriving now, Colonel. They are bringing it in directly."

Colonel Dumas smiled around his slightly damp cigar, "Good to hear it, Private. You know, most Privates wouldn't get this opportunity, but seeing as how you initially spotted the object I thought you should be able to see it to the end."

"Thank you sir."

Hacker was grateful for the opportunity but was more concerned that his new position was not going to be worth the trouble. He didn't know if it was an age thing or if the Colonel was really as dense as he put on.

The large bay door opened along its rollers.

"Ah. Here they come, Sir."

Outside stood a C5 transport, its nose cone open, spewing a whole line of jeeps and trucks that drove directly from the plane into the hanger. In the center of the enormous open room stood a small city of hermetically sealed tents acting as a makeshift research facility for the object.

The two leading jeeps peeled apart as they approached the tent city entrance. They took up defensive positions as dozens of soldiers in hazmat suits jumped out and leveled guns at the open doors, watching for anything out of the ordinary.

A large flatbed truck with a canvas top pulled up to the front canvas door. Half a dozen soldiers in hazmat suits climbed out the open back and dropped the tailgate. More officials in hazmat suits came flooding out of the tent's entrance with a large gurney. Several of them climbed into the truck. They emerged a moment later, pulling an open wood crate that held a ten foot long silver javelin. The projected image seemed as if it were part of a video game experiencing major clipping issues.

"Come on, Hecker."

Colonel Dumas rubbed his hands and marched towards the truck.

"Hacker, Sir."

"What?" Dumas barked.

"My name is *Hacker*. Sir."

Dumas threw Hacker a bit of the ol' stink eye.

"That's what I said, Private. Are you sure you're going to be able to keep up if you can't hear me properly?"

Hacker gave a half-smile of resignation, "Yes, Sir. I'll be able to keep up."

Colonel Dumas threw his cigar between his lips and approached the technicians in lab suits.

"Good. Come on. I don't want to miss this."

"Uh, Sir? Should we be getting this close to the object?" Hacker asked, concerned with the Colonel's complete disregard for containment protocols.

"Don't be such a baby, Hecker," Dumas snapped. "You don't grow hair on your balls by just sitting around. You've got to get right up in the shit if you want to learn how to lead from the front."

Dumas shouldered past a man in a hazmat suit. The man took a double take at the colonel coming in without any protective gear whatsoever.

"Actually, that's exactly how hair grows," Hacker

muttered, joined by the parade of people following the object on the cart into the tent city.

Dumas finally caught up to the head scientist, who was easily picked out due to their white hazmat suit in stark contrast to the rest of the yellow ones.

"Scientist. What do we have here?" Dumas thundered.

The person in the white hazmat suit jumped nearly a foot in the air as they were assaulted by the Colonel's bark.

Hacker was struck breathless to see a beautiful woman inside the overly large plastic hood on her suit.

"What in God's name, Colonel?" the woman asked as she tried to herd him back. "You shouldn't be this close to the object without some kind of protection on. We've yet to determine how dangerous it is."

If you were to ask Hacker if he believed in love at first sight just ten minutes ago, he would have told you that you were clinically insane - that love was the artifice of those with learning disabilities who routinely failed to keep their saliva in their mouths. After hearing this petite, brown-haired woman telling the Colonel he was insane, Hacker found himself in love in an instant.

Colonel Dumas backed off and allowed the rest of the parade whisk the object through the tent doors

Hacker kept his distance, "Scientist?"

"Yes, Colonel?" she said in an angelic, come-to-bed tone.

"I, uh, *we* need to get to the bottom of this thing before the commies get the jump on us. What do we know so far, scientist?"

She cocked her head, "Are you just calling me *scientist* instead of asking my name? Is that what we're doing, here?"

"No time for pleasantries, *scientist,*" Dumas said, enacting the treat 'em mean, keep 'em keen proliferation he'd heard so much about in his youth.

The woman leaned to the side and made eye contact with Hacker, who tried to say "*sorry my boss is such a douche canoe"* with nothing but his eyes. To his relief, the message seemed to get across. Maybe his dream of becoming a Sargent one day was possible. He had heard that eye communication was an essential skill for promotion.

The woman closed her eyes and sighed.

"Well, I suppose it's too late anyway," she said. "You're already exposed. If there is anything to be exposed to, that is."

"I can assure you that adequate protection isn't necessary," Dumas said, careful not to overstep the line with his salacious, ill-placed quip.

She took the opportunity to ignore his remark and introduce herself, paving the way for the sort of professionalism she expected, "I'm Dr. Gwen Furch."

"I'm Doctegwenfuurrj," Dumas mouthed, trying to decipher her strange sentence.

"Huh?"

"I'm Doctegewnfuuurj?"

Her patience drained away from her body, "What are you talking about?"

"What's a Doctegwen—*Furj*?"

"No," she huffed. "Gwen. My first name is Gwen. Furch is my surname. I'm a doctor. Dr. Gwen Furch"

"Oh," Dumas said with relief. "I'm sorry, I thought you had brain damage. Very nice to meet you, Gwen. I'm—"

"—Yeah," she ignored his ridiculousness and marched towards the tent. "Come on."

Hacker was still a little reticent to enter, but knew Dr. Furch - the latest object of his desire - was right. His boss had already exposed them to whatever horrors there might be.

And that tight little bum of hers was worth following, too. Though, the frumpy hazmat suit made him use his imagination more than he'd have liked.

The interior of the tent city was a mass of interconnected isolated rooms with clear plastic windows for walls. Hacker was surprised to see that the first few rooms looked like normal offices with people sitting at desks doing paperwork. Except that all the people were wearing the bulky hazmat suits. This was, after all, a government facility, and paperwork waits for no man in government.

They arrived at the main lab where a dozen or so officials with instruments took readings from the object. The diamond-skewered object had been *de-crated* and was now hovering a foot off the ground standing on end. The holograph, now unobstructed by the crate, showed just a few hours under three days ticking down. The bold words Time to Race Start pulsed vibrantly in the blue light.

Dr. Gwen Furch proceeded to explain the obvious.

"The object has been studied while on route to this facility. We don't know much, but this is what we do know."

Two suited men pulled the top off the object from a platform they rolled up next to it.

"The blue substance inside, what the recording called *Moronium*, is composed of unknown elements. Well, *mostly* unknown, we did find a bit of citric acid mixed in. We think it's for preservation. The truly amazing thing about it is that it seems to defy physics. When we dipped the tester into the substance. The two bonded and proceeded to rise."

"Rise? Like anti-gravity?" the Colonel asked, nodding along as if he knew what she was talking about.

Dr. Gwen shrugged, "Not so much anti-gravity as an actual *lift*. Propulsion. I guess that conjures the right imagery, though."

Dumas slapped her behind and licked his lips, misconstruing her last sentence as a come-on, "It certainly does, young madam."

"Touch me again and I'll remove your hands, cut off the fingers, coat them in plastic, and sell them as midget dildos on Ebay, Colonel."

"Oh," he said, disappointedly. "Very well."

She cleared her throat and turned the exchange back to the matter at hand.

"At any rate, the effect was rather pronounced. Eventually, the tester was pulled from the soldier's hand. It's now somewhere in the upper atmosphere."

"So the commies figured out anti-gravity?" the Colonel grumbled, chomping on his cigar as if the thought offended him.

"I'm sorry? The commies? What commies?" Dr. Gwen asked, giving the Colonel a sideways look.

Hacker just shook his head and rubbed his eyes in exasperation.

Dumas grumbled with assuredness, "First, the fluoride in our water. Now, the anti-gravity in the air. Commie bastards, they cheated us. Probably want us to slather the stuff all over ourselves so we can fly, then they set it off, and blow us to kingdom come."

"Uh—" Gwen muttered, evaluating the sanity of her superior, "I, uh, well, that's certainly *one* way of looking at it."

"It's the *only* way of looking at it, young madam."

"Stop calling me that."

"Oh. I apologize."

"Of course," Gwen continued. "Another way of looking at it is that it's an alien. Or, at least of alien origin."

"I see."

"And very definitely *not* commies, as you suggest."

"I highly doubt that. Although, if they have women scientists, now, God alone knows what'll happen."

Dumas stared at the goo in a daze, temporarily forgetting he was in the room.

"Colonel?" Gwen asked.

He snapped out of his catatonic state and blinked, "Huh? Yeah, what's up?"

"We think it's of alien origin, Colonel."

Dumas yanked the cigar from out of his mouth and felt

his stomach churn.

"*Beaners*? Goddamn it. No way those Sombrero-wearing *aliens*, as you call them, could get anything into space."

"No, not *Mexican* aliens," Gwen snapped. "I mean, like, proper real aliens. From outer space and stuff."

"You mean like in those films they have now?"

"Yes."

"Sir?" Hacker added.

"What is it now, Heckler?"

"*Hacker*, sir."

Dumas got the wrong end of the stick.

"*Hack her*? How *DARE* you suggest such a thing. This young lady and I have barely known each other two minutes, you vile scoundrel."

"No, Sir," Hacker said. "That's not what I meant—"

"—Ohh, spare me the apology and just speak, you sex-obsessed buffoon."

Hacker breathed a sigh of relief and recollected a nugget of trivia from a bar quiz he had attended last week.

"Mexico actually sent probes into space as early as the late 1950's, Sir."

"Fake news, Hecker. Don't believe what you read."

Hacker gave up correcting Dumas, "I think it's *don't believe everything you read*, Sir."

"That's what I said. Now, Felcher, what can—" the Colonel began but Dr. Gwen cut him off.

"Furch, Colonel?"

Dumas got the wrong end of the stick and grinned, salaciously.

"Well, that's a most generous offer, young lady," Dumas said. "But I think we ought to solve this issue of the blue goo before I suck mine out of your rectum with a straw."

Gwen's jaw dropped, "I beg your pardon?"

Dumas lifted his eyebrows with suspicion, "I'm sorry. Is there something wrong with you?"

"I was about to ask the same question, Colonel."

"What?"

"My name is Furch. Dr. Gwen Furch. Like *church* but with an F."

"That's what I said."

"No, it wasn't."

"Wasn't it?"

"No," she frowned. "And you're not the first to have made that mistake."

Hacker felt the need to come to the doctors defense, before this got out of hand. "Sir, you said *felcher*—"

Dumas held out his hands and grew impatient.

"Yeah, whatever. Would you be so kind as to realign the conversation back to the matter at hand, young lady?"

Gwen blinked and swallowed, trying to fight off the bizarre exchange the pair had found themselves in and pointed at the goo.

"We're relatively certain this is not the work of the, uh, commies. Or the Mexican space agency. We believe this is extraterrestrial in nature."

"Hmm. Perhaps you're right," Colonel Dumas growled, scratching at his jowls. "Better than I thought. So what do they want?"

Hacker and Dr. Gwen turned to the glowing hologram.

"I think they want us to race to the moon."

"But why?" he mused.

"The message referred to *fabulous prizes*, I think, Sir," Hacker supplied.

"But we've already been to the moon."

"I know, Sir."

"Indeed. We beat the commies to it, and they're unhappy about that."

"Yes, Sir."

"So, we don't need to go back. There's nothing up there but a bunch of rocks. Not even a drop of water."

"Actually there's a considerable amount of water—"

"—I mean, it's the sort of featureless cesspit that might

warrant a one-star review on VacationAdvisor, if nothing else—"

"—Colonel?" Dr. Gwen said, trying to steer conversation back to normalcy.

Dumas, once again, snapped out of his daydream and was greeted by a feisty vision of sex and love in the form of Dr. Gwen Furch.

"Yes, darling?"

"Don't call me that, please."

"Sorry," Dumas said. "You were saying?"

Gwen allowed Hacker to explain the last sentence she had tried to get out, "There's a considerable amount of water on the moon, Sir. It's all ice under the surface."

Dumas gave the private a hard stare, "Where are you getting all this fake news, boy? Water on the moon? Are you insane? Next you're going to tell me it's made of cheese."

Dr. Gwen shook her head and brought the conversation back on track.

"Four more objects were sent to major cities around the globe. There were five, but the one headed for Toronto was shot down, and presumed lost. Each of the objects gave the same message as this one, but translated into the cities native tongue. Either this is some sort of very elaborate hoax or we have our first true encounter with an alien species. Either way, we have been handed a substance that could very well change space flight forever. If we can learn what it's made of, and replicate it, we could make space travel cheaper than driving your car."

"But why the moon?" the colonel asked, still stuck on that small fact.

Dr. Gwen threw up her arms, "Because it's far away, probably. Who knows?"

A round man in one of the yellow hazmat suits raced over to the group. He gave the colonel and private a double take. "Dr. Furch. Shouldn't they be wearing hazmat suits?"

"Yes, but I doubt it'd make much difference to their brains." Dr. Gwen said, giving the men a hard disapproving stare before turning back to the newcomer. "What is it, Jeffries?"

The overweight man handed her his tablet.

"We got word from NORAD. They've spotted something out at the Moon."

She flipped through images on the tablet. A cheeky grin crept across her face as she handed the tablet to Colonel Dumas. "You wanted to know why the moon? Well, there you go. Because that's where the finish line is."

Hacker leaned over Dumas's shoulder and saw images taken by satellite.

A hoop-like structure floating several kilometers above the moon' surface took center stage on the screen. It was fairly large, at least large enough to fit a cargo plane through. Multicolored triangular flags on a white cord lined the ring like one would find in a used car dealership parking lot.

A holographic sign above the hoop that read **Congratulations! You've Earned Your Fabulous Prizes!** The text appeared to cycle the same message through several languages.

Jeffries swiped the image to the right.

"We've gotten word from Russia that they are planning to participate. They're gathering their best minds as we speak, Ma'am."

"Gathering their best minds? Between them they must have created a cretin."

Dr. Gwen folded her arms with satisfaction.

"Well there you have it, Colonel. It looks like the other countries are preparing for the race."

Dumas pulled his cigar from his mouth and accidentally crushed it as his face turned red with anger.

"There is no cock-in-bum's way in hell we are letting the Russians get to the moon first. You have unlimited resources, Doctor. Gather your team, and build a spaceship that will crush those dick-chewing commies. I'm leaving my aide, Hocker, here to make reports directly back to me."

Hacker began to protest.

"Uh, that's not exactly what I was saying. We should study the goo. Figure out how to make more. We don't need to race to the Moon to win some amorphous prize. We already have the prize," Gwen said, indicating the object and its magical goo.

"You will win this race if it's the last thing you do, Doctor. This is our chance to prove to the world that we could have won the Cold War if it weren't for that fucking hippie, *chewing-gum-foreheaded* Gorbachev calling it quits before the game even started."

Dr. Gwen raised an eyebrow. "Well, that's certainly one view of events. But, Colonel, we should use this resource to better ends than a simple race."

The Colonel turned to Gwen with rage in his face. The throbbing vein pulsing on his forehead mesmerized her.

"You will use every drop of that stupid alien goo to get us to that finish line first. Do you understand me? Our nation's pride is at stake. Make it happen, Doctor."

"Uh, okay. Yes, Sir. We will make it happen," she said, taken aback by his intensity.

"Good. I expect great things from your team," Dumas said as he turned to his right-hand man. "*Fucker*, keep me up to date."

"Hacker, Sir."

"*Hack her?*" Dumas thought aloud and planted his eyes on Gwen's chest. "Not right now, boy. Given half a chance, I'd only be too happy to do that in celebration if we win."

"Uh, yes, Sir."

Dumas threw Hacker a threatening look and inhaled, "And we *will* win. Won't we, boy?"

"Yes, Sir."

"Good," Dumas turned and marched out of the room,

"Now, fuck off and get winning."

"Yes, Sir."

Hacker and Gwen watched him go, then turned to look at one another.

"Hacker, right?" Gwen smiled.

"Yes. Dr. Furch?"

"Please, call me Gwen."

"Gwen. Cool, cool. Sorry about Dumas, by the way. Not that I'm a proponent about speaking ill of my superiors, but he's a bit spastic in the brain."

"So I see," Gwen chuckled. "So, *Hacker*? What do you know about racing?"

"Well, I come from Minnesota. So, I'm really more of a hockey man, ma'am."

She bit her lip, "Yeah, I'm from Seattle, so I'm more a coffee person. I think it's time to call NASA. You have their number?"

Hacker switched on his tablet, "Nope, but I have Google. Give me a second."

Chapter 7

Burj Khalifa, Downtown Dubai, United Arab Emirates.

"If it pleases you, Sire. They have arrived."

The Sheikh clutched his robes and ignored the advisement from his right-hand man as he peered through the window.

Jumeirah looked especially calm today.

Everything seemed so small from this high up in the mile-long skyscraper. The way it ought to be, according to the Sheikh. If you squinted hard enough, you could make out the tiny ants scurrying in slow motion across the sidewalks.

Humans, of course. But to the Sheikh they looked like insects.

Only slightly bigger were the cars on the roads, marching in single file in all directions along the cascade of roadways.

"I shall be with them in a moment," the Sheikh said.

"Very good, Sire."

Sheikh Yur-Bhutay had seem some terrific sights in his fifty-two years on the planet. His cousin had overseen the magnificent construction of his beloved land. His cousin's cousin, twice-removed on his father's side, owned the building he stood in.

The Sheikh never revealed his first name. Everyone respected him. Lately, he'd fallen on hard times. No one was to know except for his right-hand man, Akram, who walked through the door in search of the Sheikh's visitors. The deal that was about to go down would put him back on top.

Yes, he'd seen everything.

Today, however, proved to be rather different. For something had appeared two days ago, hovering above the fountain outside the mighty tower where the hourly music show took place.

Millions, it seemed, gathered to inspect the alien jewel. Tourists were always welcome in Dubai, and with them their rivers of money. The diamond pierced with a silver javelin had attracted a lot of media coverage, as well.

Akram returned to the room with two men in tow and ushered them to the central oakwood table, "They are here, sir."

"Very good."

The Sheikh turned around to see two men dressed in black. They were being frisked by Akram, the Sheikh's personal security man. When Akram was done, the Sheikh offered them his right hand to shake, which they duly did.

"My name is Sheikh Yur-Bhutay. It is a pleasure to meet with you on this fine day."

"Shalom, Skeikh," the first man said in his eccentric dialect, "Are we to call you Sheikh, or *The Sheikh*?"

"You may address me as *Sire*."

"Ah."

"And, please, if you will, do not use your Jewish epithets with me."

"What?" the man asked.

"Please, we are conducting business."

The Sheikh spotted the briefcase in the second man's hand and licked his lips.

The first pasty-faced man adjusted his pristine collar and cleared his throat.

"My name is Micah Kass," he said as the second man

placed the briefcase on the table. "This is my esteemed associate, Abba Gorin. But you may call him Goldie."

"Goldie?"

The Sheikh made eyes at the second man who'd remained silent the whole time he'd been in the room. Goldie was a mountain of a man. Obviously the muscle of his guests. "Enough with the pleasantries. Open the case, please."

CLUMP — CLUMP.

The two locks pinged out, enabling Goldie to lift the lid and reveal the contents inside the briefcase.

The Sheikh's face lit up a mysterious bright yellow, forcing a shit-eating grin to stretch across his face.

"Oh my. It is magnificent."

"It's a mitzvah, is what it is," Micah said. "I trust you find them satisfactory?"

"I do, I do."

"Then, may we expedite our attention to the transfer of monies for the procurement of our most magnificent wares?"

The Sheikh looked up and squinted at the man, "Huh?" While the Sheikh's English was good, it wasn't pompous good.

"The money," Micah said. "*Sire.*"

"Why are you talking strangely?"

"I believe I am using the English language with propriety, sir," Micah nodded to Goldie to close the briefcase.

Goldie slammed the lid shut and fastened the locks.

CLOMP — CLOMP.

"Alas, if it is your wish to terminate the transaction, we can—"

"—No, no. Please," the Sheikh clicked his fingers at his assistant and waved him over. "Akram. Pay the gentlemen."

"Certainly, Sire."

Akram produced a small device from his pants pocket

and proceeded to punch the buttons with his fingertip.

Micah and Goldie smiled at each other. The transaction seemed to be taking place.

"I, uh, understand that something bizarre is occurring down there?" Micah asked.

"Yes," The Sheik sighed. "It is causing some consternation with those who have seen it. Be careful on your way out that you are not seen."

"Discretion is our byword, my friend."

"I am *not* your friend. We are mere acquaintances," the Sheikh said. "To me, you are nothing but human-shaped wallpaper. A necessary evil with which I must dalliance to save my reputation and good standing in this hallowed land."

"Yeah, whatever you say. Hey, don't worry about it," Goldie rumbled. "We feel the same way. Just pay us our money and let us get out of here."

"The feeling is mutual, rest assured."

Everyone turned to Akram as he fiddled with his device.

"Goddamn thing is taking its time," he said, apologetically.

"Confound it, you cretin," Micah snapped at the man. "How difficult is it to transfer the funds?"

Akram knocked the side of the device against his palm, "I'm trying, I'm trying."

With each knock, the building seemed to shake.

KNOCK-RUMBLE — KNOCK-RUMBLE.

"Whoa," Micah gasped. "Your servant, here, is very strong."

A plume of dust coughed out from the ceiling and rained down around the men's shoulders.

Akram thumped the device against his palm once again, "Just give it a bit of user-friendly love."

THWUCK — KBROOOM.

The room shifted around, followed by an incessant grinding thundering below their feet. The four men stumbled as the building swayed suddenly.

"What in heaven's name?"

The distant sound of screams far below caught their attention. The Sheikh turned to the window with Micah and Goldie. The three men slowly approached it and stared at the ground hundreds of feet below.

Micah's face fell as he saw the diamond spinning around above the water. There was a flood of blue liquid flowing from it to the base of the tower. "What is going on?"

"I do not know."

The light in the room dampened as a batch of blue goo slithered its way across the window.

"Gah," Goldie spat. "What is *that*?"

"Is it raining?" Micah asked.

"Buffoon. It never rains here," the Sheikh barked and turned to Akram. "Have the men been paid yet?"

Akram shook his head and took a deep breath, keeping his gaze fixed on the plush animal fur carpet. A line of blue goo had somehow found its way through the window and slithered up Akram's leg.

"You imbecile," the Sheikh said. "What is going on?"

"Hello!" Akram yelped abrasively, "Welcome to the race!" His voice had changed, while still sounding like Akram.

"I *beg* your pardon?" the Sheikh asked, somewhat disturbed by Akram's robotic answer.

RUMBLE — RUMBLE.

A hurried sound of screaming and concern whirled into the room from the observation deck across the way. Scores of tourists ran in all directions, mostly headed for the elevators.

"In the name of Allah, what is going on—"

Akram lifted his head and faced the Sheikh and the two men. The former stopped in his tracks and looked at Akram's face. His skin had turned blue.

"Akram?"

"After careful consideration, you have been selected to participate in this wondrous event for pride, bragging rights, and fabulous prizes! You have selected your racer, and your crew! "

"Okay, that's just crazy talk," the Sheikh said.

He and the two men ran to the door, scared out of their skin. Akram waved them forward to the relative safety of the corridor.

SLAM — WHUMP.

The doors crashed shut. One by one, the men returned their attention to Akram who'd managed to close the door with only the power of his mind.

"Akram?" the Sheikh tried.

The man dropped the device to the floor and extended his blue, saliva-ridden tongue.

"Only the best of the best will make it in this grueling completion of physical endurance and mental capacity. "

"Uh, Akram?" Micah tried as he snatched the briefcase from the table. "Me and Goldie have nothing to do with this. We can return at a later date—"

"SILENCE."

Akram backed up to the window, only he didn't walk there. His heels slid along the carpet, ramming his shoulder blades against the glass window.

The blue goo spread out into an Akram-shaped mess on the outer window and seeped through the glass, smothering his body.

"Akram?" the Sheikh said. "Have you been *drinking* again?"

"Bwuck-bwuck—" Akram's neck bulged, pushing something up his throat and into his mouth.

FWOPP.

He spat the object into his hands.

Akram, for all intents and purposes, had been possessed and taken leave of his senses. In his palms sat a drool-coated miniature version of the diamond skewer from below.

"In this container is the approved allotment of Moronium for one racer. Please note that if you are caught using more than the approved allotment, you will be disqualified."

"Yeah, okay," Micah said. "You can keep the case. I think me and Goldie will fuck off with the others, now."

The Shiekh reached into his robe and whipped out an AK-47 machine gun. He pointed it at Micah and dared him to leave.

"The fuck you are, asshole," he screamed. "You move another inch and I'll blow you to smithereens. And your little bum-chum, too."

Akram groaned as what felt like an invisible hand of God had grabbed his shirt and hoisted him into the air.

"The goal? The Moon! Ze prizes fabbolos!" Akram said.

The Sheikh swung the AK-47 around and released the safety catch as Akram's body shunted across the room, preparing to launch itself at the Sheikh.

"What in the name of—"

"Yaaargggghhhhhh," the Sheikh screamed as he unleashed a round of bullets after Akram. "What the fuck?!"

RATT — TATT — TATT
WHUMP — SMASSSHH!

Akram crashed through the window, having been tossed through it by the force of the bullets going through him.

WHOOOOSH.

His body rocketed towards the ground.

The small replica dropped to the carpet, falling from Akram's hands in the carnage.

Micah darted over to the diamond on a skewer on the floor and lifted it to his face for inspection.

"What the hell is it?"

The replica buzzed to life and began to speak.

Please race responsibly. This message brought to

97

you by *SHLOOM* - The Official Beverage of Mur'kroznitck.

The Sheikh Pressed the side of his AK-47 against his chest to prevent the vicious gust of wind blowing his robe clean off his body.

Hundreds of civilians ran and screamed as Akram's body plummeted towards the fountain below. The Shiekh noted the alien object that had drawn tourists for the last few days was now gone.

"Praise be to Allah," he muttered.

SCHWOMP.

The ground became a Jackson Pollock of Akram's insides. The concrete at the impact site spider webbing with cracks.

RUMBLE RUMBLE.

The room shunted around like a toaster in a washing machine, clanging and shifting from side to side.

"Hold on to something," the Sheikh screamed.

Micah and Goldie didn't need telling twice. They dived to the floor and grabbed the leg of the table.

"What in damnation is going on?" Goldie squealed like a terrified little girl as the entire building rocked to and fro.

An almighty sound of fire and all-round apocalypse erupted from the ground below, followed by a burst of orange flames.

"What?! We're... *flying?*" Micah screamed. "Sheikh, what is going on around here?"

The Sheikh released the AK-47 and threw himself forward, clutching for dear life at the nearest table leg.

"I do not know."

TUMBLE — TUMBLE — WHIPP.

The gun bounced through the window and into the air as the horizon tilted left and right and eventually sunk below their feet.

WHOOOOOOOOOSH.

LADIES   AND   GENTLEMEN.

MUR'KROZNITCK... HAS... BEGUN!

The windows darkened in a blue hue, and a layer of goo enveloped the entire building.

Those down below by the lake watched as their beloved Burj Khalifa cracked away from the ground and launched into the air like a giant spaceship.

"Oh my God," one woman screamed. "Look at the building. It's—"

"—*Flying?*" her friend finished. "My God!"

"But there's people in that building," another man screamed. "It's one hundred and sixty floors of offices and apartments."

Hundreds of frightened Burj Khalifa occupants thumped their windows all up the side of the structure as it raced towards the sky.

A torrent of fire and smoke raced across the ground, threatening to incinerate anyone unfortunate enough to be standing too close to it.

"Christ, everyone get back," a security guard said. "Get back."

WHOOOOOOOOSH.

The poor souls on the ground had no choice but to watch the Burj Khalifa disappear beyond the clouds and out of their lives for good.

A giant, smoldering crater was all it left behind.

None of the civilians knew what to do next. The woman turned to her friend as the last of the building disappeared from view entirely.

She shrugged her shoulders, "So, *that* happened."

Chapter 8

Freeway Five Estate, Chrome Valley, United Kingdom.

The view was stunning.

As the Ford Mondeo flew through the air, Danny could see the five apartment blocks looming in the horizon, silhouetted by the dusk sun.

Chelsea shifted in her seat, careful not to touch the blue goo seeping in through the partially-opened passenger side window.

"Wow, look at it," she gasped. "I've never seen the valley from this high up before."

"Yeah, man," Danny added. "Look, there's my house."

Baz gurgled and dribbled, still unconscious in the back, "Ughh, my head."

Danny hollered over his shoulder, "Wassup, Baz? You're missing all the good shit."

"Wuh?"

Baz lifted his eyelids and launched into a panic attack when he clocked that the car was flying.

"Fuck man."

"Hehe. Pretty safe, innit?"

Chelsea lifted her legs and planted her knees on the seat. She gripped the backrest and winked at Barry.

"You okay?"

No, Barry was *not* okay. Worse for wear, he gripped the

101

door handle as the grid of streets rolled scores of feet below the car.

"What's happening?"

"Dunno, mate," Chelsea said. "We found this slimy blue shit and it made the car fly."

Barry gulped at the news.

"Wuh-wuh?"

Chelsea turned to Danny, "Man's trippin' out, you know."

"Yo, Baz?"

Barry turned to Danny and tried to stop himself from hyperventilating, "What?"

"Calm yourself down, innit? It's just a flying car. We're cool."

Barry noticed one of their friends was missing and scratched the empty seat next to him.

"Wh-what happened to Stevie, man?"

Danny peered at Barry in the rear view mirror.

"He fell, innit."

"Fell? Fell from what? What happened?"

"Check it out, man. *Bare* weird shit went down at Burger Face. Some fucked up diamond thing tried to thief the car, and made it fly. Don't get no blue shit on you 'coz it makes you fly."

Barry shook his head as his friends chuckled. He couldn't believe a word of what he'd heard.

"Nah, man, I must be still sleepin' or sumthin'."

"Straight up, this is *real* shit," Danny said. "Something about some race. We need to get this ride hidden."

"Where we going?" Chelsea asked.

Danny winked at her and pointed at a semi-detached house on the west side of the valley.

"Home."

Five Minutes Later.

The Ford Mondeo lowered itself towards a small backyard with a climbing frame and paddling pool.

The car's nose drifted down and banked to the left in an attempt to settle onto the ground.

"Fuck's sake," Chelsea squealed. "Danny, man. Calm it down."

Danny pulled the steering wheel back.

"Still getting used to the controls—"

WHUMP.

The four tires crunched through the climbing frame, splitting its moorings away from the ground and bending the structure into a stack of falling cards.

CRUNCH — SQUISH.

"That's your baby sister's thing, man," Chelsea said.

"Yeah, fuck that. We've got a flying car."

Stevie pushed his feet underneath the passenger seat to stop the impact racing up his spine.

"Fuck, slow down—"

KEERRRAAACKKK.

The last of the steel climbing frame structure blasted in all directions and punctured the side of the plastic paddling pool, which puked water across the grass.

WHUMP.

The Mondeo settled into the mud.

Danny turned the key in the ignition and shut off the engine.

"Got the bastard. We're home."

"Safe, man," Chelsea giggled. "Now, what are you gonna tell your mum?"

Danny hopped out of the car and slammed the door shut. He surveyed his back yard.

A bit of a mess stood before him.

A destroyed climbing frame, paddling pool, and grass and mud splattered up the two side fences.

"Shit."

Chelsea stepped away from the car with Stevie, both acutely aware of the blue goo slurping around the entire vehicle.

"Yo," Danny said. "Don't say shit to my mum, okay?"

Chelsea chuckled to herself.

"Mate, it's not exactly inconspicuous, is it? Look at it, if she looks out the kitchen window, she'll see—"

KKERRAAACCCKKKKK.

The roof of the car split apart like a giant snapping a baguette. The crack daggered from the back end of the car to the front, and produced a javelin with a diamond-shaped middle.

"The fuck?"

Danny stepped forward and watched the diamond spin around. A deafening static sound rocked the car as the dashboard came to life.

The screen produced a bizarre frequency and turned up the volume in the speakers.

Congratulations, user. You have been selected to take part in the ultimate SPACE RACE. Please race responsibly.

"That's some fucked up bollocks," Barry said. "What race? What's going on?"

"Dunno, must just be some prank or something," Danny said. "Look, the car's hot, man. I already had some pigs trying to pull me over before I picked you up."

Chelsea looked at the back door of the house. A knocking sound had caught her attention.

"Danny, man. I think your mum is home."

He looked around for answer to his predicament. The car needed disguising, somehow. His eyes trailed around the messy fence and arrived at the deflated plastic that had once acted as a paddling pool.

"Ah, I got it."

"Got what?"

"Help me, man," Danny barked as he picked up one

end of the tarpaulin-like paddling pool plastic. "Get the other end, innit?"

"Cool, cool."

Barry squelched his way to the adjacent end and grabbed the plastic in both hands.

"The fuck you two gay boys doing?" Chelsea asked.

"Move."

Danny and Barry hoisted the ten foot long sheet of drenched plastic and prepared to launch it over the car.

"Okay, on... one, two, three."

WHUP — SLAAPPP.

The plastic launched over the roof and splatted down either side of the car, and the javelin.

Barry wiped his hands on his shirt and observed the final result.

"Mate, it looks like someone tenting in their trousers," he said. "Look, that sharp thing is pushing the thing out like a dick through your trousers."

Chelsea burst into a fit of laughter, "True dat."

"Whatever," Danny said. "At least it's out of—"

"—*Daniel Hook*," came a voice from the kitchen door. "What on Earth do you think you're playing at?"

One by one, Danny, Chelsea, and Barry turned to whoever had just spoken. They knew the voice very well - a raspy tone indicative of decades of smoking.

The attitude behind it signaled to them that it could only be one person.

Deondra - Danny's mother.

"All right, mum?"

"What are you doing out here?"

"Hello, Mrs. Hook," Chelsea offered.

Deondra stormed across the broken patio and placed her hands on her hips with disdain. She eyeballed Chelsea and snorted at her jean skirt and low-cut top.

"Ms. Handler. Up to no good again, I see."

"Sorry, Mrs. Hook," Chelsea said. "I was just helping

Danny."

"Daniel?"

"Yeah, mum?"

Deondra stormed over to the boy and clipped him round the ear, "Don't *yeah* me, you little shit," she yelled. "You are meant to be at school."

"I *was* at school, innit?"

"Oh no *you was not,*" she barked. "Three times, now. *Three.* Three calls from the principal asking where you are, and I don't know what to tell them."

She turned to Barry and Chelsea and fumed.

"I suppose you were out? Gallivanting with these juveniles again?"

Danny hushed his voice and begged the woman to allow him some dignity.

"Tch, *mum.* Allow me, man."

Deondra's face fell. A good and proper accosting was about to take place with two audience members.

"Daniel?"

"Yeah?"

"You call me *man* again and I will ground you for life. No Wifi, no video games. No phone—"

"—Allow me, mum."

"—No!" Deondra continued, finally realizing that the back yard was well and truly totalled. "I shan't *allow* you anything, you insolent little shit—Hold on. What happened here?"

Chelsea thought on her feet and rustled up a lie that she felt might work.

"The paddling pool got hit by lightning, Mrs. Hook."

Deondra turned to Barry for confirmation, "Is this true?"

"Uh. Yes, Mrs. Hook."

"Right. Get this mess cleaned up, you hear me?"

"Yes, Mrs. Hook," Chelsea and Barry said in tandem.

Deondra slapped Danny in the face.

"I wasn't talking to you two, I was talking to this useless mound of flesh and bones, here. Daniel?"

"What?"

"Get this mess cleaned up. You're grounded. And when you and your little friends are finished, you come in for your dinner."

"But mum—"

"—No, no, Daniel. No buts," she finished and walked back to the house, "The only *butt* I will allow is yours getting kicked when we have a little talk later."

"Pfft."

Deondra slammed the door shut, leaving Danny alone with Chelsea and Barry.

"Fuck, man, your mum is a feisty bitch," Barry said.

"Don't talk about my mum, mate."

"She's kinda hot when she's angry."

"I said don't talk about my mum, innit," Danny said. "That was out of order."

Chelsea lifted the edge of the paddling pool plastic and peered underneath. Her face dropped the moment she saw what was going on.

"Uh, Danny?"

"What?"

"Look at this."

***

Panzer Tank Strip Club, West Virginia, USA
32 hrs 47 min Till Race Start

The sun had gone down an hour ago and a brisk chill was in the air.

Bucky stood in the parking lot with a blindfold around his eyes, waiting for something. All he could hear was the hustle and bustle of people chatting, smoking, drinking, and laughing.

"Okay, this is gettin' real old, now," he said. "When can

I take this off?"

"Hold your horses, dude," Satchel's voice bled into his eyes.

VROOOM. VROOOM.

A sound of tires screeched across the tarmac as the truck pulling the camper positioned itself by th wall of the club. An insanely tacky ridiculous William Tell Overture car horn announced its arrival.

"Man, this is awesome," Skeez's voice whirled into Bucky's ears.

"Skeez? Where you at?"

Bucky felt a soft hand creep across his shoulder.

"Bobby Jo?" he asked. "That you?"

"Sure is. I think you're gonna love this," she chuckled.

"Okay, come on, now. Show me."

He felt a pair of finger nails pinch the fabric just above his right cheek.

"Here we go. Check it out."

WHUP.

Off came the blindfold.

"Ta-daa!" Satchel said as Bucky's pupils adjusted to the harsh neon lights emanating from the night club.

A crowd of drunk men in jeans and half a dozen female patrons in skimpy underwear surrounded the defaced camper. Their faces were masks of confusion and revulsion.

Bucky felt exactly the same way and blinked, trying to ensure himself that what he was witnessing wasn't some kind of crass joke.

"Panzer Tank?"

"Yeah-huh," Satchel said. "What you think?"

If you were to ask any reasonably sane person what they thought of the newly sponsored camper sitting proud in the middle of the lot, they'd probably concoct a list of adjectives as follows:

1: Tacky.

2: Crass.

3: Unfit.

The side of the camper had Panzer Tank daubed on the side in big, blocky letters. A drawing of a ridiculously well-endowed teenage girl wearing next to nothing adorned the broadside of the camper.

Bucky's tastes in sponsorship had been well and truly tested. He remained silent as he inspected the back.

A bunch of stars, planets, and the sun had been painted on the back - from the looks of it, by a three-year-old child.

"So, whaddya think?" Satchel asked. "Pretty cool, huh?"

"It's, uh, not what I had pictured in my mind."

Bobby Jo giggled and took out her cell phone.

"Bucky, come on. Let's get a picture."

"Yeah, good idea," Satchel said. "Get a memento of this monumental occasion."

Skeez hit the car horn again, rousing the crowd into a drunken, jubilant stupor.

Reluctantly, Bucky allowed himself to be pushed forward as Bobby Jo held her cell phone out at arm's length for a selfie.

"Smile for the camera, Bucky."

CLICK.

An image of an excited Bobby Jo, Satchel, and Skeez appeared on her screen. Wedged in the middle was a less-than-impressed Bucky sporting a defeated frown.

Woohooo! The crowd cheered and sloshed their drinks around. The girls in the group smiled at Bucky and blew him a torrent of kisses.

"Good goin', Bucky," they said.

"Yeah, thanks."

Satchel noticed Bucky's mood had taken something of an unexpected nosedive.

"What's up, Bucky? You seem down."

"Nothing. It's just that we're going to be racing, and I

kinda had a bit of a NASCAR vibe in my head."

"Yeah?" Skeez said. "Check this beast out with that blue shit, and it'll be faster than an Ethiopian running for fresh water when we start."

"But, fuck," Bucky frowned, unable to contain his disappointment. "I wanted it to look... *cool*, you know?"

"It *does* look cool," Satchel said. "I'm tellin' ya, people are gonna notice you. Notice us."

"Yeah, that's what I'm afraid of."

Bucky folded his arms and accepted his fate. It was too late to go back, now. He'd already done the deal with Satchel. And it was just a matter of hours until that silly countdown thing reached zero back at Bucky's yard.

"I guess it'll have to do," he said. "Let's get this heap of pornographic junk back to my place and get ready."

Skeez clapped his hands together and jumped into the driver's seat of the truck, "Hell yeah. Let's win this thing."

Bobby Jo ran after him and climbed into the back.

Bucky hung his head and muttered, "I'm sorry, pa."

Chapter 9

"Got *dayum*, this thing fancy as hell!" Skeez said as they climbed into the trailer the next morning.

They had hitched it up to Skeez's truck and brought it back to Bucky's place. At first, Bucky wasn't all that sure about using the trailer, especially after seeing Satchel's sponsorship paint job.

The more he thought about it on the trip over, the more he thought about all the things he was *not* going to need to figure out because it was already taken care of in the trailer. Like a place to go to the bathroom, and sleep, and make snacks for the long trip. He just hoped it was nice inside, unlike the rotting trailer Satchel had for a home.

Bucky was not prepared for what he found. The interior resembled a mansion. It was brand, spankin' new. Leather everything, and wood everything else - and if it wasn't wood, or leather, it was chrome.

A curved set of windows lined the front of the trailer above a leather couch. Through the middle, a kitchen stood on one side and the inbuilt dining room table on the other. A leather couch sat beside the door to the latter.

After that was a bathroom on one side, and a shower on the other. The bedroom lay the back-end, with a queen size bed fit for a, well, *queen*.

113

"This is fuckin' nice as dollar beer night," Skeez quipped. "Did you see that shower? It's nicer than mine at home."

He opened the fridge and frowned at the distinct lack of alcoholic beverages.

"Skeez, this trailer is nicer than all three of our houses combined," Bobby Jo said, flopping on the front couch, and sighing at its supple feel.

Skeez turned the stove off and on again. It clicked and a blue flame shot out in an instant.

"I can't believe Satchel is just giving this thing to us."

"He ain't," Bucky said. "He's going to have something embarrassing painted on the side in less than a day, mark my words. We're going to pay for this, but it'll be worth it."

The sound of a beer cracking open brought Bucky back into the room. He turned to see Skeez lounging on the front sofa, sipping on a Rollneck.

"I see you brought your own supply?"

"Damn straight."

"Whatever," Bucky said. "First things first. We need to figure out how that alien goo works. Skeez, come with me. Bobby Jo, make a run down to the liquor store. We're going to be needed some fuel for the work."

"You got it," Bobby Jo chimed and pulled the insides of her extremely short pockets inside out to illustrate. "You have any cash? I couldn't jump over a nickle to save a dime, at the moment."

Bucky pulled his wallet out and handed it to her, "Here. Be sure to grab some snacks too."

"Get some of them flamin' Cheetos. And some sour gummies," Skeez hollered at her as she stepped through the door. "And some corn chips."

"Is that it?" Bucky asked, rolling his eyes.

"And some Ho-Ho's," he shouted.

So far they had lost three spoons trying to scoop the

blue goo into a green Tupperware salad bowl. After the fourth scoop the spoon ripped itself from Bucky's hand and flew off into the sky.

"Fuckin' hell. I'm going to run out of spoons at this rate."

Bucky reached for another spoon from the pile he'd brought from the kitchen.

There were only a few left.

"I think we got enough for now." Skeez said, eying the goo as he held the bowl. His head was to the side so he could keep his cigarette's ash out of the bowl.

"You want me to ash that thing for you?" Bucky asked.

"Naw, s'all good," he mumbled around the filter. "I can take it."

"Okay, so why isn't the bowl floating? The spoons didn't have a problem gettin' gone."

Skeez shrugged, "Maybe because they're made of metal? Like how magnets don't work on clothes."

Bucky shook his head, "Naw, can't be. It worked on Bobby Jo's shirt earlier."

"Fuck yeah, it did." Skeez said, his lips smiling around his cigarette.

Bucky's eyes widened at a stick on the ground, "Holy sheeit. I think I got it."

He poked the end of the stick into the goo then pulled it out and held it up to his face staring at it. After about thirty seconds he let go, and the stick floated upward.

Skeez spat the spent cigarette butt from his mouth, "What the fuck, man? That was a perfectly good stick."

"I think the stuff needs to dry to work. When it's all wet it don't float, but I saw it dry on the stick and that's when it took off."

Skeez regarded the blue stuff in the bowl in his hands. "That kinda makes sense. So, what? We just paint the trailer with this stuff and we got's a spaceship?"

"If we just paint the stuff on then it will float our trailer off and we'll be up shit creek. We need to figure out how to use it. Make it go where we want."

"Well," Skeez said, awkwardly climbing out of the crater while still holding the Tupperware bowl in his hands, "Let's start tying stuff."

An hour later, Bucky and Skeez sat in the rusty lawn chairs on Bucky's porch. The offending bowl of goo sat a few feet away. Scattered around it were the remnants of their tests.

A blow torch.

A jar of mayo.

A drill with a dildo attached (Bucky didn't ask why Skeez had that in his truck, and Skeez didn't say).

Several empty cans of beer they had poured on top of the stuff. A large magnet. And various other things.

Nothing had worked so far.

About the time they were cracking their third beers, Bobby Jo pulled up in her truck. She slid out, giving the boys a good showing of tanned thigh before elbowing the door closed. She hulked a case of beer with a plastic bag of snacks on top across her arms.

"Is that all the beer you got?" Skeez asked, insulted at her lack of planning.

"Naw, there's two more cases. Why don't you get off your lazy ass and get them for me?" Bobby Jo said.

Skeez got up, muttered something, and downed the rest of his freshly opened beer. He tossed the can at the bowl of goo in frustration as he walked past, missing the Tupperware completely.

Bobby Jo put the case of beer on the porch and pulled it open to grab a beer for herself. She plopped down in Skeez's vacated chair, and cracked it open. "How's it going here?" she asked, eying the drill dildo combo with a look Bucky couldn't quite place.

"Frustratingly, I'd say," Bucky grumbled and slouched into the lawn chair. "How was the run into town?"

"Fine."

As she cracked open a cold beer, she scanned the discarded tools scattered across the ground.

"How'd you get on?"

"We're trying to figure out how to make this shit do want we want. We need to figure out how to make it do stuff other than just float."

"Have you tried electric?" Bobby Jo asked, sipping her beer.

Bucky cocked his head, "Uh, no. We probably should have, huh?"

Bobby Jo jumped up and jogged to her truck, passing Skeez as he struggled with two crates of beer stacked one on the other.

"I have just the thing."

She rummaged in the cab of the truck till there was a squeal of delight and she emerged with a black and yellow taser gun.

Bucky sat up straight and raised his eyebrows, "Where the hell did you get that?"

She swaggered back towards them and waved the taser at the sky, "A cop pulled me over the other day. He dropped it when he was layin' across my seat."

Skeez opened a can of Rollneck in his left hand and tipped the froth to the ground, "Why was he layin' across your seat?"

Bobby Jo smiled, "Call it community service."

"Huh?" Skeez finally clocked on to what she had *referred to*. "Ohhhh, I getcha, now. Nice, nice."

"Yeah.

"Lucky-ass cop."

"Uh, guys?" Bucky frowned. "Let's give the taser a try?"

Bobby Jo lined up her shot from about five feet away and squeezed the trigger. There was a snapping sound as two hooks attached to thin wires shot out of the cartridge and buried themselves in the goo.

A clicking sound emanated from the gun as Bobby Jo

held the trigger down, sending thousands of volts of electricity into the alien substance.

At first nothing happened except the goo jiggled in the Tupperware bowl as current passed through it. Just then, the bowl pushed into the ground as if a great weight had been applied to it.

Skeez jumped up and down, as everyone began whoopin' and hollerin'.

"*Gawd daaaayum*. You figured it out, Bobby Jo. Yee-haw," Skeez yelled, sloshing the beer from his can as he did a jig.

Bobby Jo released the trigger and the clicking sound stopped, "Well, *fuck me*. That seemed to work right nice, there."

"That's right! Fuck you, you fuckin' alien goo." Skeez shouted, throwing his can to the ground and stepping up to the bowl. He unzipped his cargo pants, and whipped his shlong out. "Take this, you fuckin' piece of alien shit. No one makes me look the fool for tryin'."

A golden stream of piss spurted out, splashing into the bowl of goo.

"What the fuck, Skeez?" Bobby Jo said, averting her eyes.

"Jesus, Skeez," Bucky snapped. "Exercise *some* decorum, huh?"

"Fuck that," Skeez screamed. "I'll *exercise* this motherfucker with my hot piss. It needs to know who's boss."

The goo vibrated again. This time, it was far more violent. There was a squelching noise as the goo flopped back and forth as Skeez's thick, yellowy urine embraced the alien substance.

"Uh, oh shit." Skeez said, his eyes going wide as his stream of piss weakened down his pants leg.

The goo continued to flop and convulse, then it stopped, settling back down in its bowl.

A big toothy grin split Skeez's his face, "Whew. I

thought it was going to do something crazy, there, for a minute."

At that exact moment the goo flew out of the bowl and directly into Skeez's crotch. It hit him at an incredible speed, doubling the skinny man over as it pushed him across the porch and slammed him ass-first into the cabin.

"Yaaooww," Skeez groaned in pain four octaves higher than normal, "Help."

Bucky ran to his side but didn't know where to grab him. He didn't want to get his hands too close to Skeez's junk.

Before he could decide, Bucky was forced to jump to the side as the goo shot away from Skeez and released him from his crotchal prison.

It hit a tree at incredible speed, cracking the trunk, then rebounding to hit the ground in a spray of dirt. Bucky hit the deck as the ball of goo shot right at him. He got down just in time for the ball to pass over him and crash through the rickety front door.

There were a few minutes of crashes and shattering glass as the ball of goo did its best to destroy the interior of Bucky's cabin.

Finally, in a ripping nightmare crash, the ball shot out of the roof sending a shower of shingles and splintered wood down into the yard. The ball shot into the sky, and was soon out of sight as it streaked upward like a bat out of hell.

"What the actual fuck?" Bucky said, eyes wide.

"Hungggh." Skeez agreed.

"Your piss sent that thing nuclear." Bobby Jo gasped.

"Well, I think that answers the question of how we use the stuff." Bucky said.

"It's a little unpredictable," Bobby Jo said as Bucky returned his behind to the lawn chair.

"Then we'll just have to make it predictable."

"I think I have a few ideas on that front."

Skeez grasped his crotch and rocked back and forth in

the fetal position in some agony.

"Hngggg."

Bucky winked at him and enjoyed his friend's theater of pain. He held up his half-drunk can of Rollneck and offered him an evil salutation. "Exactly, Skeez. Now, stop playin' with yourself and get back up. This spaceship ain't gonna launch itself."

Chapter 10

Khamovniki District, Moscow, Russia.
12 min Till Race Start

Yulia gripped the steering wheel hard.

She leaned towards the windscreen and brushed her silver-haired brow away from her eyes. Her fingers pinched the microphone hovering in front of her chin.

"A. I think it is them," she said in her thick Russian accent. "Get ready."

A voice came into her ear via her headgear.

The one-second delay came from a man in a car parked on the adjacent side of the street.

"Understood, Y. Can confirm package has arrived. Standby"

"Good."

Yulia turned to her associate sitting in the passenger seat - a stern-looking young man by the name of Ivan.

"You ready?"

Ivan lifted his pistol and inspected the side, "I am always ready."

"No funny stuff," Yulia said. "We are out, we get what we want, and we're back in."

"We're going to be rich," Ivan said.

"Indeed."

"What are you going to do with your cut?"

Yulia squinted at the driver of the silver car across the road and gave him the thumbs up, "We have not got it, *yet.*

No time to chat, let us go."

VROOOM.

A reinforced white-and-gray security truck lifted over the road in the horizon, headed straight for Yulia's stationery vehicle.

"A, they are here. ETA twenty seconds. Let's go."

"Understood."

She booted her door open and jumped out, "Go, go, go."

The burly man in the other car exited and swung his machine gun at the approaching truck.

"Get ready."

Andrei focused his attention on the front of the truck, "That's right, *morons*. It is a gun. Now, *come to Daddy*."

Inside the truck, the two security guards flipped their visors and scanned the road ahead.

"Is that *a gun?*"

"Oh shit, no," the driver said. "We must stop."

He slammed on the brakes, forcing the tires to lock dead and screech across the cement.

SCREEEEECH.

"This is dispatch."

"Dispatch, carrier three," came the response. "Please advise."

"Potential security breach," the driver said into his walkie talkie. "We must change route. Standby."

He flicked the talkie off and replaced it on the dashboard clip.

"I do not like the look of this.

Yulia, Ivan, and Andrei sprang into action.

Their faces covered in cloth - unrecognizable. They ran towards the security truck and aimed their weapons at the windscreen.

"Remove your hands from the wheel," Yulia ordered. "Do it."

The frightened driver and his colleague lifted their hands in the air and begged their assailants for mercy.

"Get out of the fucking van," Andrei said. "I won't tell you again."

Both doors of the truck opened, and out came the driver and his colleague with their hands in the air.

"Please, do not kill us," the driver said.

Yulia buried the end of her machine gun in the driver's temple.

"Keys."

"They are in the truck."

"Good."

Yulia waved Andrei over to the opened driver's door. He nodded, climbed inside and took a look around the dashboard.

"We are all set, Y."

"Please, do not take the van," the driver's colleague said. "You do not know what is inside it."

"How much are you carrying?"

The two security men frowned and turned to each other.

Ivan lost his temper and kicked the driver in the back, "Goddamn it, tell us. How much are you carrying?"

"It's not what we're carrying. It is not a matter of how much, but *what*."

"But what?" Ivan asked, confused.

"Yes. We do not kn-know what it is—"

"—Damn it," Ivan screamed as he grabbed the back of the driver's collar and lifted him to his feet.

"P-Please d-don't—"

"—I ask you one time more," he whispered in the man's ear. "You tell us how much you carry or I paint the road with your brains."

The driver's legs turned to mush, forcing his bodyweight to his feet, "I'm telling you, I—"

"—Do not say you do not know—"

"—I do not know—"

KERSPATCH!

Ivan blasted the driver's head clean off his shoulders like a busted watermelon. The bullet rocketed into the sky, taking what little remained of his skull into the clouds.

Ivan turned his attention to the second security man and released the driver's body to the ground.

FLUMP.

"Oh, p-please, no—"

"—What are you doing?" Yulia yelled at Ivan. "That was unnecessary."

"He did not tell us what they have."

"Please," the security man said. "You do not understand."

Andrei booted the back doors open from inside the truck and hopped out.

The left door banged against the side of the truck, revealing a big, black number three stenciled on its exterior.

"I think you'd better have a look at this."

Yulia raced over to join Andrei, leaving Ivan alone to terrorize the poor security man with his shotgun.

"What is it?" she asked.

Andrei pointed into the back and smiled. "We have hit pay dirt."

Ivan slapped the security guard's face and hollered over his shoulder.

"What the fuck is going on?"

"Hold on," Yulia said as she walked around the back of the truck and looked inside.

Dozens of tiny white shafts of light danced around her face, reflected off the object within the van.

"Oh my God. It's beautiful."

"Yes it is," Andrei said."

"Damn it. Tell me, what is it?" Ivan shouted.

"Leave that poor fellow alone and come and see this, Ivan," Yulia gasped. "It is unbelievable."

"Stay here on your knees and do not move or I will shoot you," Ivan said to the security man as he raced over to the truck. "Okay, what is so special?"

"Look."

Ivan got a good eyeful of the interior of the truck.

A giant diamond hovered in the center of the cage, held into place by two javelin ends daggered into the floor and roof.

"A diamond?"

"A girl's best friend," Yulia beamed as she climbed into the car. "Perfect for our wedding."

Andrei looked at the ground. Now wasn't the time to start sending out invitations.

"Please, let us just take it and—"

"—No!" the security guard squealed. "Do not do that. Do not touch it. We do not know what—"

FWUMP.

Yulia's feet stomped into the back of the truck. She held out her gloved hand and caved into her temptation to touch the diamond.

Her fingers moved closer and closer...

"Gentlemen, we *are* rich, now."

Andrei and Ivan had little choice but to watch the woman fall in love with the giant jewel.

She widened her eyes as the stone began to spin around.

"You are very precious," she whispered. "My-oh-my, where did you come—"

Hello!

Welcome to the Race.

The diamond's sudden announcement startled the woman. She lowered her hand and backed up to the doors of the truck.

"It speaks. It speaks."

Andrei and Ivan pointed their guns at the diamond body.

"What the fuck?"

It continued to emit a bizarre voice, caring little of the threat of their weapons.

"What did you say?" Yulia asked.

After careful consideration, you have been selected to participate in this wondrous event for pride, bragging rights, and fabulous prizes!

The security guard picked himself up to his knees and begged the three robbers to vacate the truck, "Get out. It is not safe."

You have selected your racer, and your crew! Only the best of the best will make it in this grueling completion of physical endurance and mental capacity.

"Huh?" Yulia asked. "What physical endurance? What mental capacity?"

Ivan hooked his finger around the trigger and aimed at the monstrosity, "This *thing* is mental in its head."

He fired three shots at the bizarre object.

BLAM — BLAM — BLAM.

The three shotgun shells bounced off the diamond, failing to put so much as a dent on its surface.

"Huh?"

Now, now, *comrade*. Play nice. You don't want to be disqualified, do you?

A fountain of blue goo raced out the opening at the top of the javelin and slimed its way down the beautiful structure, filling the back of the truck at speed like a swimming pool.

In this container is the approved allotment of Moronium for one racer. Please note that if you are caught using more than the approved allotment, you will be disqualified.

"Oh fuck me," Yulia said. "Get out. Get out."

The goal? The Moon!

The Prizes? Fabulous!
The time? Now!

Yulia and Andrei jumped out the back of the truck and raced to the front.

Ivan trained his shotgun on the diamond, seeming to stare into its very soul.

"What are you?"

Yulia jumped into the driver's seat and started the engine.

"Ivan, get out of there."

WHUMP — SCHLUMP.

The two back doors slammed shut, sealing Ivan inside the cocoon of quick-filled blue goo.

"Yulia, my sweet," Andrei said. "We cannot leave him inside there."

Yulia slammed on the gas and lifted the handbrake, "Shut up, darling, and fasten your seat belt."

VROOOOM. VROOOOM.

"Noooooo," the security guard jumped into the path of the truck, thinking the woman would apply the brakes.

She didn't. Instead, she just sped up.

BLAAARREE.

"Move out of the way, you shit—"

"—Wait. *Stop.*"

The security guard trailed into the path of the truck and held out his hands, desperate for her to stop.

"Nooooo—"

KER—SPLAAAAATCH!

Yulia and Andrei turned away as the front of the truck smashed into the security guard, splattering his guts and flesh up the windscreen.

"Ugh," Yulia said. "Cretin."

The truck shot off down the road.

BAM — BAM — BAM.

A thunderous banging came from the compartment wall behind Andrei's shoulder. He turned around and listened closer.

"I think it is Ivan."

A muffled cry of desperation came from the back of the truck as it joined the freeway.

"Help. Help me," Ivan's muffled cries rumbled through the compartment wall and across the two front seats.

"We need to pull over," Andrei said. "We cannot leave him there."

"No. We must not stop."

Yulia hit the gas and turned into the fast lane.

"This vehicle is too hot. I'm sure he can look after himself, he is a big boy after all."

The goop had filled the back of the truck. Ivan was now waist-deep.

The blue stuff kept frothing from the diamond and showed no sign of abating.

"Please, Yulia," he begged as he banged on the wall. "I am going to be submerged in this... *stuff*."

No response.

He released his already-submerged shotgun and watched it sink to his feet in the pool of blue goo.

The diamond revolved around one hundred and eighty degrees and appeared to stare into Ivan's soul.

"Wh-what *are* you?" he asked as if witnessing the arrival of the second coming.

The diamond slowed down and shimmied.

Please race responsibly.

Then the voice went silent, and a timer appeared in the hologram reading 9 minutes 32 seconds. **Time to Race Start** appeared above the timer as it began to tick down by the second.

"A race? What race?" Ivan asked as the top level of the goop threatened to reach up past his face.

"Arrgghhhhh."

GLUB — GLUB — GLUB.

Ivan sank into the sticky mixture and thrashed his

limbs around. Wading through the substance proved to be as fruitful as trying to swim through jam.

Ivan's lungs wanted air. His mouth yawned open and took in a chestful of blue goop.

"Gwwurgghhh."

Blindly, he kicked his left foot forward and hit the trigger of his shotgun.

BWULP.

The bullet had no difficulty careening through the thick liquid and chewing through his groin.

BWLATCH.

"Gwuurrr—"

His eyelids panged open and his eyeballs crossed together - his ass well and truly drowned. A thick streak of black blood waded out from between his legs and darkened the mixture as his body slumped to the ground.

The diamond revolved once again on its javelin-like skewer.

This message brought to you by *SHLOOM* - The Official Beverage of Mur'kroznitck.

Yulia sped past the other vehicles on the freeway and glared up at the moon in the night sky.

"He's gone quiet back there."

"I know," Andrei said. "Perhaps he has figured out what that blasted contraption actually is?"

"I wouldn't count on it, darling. The man is several sandwiches short of a picnic."

Yulia released the gas, but saw that the speedometer climbed higher.

"What? What's going on?"

"What is wrong?" Andrei asked.

"The counter says we go faster, but I am trying to slow down—"

KERRAA-AAA-THWWAAMMMM—MM.

The truck's back doors swung open and released an ocean of blue goo onto the freeway, forcing the security truck faster along the freeway.

The tires lifted away from the ground and pushed the vehicle up at a forty five degree angle.

"We are lifting!" Yulia said. "Darling! We are lifting."

"Good," Andrei said. "It means police cannot catch up to us."

"The father-fingering air force will not be able to catch up to us if we keep going like this!"

The car in front screamed towards the truck.

"Shiiiiiiiiit!" Andrei squealed like a girl as he clung to the overhanging bar in the passenger side.

"Darling, *please*," Yulia quipped, taking control of the situation as best she could. "Try to be a man."

"I am, I am—"

CLIP — BWUMP.

The two front tires bopped off the roof of the car in front, forcing the back end of the truck to expel everything but the diamond onto the road.

Ivan's corpse rumbled across the floor and bolted onto the freeway.

WHOOOSH - SCHWUMP.

The body hit the windscreen of the car the truck had flown over, causing it to screech and spin around to a halt.

Dozens of speeding cars slammed on their brakes - but it was too late.

One by one, each car slammed into the back of the overtaken vehicle, pulverizing it - and Ivan's body - to pieces.

Yulia rolled the window down and poked her head out. She laid eyes on the carnage dozens of feet below as she and Andrei rocketed towards the Moon.

She could see that the blue goo was still attached to the back of the armored car. A long string if the stuff hung between them and the freeway below. As she watched the string thickened and the blue goo began to race back into the truck.

SWISHHH -BRRRRRR.

The communications radio sprang to life on the dashboard.

LADIES AND GENTLEMEN.
MUR'KROZNITCK... HAS... BEGUN! **Please enjoy the complementary life support.**

"What the fuck is going on?"

Yulia yanked the driver door handle in an attempt to escape. Andrei grabbed her shoulder and pinned her to her seat.

"What do you think you're doing?" he snapped with sarcasm, "*My sweet?*

"We need to get out," she squealed. "I do not know if you have noticed, *darling*, but we are *flying*."

"So, what? You will jump to your death?"

Yulia took a deep breath and decided that the drop would kill her. They were far too high to escape.

"What do we do now?"

"I do not know."

The radio volume dialed up and caught their attention.

You want the moon? "You got it", as you Earthlings say. Ten minutes until departure from Earth's atmosphere. Good luck, and may the best team win.

"What best team win?" Yulia screamed and thumped the steering wheel. "What about Earth's atmosphere?"

"Uh, my sweet?" Andrei said, clinging to her arm.

"Yes, darling?"

Andrei pointed to the window.

HERE... WE... GO!
The race has begun. Good luck.

Yulia saw a film of blue goo crawling over the surface, encasing the truck in a thin film of the stuff. She glanced at the rear view mirror. All the goo had been sucked back onto the truck from the freeway.

"Where the hell is this thing taking us?" she yelped.

Andrei pointed at the big hunk of white cheese hanging in the night sky like a bad smell.

"I think we are going *there*."

"You think *what*?"

The moon seemed to smile at them, daring them to visit it.

Yulia looked through her window to see in the distance a colossal, skyscraper-shaped *building* racing alongside them.

Andrei's jaw dropped the moment he laid eyes on the flying structure.

"My sweet?" he asked, disbelieving his very eyes.

"Yes, darling?"

"Is that... *the Burj Khalifa*?"

"Huh?"

Yulia pressed her hands over his lap and took a good look through the window.

"Jesus *fucking* Christ," she gasped. "Yes, it is. I think it is."

The security truck blasted through the sky and into the clouds, racing next to the skyscraper.

Chapter 11

Bucky slid into the stained lazy-boy recliner they had bolted to the floor of the camper tailer. The curved windows around the front couch served as a windshield once the couch had been removed.

Skeez, in a rare flash of brilliance, had moved the couch around behind the lazy-boy, which meant there were multiple seats looking out the front of their spaceship, theater style.

Bucky reached out to the "controls" they had rigged up, and tried to get acquainted with their set up.

It turned out Bobby Jo had served her community service early quite a few times.

At least six of them - probably more.

She had a small stockpile of six tasers in her truck and Bucky had the brilliant idea to use them as their steering components.

The tasers were attached to a 2x4 that rested across the Lazy-boy's arms. Six pistol grips that, in theory, should be able to control the camper trailer.

The thin wires snaked all through the camper, and fed into holes they had drilled through the walls, sealed with some leftover tar Bucky had from patching his roof.

"How's it feel, racer boy?" Bobby Jo asked, leaning over the back of the recliner.

She had gone home and grabbed some things, so she was back in one of her tied-off red and black flannel shirts and daisy dukes.

Bucky considered the six pistol grips, "Not exactly what I pictured. I was thinking more a joystick."

"I'm holding your joystick right here," Skeez shouted from the bathroom. He grunted over the distinct sound of shit hitting the toilet water.

"The only ship that stick is flying is the butt plug you keep tucked up in yo' ass," Bobby Jo yelled back at him.

Silence befell the camper as they all thought about what she'd just said.

"Sorry, Bobby Jo. It was a good attempt, but that don't make no sense," Skeez said from the crapper in a vain effort of sympathy.

Bucky chortled and adjusted his hat.

"I have to agree with Skeez. I mean, if the butt plug is the ship, how would his dick control it?"

Bobby Jo conceded.

"Yeah. If anything, *he* would be the spaceship and the butt plug would be the passenger."

"What?"

Bobby Jo thought aloud.

"Well, think about it. If you want to control someone like Skeez, you would do so with his dick. So, that would make the butt plug a passenger in the ship that is Skeez, who is controlled by his own joystick."

"I'm uncomfortable with this conversation, now." Skeez said, quietly before there was another watery plop.

"Me too," Bucky said.

Bobby Jo cleared her throat, "So, how does it feel to be in the captain's chair?"

"I've got a captain's log for you," Skeez yelled, followed by another splash and a chuckle.

"Just ignore the retard back there," Bucky said as he switched between grips and pretended to fly the ship. "It ain't bad. I think Yonder's gonna work just fine."

"Yonder?" Bobby Jo asked. "What's that?"

"New name for our vehicle. *Yonder*."

"Yonder, huh? I like it."

"Good."

"I guess now all that's left is to get the space goo slathered on," Bobby Jo said.

"Yup. I guess so. No time like the present," Bucky turned to the bathroom, "Yo, Skeez. Get your stinky ass out here. We're paintin' the goo on Yonder, now."

"Paintin' Bobby Jo's breasts with my goo," Skeez yelled. "What kinda faggy name is *Yonder*, anyhow?"

"You'll figure it out, my friend."

Bucky climbed out of the recliner and waved at Bobby Jo.

"C'mon. He can catch up to us later."

Bucky jerked the thick tow chain to make sure it was secure.

He figured it was good to go.

They had decided the best thing to do was chain the camper down to the four largest trees in Bucky's yard, and hope that the goo wouldn't pull them out of the ground before they could get the trailer painted with the weird blue stuff.

Bucky had painted 'Yonder' across the front fender - an appropriate name, given that the 'ship' would be traveling to the great *yonder* very soon.

Bobby Jo stood on top of the trailer with just her bare feet for grip. She used a long-handled roller to coat the aluminum finish with a glossy translucent blue.

She needed to work fast so that the roller wouldn't dry out, forcing whatever it covered to float off before the job was done. So far she was doing a bang up job - nearly half the top had a coat of the alien stuff on it.

"Lookin good, Bobby Jo," Bucky yelled, meaning it both ways.

She gave a wink and blew him a kiss before going back

to work with the pole in her hands.

"I'm doin' all the work here, you know."

Skeez, on the other hand, was having a little more trouble. He worked his way down the side of the camper with a brush and the green Tupperware bowl.

He'd lost three brushes when he would take breaks to drink beer. Worse, he'd lost three beers to the sky when he accidentally got goo on the cans.

Bucky glanced at the hologram timer above the thing spiked into his yard, "Shit. Get'er done, Skeez. We don't have much time left."

"I'm workin' on it, man."

Skeez sat his beer down and reached for the floating brush that was now twenty feet in the air.

"C'mere, you little runt."

As Skeez cursed at the floating brush, his can of beer lifted off behind him.

Bucky made for the shed that doubled as his workshop. "Keep at it guys. I have an idea I want to try."

Rummaging through old milk crates full of car parts, Bucky finally found the one he was looking for. He grabbed a 2x4 and a decades-old coffee can full of nails.

And a hammer.

He found a spool of wire behind a broken wooden crate with four old tires in it, and threw it in the milk crate along with everything else, and dragged his haul out into the yard.

"What the hell are you doing?" Skeez asked, slapping more goo on the trailer.

"I was thinking about power."

"Oh, yeah?"

Bucky wrestled a couple of old car alternators out of the crate.

"Uh-huh. We're gonna need to do something to keep the lights on while we're up there. Plus, I think it might help with a booster of sorts."

Skeez dropped his new brush in the blue goo, and scratched his balls.

"Skeez, be careful you don't get any of that blue spunk on your balls."

"Never mind that. You know this thing don't have an engine, right?"

Bucky rolled his eyes, "I'm aware, Skeez. But you don't need one to make these work. They just need to spin. Bring that bowl of blue shit over here. I want to give this a try."

Bucky nailed the alternator to the board so that the belt wheel faced him. He then cut two lengths of wire and attached them to the hook ups.

Skeez sauntered over and fished a fresh Rollneck from his pants, "You know what the hell you're doing?"

Bucky shot him a frown, "Yeah, I know what I'm doing. *I think.*"

"I hope so."

Skeez watched Bucky add a few wires here and there, then went back to the shed for a further rummaging.

"Ahh, I know I got one here, someplace. Aha."

Bucky found a car battery and attached it to the alternator, and sat back to make sure he hadn't missed anything.

Satisfied, he reached for the Tupperware bowl.

"Give me that splodge stuff."

Skeez gladly handed it over and used his free hand to crack open the beer. "Why are you hooking up a battery?"

Bucky slapped an inch of blue goo onto the pulley with his brush.

"It needs power. This should work," Bucky said as he unzipped his pants.

"Whoa, dude! What the fuck?" Skeez said, spinning away from Bucky's freed penis.

"Don't flatter yourself. You're not my type."

Bucky pushed his muscles till a little spurt of piss shot out and splashed against the alternator.

"God dammit. Always the way, huh? When you need to piss, you can't, and when you don't—"

"—You can?" Skeez finished.

"Heh, yeah. Hold on," Bucky said, grunting a little more piss out.

"Uh, I'd rather not hold yours."

SPRIISSHHH.

Success - this time, a healthy jet of orange, beer-infused pee hit the pulley.

Skeez turned back around when he determined it was a cockless view once again, "Okay, it's been a second. You done pissin', yet?"

Bucky frowned. "Huh. I thought that would have worked. I should have…"

He was cut off when the pulley began to shake. It stopped shaking for a second before rotating slowly counterclockwise.

Then, in a sudden move, it reversed direction and spun like it was running from the devil himself. A whine of ball bearings began to emanate as the pulley spun faster and faster.

"Woohoo!" Bucky whooped, jumping up and down. "It fuckin' worked."

Skeez took a few steps back. "What the heck? How's it doing that?"

"Remember when you pissed in the bowl? How it reacted so violently? Well I figured why not make it work for us?"

Skeez unconsciously rubbed at his still-bruised crotch, "Yeah, I remember. How can you tell if it's producin' power?"

Bucky picked up the two wires attached to the leads and held them close together. A blue arc of electric snapped between them.

"We're in the power business, now. This is going to be great."

Skeez dipped the corner of the can in the goo.

"Whatever, man. I'm going to finish painting this stupid alien jizz on the trailer."

He tossed it as he sauntered his way back to the camper. The can never hit the ground, instead it arced down then took a sharp turn upward before it had the chance to hit the ground.

"Heh. This stuff is pretty useful."

"Power?" Bucky asked from the command lazy-boy.

Bobby Jo looked at the half dozen spinning alternators nailed to the kitchen counter. "Check."

"Beer?"

"Check."

"Snacks?"

"Check."

"Space jizz?"

Bobby Jo shrugged, none-the-wiser at the command, "I mean, we painted it all on the outside. So, *check*, I guess?"

"Uh. Toilet paper?" Bucky asked, quickly running out of systems that needed checked.

Skeez leaned into the small bathroom, "Check."

"Okay, awesome. I guess we're ready to go. Just need to wait till the countdown reaches zero. How much time is left?"

Skeez looked up at the ceiling. They had dug out the spear with the diamond in its center out of the crater, and failing to find a good place to store the nearly fifteen foot object, they had duct taped it to the ceiling. The blue hologram was now flat against the ceiling. "It says we still have a few hours to go."

"How many?" Bucky asked.

"Uh, twenty six."

Bucky performed a slow calculation in his head. His two chums watched on, prepared for some kind of genius revelation.

"That's, like, one full day?" Bucky said. "Yeah, like a whole day. I thought there was only a few hours left this afternoon?"

Skeez shrugged and flopped into the booth.

"What can I tell ya? Don't shoot the messenger. It says twenty six."

"Huh. Well. You guys want to fly over to the strip club and show Satchel what we did? We should probably get some practice flying in anyway."

Bobby Jo and Skeez looked at one another, the enormity of of their endeavor sitting in hard.

"I guess that's not a bad idea," Bobby Jo said.

Bucky squeezed the trigger of the taser that had a piece of masking tape that had 'DOWN' written on it.

"Okay. I'm going to hold her down. You two unhook the chains."

The camper suddenly dropped a few feet, bouncing on the tires, and sending Bobby Jo tumbling to her ass.

"Oww. Be careful, Bucky."

"Sorry. I guess the controls are a little *all-or-nothing*."

Unimpressed, Bobby Jo brushed her ass as she climbed to her feet, "If it's gonna attack us like that, I'm happy with the *nothing* part."

Bucky snorted and rubbed his hands.

"Okay, get those chains free. Let's take this *sumbitch* out for a spin."

Chapter 12

Unknown Location: Somewhere on the Moon

A particularly massive spacecraft *thing* that looked like a pair of chrome wings attached to a metallic ball sack hovered a quarter mile above the Sea of Tranquility.

Its steadiness above the moon was eerie.

You could have sworn it was attached to an invisible pole sticking right out of the ground, it didn't move even that much.

The sunlight reflecting off the moon's surface glared over the beautiful, pristine windshield on the front of the vessel. To its left, a giant ball of blue and green reflected off the surface.

***

A giant alien with twenty-five tentacles stood at the flight deck, ogling the planet Earth from inside the ship.

The interior was beyond futuristic - the likes of which no human had ever seen before, which makes describing the fucking thing really difficult.

The walls were a dark gray. So dark, in fact, that they were almost black. The occasional strip lights indicated where the walls met the ground.

The alien being placed two of its twenty-five tentacles on its hips and tilted its head.

"It is time. They've left."

He (presumably it was male) turned around and nearly smacked the flight deck with its tentacles.

"Shit."

The alien's name was Arg-Ned. A big bastard of an alien. He stormed over to the central command table, threw his fifth tentacle forward and extended a cuticle.

"Gentlemen and ladies. The race has begun."

BOP.

His cuticle hit a button on the panel, forcing a 3D projection of Bucky and his team rocketing through Earth's atmosphere.

Arg-Ned spoke to the four other aliens sitting around the table.

"This is my team. Observe."

Bwip.

Yonder, Bucky's camper - with the name *Panzer Tank* scrawled across the side - flew across the stars.

"I believe my team will win," Arg-Ned said.

An especially ugly motherfucking alien to Arg-Ned's right leaned forward on the table with twelve of its tentacles and used one of them to swipe the image.

"Arg-Ned?" he said.

"Yes, Bar-Fys?"

Bar-Fys scissored his cuticles and brought up an image of Danny, Chelsea, and Barry in the Ford Mondeo.

"My team."

"What odds did you take?" Arg-Ned asked.

"4-1," Bar-Fys said. "These guys are mean fuckers."

"They had better not cheat."

"I'm sure they won't—" Bar-Fys said before finishing his sentence, his attention drawn to another alien sitting at the far end of the command console. "Thum-Kramp?"

The dark green version of the alien looked up from his lap, pretending not to have been caught fiddling with himself.

"What?"

"Your team is about to leave," Bar-Fys said. "Stop

playing with your parts and pay attention."

"Sorry."

Thum-Kramp clicked his cuticles and brought up an image of Tempura-Four, sitting on the launchpad. The time for the race to start had come and gone, but there was no crew so the Moronium had not started the engines yet.

"Massive technology," Thum-Kramp said. "My team will win."

"I don't think so, they will be coming from behind." said the feminine, pink alien sitting to his left. Her name was Gwar-Gull, and appeared to be the less-threatening of the bunch.

"True, but as far as I can tell they are the only ones using an actual spaceship."

Gwar-Gull fluttered all twelve of her eyes and yawned, forcing her vagina-shaped lips out and producing a gust of stale womb into Thum-Kramp's face.

"Eurgh, that's disgusting."

"I'm sorry, I'm just tired of you boys fighting all the time," she said. "Besides, my team will win. Look."

SCHWIP.

Her tentacle slapped through the holographic image and displayed the Burj Khalifa rocketing through space.

"Mmm. Big, juicy, very solid. A giant mass," Gwar-Gull said. "Surely my team will win. Many, many participants."

"Many *piss-ants*," the last of the five aliens said.

Dick-Lyss sported a pair of cool shades over his sloppy slit for a face which covered *most* of his six eyeballs.

"Observe, my team," he said, revealing a live 3D holographic feed of the security truck containing Yulia and Andrei. "I understand that this part of the planet contains some of the most ruthless and mean motherfuckers of all their kind."

WHUMP.

Arg-Ned slammed five of his tentacles on the desk, forcing the others to jolt to attention.

"Silence."

Arg-Ned appeared to be the leader, by all accounts. The others knew it.

"I don't give a shit what odds you got. It's who wins that matters. Watch my guys, here. They are far more thorough."

He splayed his tentacles open to produce a giant fifty-foot-wide rendition of Bucky and crew's pre-flight checks.

Bucky shuffled in the lazy-boy and cleared his throat. "Power?"

Bobby Jo watched the six alternators spin from the kitchen counter. "Check."

"Beer?"

"Check."

"Snacks?"

"Check."

"Space jizz?"

Arg-Ned swallowed, embarrassed, and caught Gwar-Gull's eye.

"Space *Jizz*."

Her twat-shaped hole fanned out like strings of paper attached to a cooling fan.

"Come here big boy. If you lose, I get to suck you dry."

"Shut up."

Arg-Ned dropped into a bad mood. He folded half of his tentacles across his body and walked back on the remaining, unfolded tentacles.

He lifted a small red, Mars-like globe with his tentacle and stared into it. "Fabulous prizes."

"Fabulous prizes," the others gurgled in alien snot.

Arg-ned whipped the rendition of the red planet away from his tentacle.

"May the best team win."

Gwar-Gull, Bar-Fys, Thum-Kramp, and Dick-Lyss murmured amongst themselves in agreement.

"And may the losers *fucking die*," Arg-Ned finished, as if laying out the stakes right at the mid-point of a sci-fi movie.

Chapter 13

Freeway Five Estate, Chrome Valley, United Kingdom.

Danny marveled at the newly reformed Mondeo. "Shit, man. It's all, like, brand new."

The dashboard radio screeched to life.

Your Racer has been reformed to accommodate your team. Please take your seats and be prepared for takeoff in thirty-six minutes.

Barry's eyes widened.

"What the fuck?"

A slick of sweat rolled down his brow. He looked like he was about to vomit.

The Mondeo remained roughly Mondeo-shaped. The roof had been split open, allowing a new higher roof to form where the javelin had been. It looked like there was just enough room to stand in the back seat.

"Yo," Chelsea said, as she squinted at the new design, "Kinda looks like that ride the Pope had, yeah?"

"The Pope?" Danny asked, confused.

"Yeah, the Popemobile. I seen it. A picture of it on my mum's dresser," Chelsea thought aloud. "But this one's blue and not as *gay*."

Barry looked like he was about to run.

"Ain't no way I'm getting back in that thing."

The team has been chosen. All participants are registered. Failure to participate will disqualify the

team, and racer will be repossessed.

Barry and Danny's eyes met.

The former saw the determination in latter's gaze. He needed to run, and do it now.

Unfortunately for Barry, Danny knew what a cowardly shit his friend was and had anticipated him running. So it was that Danny made the first move.

He launched himself across the gap just as Barry began to turn, and tackled him to the ground.

"Allow me, man. I ain't getting in that messed-up ride."

Danny flicked his blade out and pressed it at Barry's throat, "Oh yes you *is* getting in that ride. Swear down."

"Swear down?" Barry stuttered with fear.

"Flying car, innit? You wanna ruin a fuckin' flying car just 'coz you're a coward, mate?"

"Nar, man."

"So, no more gay chat, yeah?"

Barry froze still, not wanting his throat slit, "Y-Yeah, safe. T-Take it easy, man."

"Ugh, Are you two gonna kiss or sumfin'?" Chelsea said, rolling her eyes. "Hey, Barry. Bad man's fuckin' bottling it, is it?"

Danny rolled off Barry and pocketed his blade, "Nah, batty boy's changed his mind. He's coming with."

"So, what now?" Chelsea asked

"Now, we get ready for the race. Innit? Go to the Paki shop and take Baz with you. Get some stuff for the race, yeah?"

"Like what?" Chelsea asked.

"I dunno. Fizzy Blue Panda Pop," Danny spat. "Proper snacks and 'ting. Sugar. Crisps 'n' sweets. Keep us goin', innit?"

"Cool, cool."

Danny frowned at the back door to the house and the fight he knew was waiting for him.

Barry and Chelsea started down the drive when Danny yelled after them, "I swear down, man. If you ain't back in time to take off I'mma fuckin' open you up."

He waved the blade at them, threatening to cut them.

"Fuckin' *chill*, mate," Chelsea said with a wink. "We'll be, like, five minutes."

***

Panzer Tank Strip Club, West Virginia, USA
20 min Till Race Start

"Pull up."

WHOMP.

The camper bounced once then again before sliding sideways to a stop in front of the newly christened Panzer Tank Strip Club. The camper rocked, sending anything that wasn't bolted down skittering across the floor.

"*Fuck.* I think I shit in my pants a lil' bit," Skeez groaned from under the kitchen table. He had started in the booth seat, but the rough landing forced him to the floor.

"How would you be able to tell? You smell like shit all the time," Bobby Jo said, holding onto the arm of the couch behind Bucky's recliner.

"I resemble that statement, Bucky," Skeez groaned.

"I think you mean *resent.*"

"Yeah, that too."

Bucky could barely contain his excitement - the ship had flown better than he ever imagined. The controls were a little crude for fine-tuned flying, but he figured there'd be enough room to maneuver in space

"That was awesome."

Skeez crawled out from under the table.

"It was pretty amazing, if not completely *bowel-emptying-ly* terrifying."

Ten minutes later, they showed off the ship to Satchel. A ragtag group of women with little more than panties on along and a few men you wouldn't want to find yourself in a dark alley with had congregated around the ship.

"Pretty fuckin' sweet, man. How's she fly?" Satchel asked, sipping his Rollneck, before sucking down half a cigarette in one go.

"A little hard on the ass." Skeez said.

"Why are you always talking about ass?" Bobby Jo asked.

Skeez shrugged, "It's what connects us all. Everybody poops, Bobby Jo. Everybody poops."

"Gross."

"When do you leave?" Satchel asked, a cloud of smoke billowing out of his mouth with the words.

"About twenty-six hours from now."

"How y'all figure that?"

"It's what the countdown says," Bucky said.

"So, y'all have plenty of time before you launch?"

Bucky shrugged and looked at the sky, "I guess so. I just want to get out there."

Satchel finished his cigarette. In a surprise move, he didn't immediately light another, "I hear ya. Speaking of some time and ass."

"Gross. No one wants to fuck you, Satchel," Bobby Jo said.

He turned and glowered at her, "I ain't talking about fuckin' no one. I need to take a shit. And I ain't even seen the inside of this baby yet. Time to christen the throne."

Satchel rubbed his hands together like he was trying to start a fire.

"Too late." Skeez said, with a smile.

Satchel frowned, "Well, I'm still checking it out. Why don't y'all go inside and get a drink while I'm taking a dump?"

Panzer Tank was everything one would expect from a strip club tucked away in the mountains of West Virginia. Dark, a slight smell of mold, a less slight smell of fish, and women whose use-by date for stripping expired decades ago.

To the forty-something-year-old behind the bar, the job was nothing but a paycheck.

"The fuck y'all want?"

"Kojack, woman," Skeez said. "Bring on the *Rollneck*."

"Free drinks, and you order the same thing we have on the camper?" Bucky asked.

"What can I say? I like what I like."

"I'll have a whiskey," Bucky said to the woman.

"Vodka cran," Bobby Jo said.

"Ooo! Vodka cran? Gettin' fancy are we?" Skeez asked, taking a swig of the beer the bartender slid his way.

"Get fucked, Skeez," Bucky said.

Skeez puffed his bare chest out so he could rest his elbows on the bar behind his back.

"Way ahead of you there, my friend."

Bobby Jo squinted at a saggy-boobed woman greasing herself around the stripper pole. N.E.R.D's *Rockstar* played at a full volume through the rickety old speakers, enabling the elderly woman to dance in time to the music.

"Hey. Ain't that your mom on stage?" Bobby Jo asked Skeez.

"Ah, *fuck*," Skeez frowned, registering the stripper's mole-ridden face. "Yeah. That's her signature move. She's still got it going on."

Bobby Jo and Bucky stared at Skeez as he watched his mother dancing up a storm for a few guys in overalls.

"The fuck is wrong with you?" Bucky asked.

"What?" Skeez shot back a little too forcefully. "It's an honest living, ain't it?"

"It's your mom. Why are you watching?"

Skeez shrugged, "I can appreciate her without it being weird."

"I'm pretty sure that's the definition of *weird*, Skeez."

"Nar, Bucky. See, I got this ability to look at stuff. It's called disassociation or some shit. I got this button in the back of my brain."

Skeez mimed the flicking of a switch behind his ear.

"Whoop. Just like that. Turn it off, and I can enjoy whatever it is without it being weird."

Bucky chuckled and shook his head. "Like your mom whoring it up for money-less drinkers?"

Skeez chuckled and shuffled his hips in time to the music. "Shit, yeah. She's got it goin' *on*."

"I think you're confusing this *ability* with the prognosis from the infirmary, you retard."

"Retard?"

Skeez scanned the room to find sets of eyeballs from the patrons looking at him for a response.

"Fuck you, man," Skeez spat. "I'm going to go find some tacos that need supremed."

He pushed himself away from the bar and headed over to a group of strippers.

"*Supremed?*" Bobby Jo said.

"Add sour cream," Bucky said, apologetically.

Bobby Jo considered that as she took a sip of her drink. "He's a real shit, isn't he?"

Bucky took a sip from his drink. "Yup. Though, that's a bit unfair on *genuine* shits."

Ten minutes later, Skeez passed by with a stripper on his arm.

"Hey, Bucky. I'm going to show my friend, here, the ship. Be back in a minute."

"Hey, man," Bucky winked at the octogenarian's botox-riddled face and nodded at Skeez. "What's her name?"

"Who cares?"

"It's Candy," the woman said over the music.

Bucky chuckled.

"Is that all the longer it's going to take? I figured with how tight you keep that ass of yours it'll take her at least that long to get her dildo in there."

"Fuck you," Skeez said and turned to Candy. "I don't like butt stuff, by the way."

"Tee-hee," Candy giggled. "I don't mind if you do, honey."

"Nah, I ain't gay. Ain't ever been with no man before."

Candy snorted, failing to concentrate on the conversation for more than two seconds, as she and Skeez walked arm-in-arm to the exit.

"I can't believe that guy actually got a woman to follow him to a secondary location of her own free will."

"He's got a way with the ladies. For some reason. Honestly, I don't get what they see in him."

"An early death and whatever remains of his estate going their way, I guess."

"Yeah, I guess."

"Are you excited to get up there?" Bobby Jo asked, changing the subject.

Bucky grinned like a pervert in a primary school. "You have no idea. This is like every dream I've ever had all rolled into one."

"*Every* dream?" she said with a wink.

He set his whiskey down and leaned in, thinking over his next sentence.

"Well… there is one more."

"Ya-huh?"

"Uh huh."

"And what's *that*?"

"Well," Bucky whispered, scratching the bar with his nicotine-stained fingernail. "It's just that—"

"—Oh. *Bucky*," she moaned, setting her own drink down and coming in half way to meet him.

Bucky felt her hot breath - and cherry chapstick-laced halitosis - on his face.

"Bucky! Bobby Jo! Holy shit! We done gon' fucked up," Skeez screamed, stumbling back in through the door.

"God dammit Skeez! What the fuck is so goddamn important?" Bucky growled, angered by the interruption.

"The clock didn't say twenty-six hours. I misread it. It said twenty-six goddamn ass-lickin', motherfingerin' *minutes*."

"What?" Bucky squealed like a prissy little bitch at the news. "Twenty-six goddamn ass-lickin' motherfingerin' minutes?!"

"Ya-huh. The clock just hit zero," he said, wide-eyed.

Everyone looked at one another for a few beats before they all ran for the door at a full sprint.

Bucky slid into the camper's recliner. "Power?"

"What?" Skeez said.

"I'm going through the checklist, dumb ass."

"Oh. Cool, cool."

"Yeah. So, *power*?"

Skeez flopped onto the couch with Bobby Jo. "Forget the checklist. Just go. We were flying this thing fifteen minutes ago."

"I agree, Bucky," Bobby Jo said. "Just go."

Bucky nodded, none-too-happy with the expedition of events.

"Okay, philistines. Let's just fucking go, then, huh? Clench them sphincters. We're going to space."

With that, Bucky pulled the trigger for the 'UP' taser. A clicking filled the camper as the taser engaged. A second later they were smashed down into their seats as Yonder shot into the air.

SWOOOOOOOSH.

They gained altitude rapidly. The trees flashed past, then a second after, they passed through a thick bank of clouds.

Bucky pulled a second trigger labeled 'GO' and they shot forward at the same time they still climbed.

"HOOLLYY SSHHEEEIIIITT—" Skeez screamed all the way through their rapid ascent.

Bucky let go of the 'UP' trigger and pulled the 'LEFT' one, slamming them to the side of their chairs. The ship turned towards the low round Moon coming over the horizon.

"It's getting dark out there," Booby Jo said through clenched teeth.

"Quieter too," Skeez added.

Bucky realized they were right.

The higher they got, the less the air held them back and the less light was being reflected by the atmosphere. Earth's blue and green sphere fell away.

"Is it getting harder to breath?" Bobby Jo asked, her voice sounding distant in the thinning atmosphere.

Bucky hadn't noticed because he had been holding his breath, but she was right.

It got cold, as well.

"Oh, fuck."

Bucky realized that the camper wasn't air tight, and about fifty miles too high to do much about it.

The radio on the kitchen counter buzzed to life all on its own. The same game show host voice boomed out, a little higher pitched in the thin atmosphere.

Congratulations! You have re-established communication! This vessel has been deemed an acceptable contender. Restraints have been released. Please enjoy your race!

"What the fuck?" Skeez yelped, scooting away from the offending radio.

And *no* fucking cheating, or we'll have to issue a penalty.

"What does that mean?" Bucky asked, looking around the camper with jittery jerks of his head.

Bobby Jo tilted her head back and pointed at the ceiling. "Look at that."

The diamond speared on the javelin squelched into a silvery blue liquid and flowed across the wood paneling. It didn't get far before it was absorbed.

Seconds later, the entire thing was gone. The only evidence that a lack of oxygen wasn't making them

161

hallucinate was the three loops of duct tape stuck to the ceiling.

There was a hissing noise and suddenly it was easy to breath once again.

Bobby Jo took a deep breath. "Well, *ride me sideways*. We're lucky that spear thing brought air with it."

Bucky felt like an idiot for not thinking of that sooner.

Please enjoy your complementary life support.

"Well, I guess that sort of makes sense?" Skeez said.

A colossal banging sound came from the bathroom, followed by a groan.

HHHUUUNNGGG.

It sounded like a stowaway zombie.

"The fuck is that?" Skeez asked, quietly.

Bobby Jo held up a fresh taser.

"You got me."

"Where the fuck did you have that hidden?" Skeez asked. He looked over her skin tight shorts and mid-riff flannel.

"Wouldn't you like to know?"

"I mean, uh, *yeah*. I would like to. You have, like, zero extra cargo space on you."

"Shut up," Bucky said. "Go find out what that was."

Nervous, Skeez pulled a Rollneck from his pants and cracked it open.

"*You* go find out what it was."

Bucky was sure Skeez hadn't even realized he had done it.

"I can't. I'm driving," Bucky said, showing him the 2x4 with the tasers taped to it.

"Fucking likely story," Skeez grumbled.

"Goddamn it."

Bobby Jo got up and made her way to the bathroom door, shaming Skeez into action.

He went past the door and grabbed the handle while Bobby Jo pointed the taser at it and gave him a nod.

In one quick motion, Skeez turned the knob and jerked

the door open. Bobby Jo screamed and pulled the trigger. There was a pop as the electrodes shot out. Then the familiar clicking sound followed as Bobby Jo continued to scream while tasing the shit out of whatever was in there.

GAAAACCKKKKGH.

A man covered in shit and toilet paper fell out into the hall, stiff as a board while the electrical current seized his muscles. Bobby Jo kept the trigger pulled, but jumped back as the man flopped over onto his back.

"Bobby Jo," Skeez shouted over the screams. "Let go of the trigger."

"Huh?"

"It's *Satchel.*"

She released the trigger. A shit-covered Satchel shape relaxed with a groan. "Ughn, wha eh fuck?"

He barely got out.

"What are you doing here?" Skeez asked as he squatted next to Satchel.

"Oh. Poo."

The smell of shit hit him and he stood back up.

"Why are you covered in shit?"

"Ugh, fuck me," Bucky grunted with disdain. "That's one more prick we got on board, now."

"I was in here taking a shit. I told you assholes that when you got to the Panzer Tank," Satchel said as he spat out flecks of feces.

He'd come around just enough to reach into his shirt pocket with a shaky hand and pull out a cigarette. The end landed in his mouth as he searched for his lighter.

"You can't smoke in here. We don't know how much air we have."

Satchel was still pretty out of it. A few unsteady hand holds that left shit stains on the booth seats and kitchen counter as he got to his feet. His eyes didn't seem to focus. He stumbled past Bobby Jo, who jumped back so as not to be smeared with shit. He leaned on the wall beside the door and took a few deep breaths.

Bobby Jo felt bad for his condition.

"You okay? Sorry about the taser."

He held up a hand to forestall further question. He took a few more breaths seeming to gather himself further. "Fuck. I need a smoke."

"Not in here, man. We can't be using up oxygen for that shit," Bucky said.

"No, no. It's fine," Satchel said. "I only bought the thing, but that's fine. I don't have to smoke in here." Satchel opened the door and stepped out.

"Satchel, NO!" everyone screamed.

Chapter 14

Danny slid off the Mondeo's-Popemobile hybrid and nodded at Barry.

"Where you been, man?"

"Should you be touching that blue shit?" Barry asked, his arms laden with plastic bags from the corner store.

"It's all good. Shit dried off. You ready to get the fuck out of here? We got, like, five minutes to get in the car."

"What about your mum?" Chelsea asked. "Don't she want you to go in for dinner?"

"I'm not missing this for another night of microwave chips, man," Danny said. "This is a fucking flying car."

BANG.

The sound of the back door slamming open made everyone jump.

"I thought I told you to clean this mess up, Daniel? Am I going to have to come down there and smack you upside the head?" Deondra asked, holding a spatula like a short sword.

Danny hung his head in supplication.

"No mum. I'll be in in a minute. Just saying goodbye to my friends."

"Don't give me any of your nonsense, young man. Get all this cleaned up—" she stopped berating Danny and looked past him. "Daniel?"

"What."

"Don't *what* me, you prick."

Danny hung his head and made damn sure his mother knew he was apologetic.

"Sorry, mum."

"Where did that car come from?"

"Dunno. We found it."

Deondra didn't buy a word of his explanation. His face seemed to suggest he was lying his teeth off.

"You found it?"

"Yeah."

"As God is my witness. If you stole a car, Daniel Hook, I will tear the flesh from your arse."

His face had gone crimson and she was stomping down the path right at the teens, her spatula raised in a threatening manner.

"Oh shit, boys. She's gonna murder us. Get in the car," Danny said, backpedaling.

Barry and Chelsea were two steps ahead, and were slamming the doors closed by the time Danny had his open.

The fires of hell blazed in Deondra's eyes, "Don't you dare run from me, now."

"Sorry mum," Danny squeaked.

He jumped into the driver's seat and slammed the door just in time to miss the business-end of a spatula.

Deondra tried the handle, but Danny locked it just in time. She began pounding on the window.

"Open the door, Daniel. Open it."

"S-Sorry mum."

Danny tried to hot wire the car, but it didn't work. "What the fuck?" he tried to kick the panel out again.

The car had been rebuilt by the diamond. Something had made it stronger, the result being that he couldn't get through.

Deondra hit the glass with the metal spatula. Danny was shocked that the window didn't break right then and there.

"Oi, in the ignition. There's keys," Chelsea said, helpfully.

Her voice shook with fear at the motherly display on Danny's side of the car.

"Cool, man," Danny said, chalking it up to the remake of the car. He gave the key a twist and the engine roared to life.

Deondra reached back with the spatula for a final blow.

"Don't you dare drive away from me, Daniel!"

Before the hammer fell on the driver side window, Danny stomped on the gas and pulled the steering column back.

"YOU ARE GROUNDED!"

Contrary to his mother's statement, the car lifted up and shot into the air. The house came up fast, and the three in the car cringed thinking they were going to smash right into it.

Luckily, the tires were the only thing to make contact.

BOP - SCHLINK.

The two front tires dislodged a few tiles and sent them crashing down around Deondra's feet.

"A trio of pricks. I hope they crash and burn."

The Mondeo drove right over the roof and shot off into the open sky.

Danny looked in the rear view mirror to see his mum standing slack jawed in the muddy back garden.

"Fuck, man. That was *bare* close," he mumbled, not sure if he meant the roof or the spatula, but probably both.

They cruised over the valley in silence.

Danny was fuming inside.

The other two didn't know what to say.

Finally the car broke the silence.

LADIES AND GENTLEMEN. *MUR'KROZNITCK... HAS... BEGUN!* Remember, first to the finish at the Moon - in one piece - wins!

Barry freaked out in the back seat.

"The fucking Moon? Did that thing say the Moon? What the fuck is happening?"

"Fuckin' allow it, man," Danny barked. "You wanna be at school? Or in a fucking flying car?"

Barry sat back in the chair and sighed. He'd definitely rather be in a flying car. Danny sucked his teeth and exhaled through his nostrils.

"Tch. Yeah, that's what I thought, *nigga*," Danny threw his friend a callous glance via the rear view mirror. "You're a fuckin' batty man. Allow that shit, bruv, you're in a *flyin' fuckin' car.*"

Danny thumped the steering wheel and beamed with glee. "A fuckin' flyin' car, man. Swear down, bruv."

"This is some next shit," Barry blurted. "I mean it's better than school, but still. We're in the fucking sky, man."

"I say we wreck this race. Show 'em all what a proper thrashing looks like," Danny said.

Chelsea smiled, "Tryna be a bad man, Danny? I got your back on that."

"So, what we doing?" Barry asked, more inclined to play along if it was something that would light Chelsea's fire.

"I dunno, man. See what's up. Looks like this car is going to fix itself. We can take advantage of that for sure. Maybe we ram the fuckers?"

"Could do, man," Barry said.

"Right. Let's bounce."

Danny pulled the wheel back, tilting the car up towards the sky and the Moon. He slammed the gas pedal down and, with a roar, the car lurched forward like it was on rockets.

"*Shiiii-iiit*, bruv. This ride can fuckin' *move,*" he said, feeling the rush of power flow through him.

Chelsea peered through Danny's window. "Is that a building?"

"I think there's a caravan over there," Barry said, looking out the other side of the car.

Danny smiled and muttered at the adjacent vehicles, angering himself for war. "Fuck 'em. That's right, you little *beeyatches*. Check this shit out."

***

Stereotype Industries Inc, Harajuku, Japan.

"Laskar, あなたは彼と一緒に行きます," Kenzo said.

A pair of medics carted Dr. Krutch's melted body and most of his wheelchair out of the room.

Laskar's eyebrows rose. "Sir. Why? I know nothing of Tempura Four. How I help?"

"*Transration*, if it please," he said, struggling with the words.

Geoffrey looked between Kenzo, his boss, and Laskar, Kenzo's aide. "Uh, excuse me. What is going on?"

They ignored him for the moment.

"私たちはジェフリーとその船と話す必要があるでしょう、しかし彼は彼の西側の育成によって毒されました.彼は道を見失ったが、彼は私たちの唯一の選択肢である," Kenzo said, throwing enough looks at Geoffrey to let him know they were talking about him.

Laskar gave Geoffrey a quick glance, then bowed to Kenzo.

"頑張ります、サー."

"So, what's up?" Geoffrey asked the diminutive woman.

She rolled her Rs to a ridiculous degree. "Jeffwey. To work transr-r-r-ration. I will be riding you."

"Oh?"

"Me and you ride together. Very hard and fast."

Geoffrey mined the comedy from her attempt at

171

English, "That's very kind of you. But don't you think we should race first?"

"I pardon your beg?" Laskar asked.

"Never mind."

An awkward silence fell between them. Laskar didn't move, thoroughly confused by the event.

Geoffrey raised his eyebrows. "So, translation, eh? That will be helpful, I suppose. Glad to have you aboard."

"About half past three," Laskar said.

"あなた二人はあなたのスーツを着るsushi-roll必要があります.起動時間は1時間以内です," Kenzo said

He gave a curt bow and then headed for the control room.

"What was that all about?"

"I need suit of space," Laskar said and took yet *another* bow. She mimed pulling a helmet over her head. "For riding you *hard.*"

"Oh."

"Yes," she continued and pointed at her nose, "Giant *helmet* in my face."

Geoffrey ducked his head and wondered if handing in his resignation might be a better idea.

"Oh dear."

Laskar, completely unaware of her amusing miscommunication lifted her left leg and pointed at her thigh, "Strap. On."

"You what?" Geoffrey blinked and connected the dots a second too late. "Ah. You mean a space suit?"

Laskar nodded and mimed what looked like a blow job with her fist. She dug her tongue into her cheek, which really didn't help.

"Choke," she added. "Fewer air."

"Good guess," Geoffrey amused himself, quietly. "Oxygen, you mean?"

She mimed a choking fit, "Gag. It too big."

"Who told you?" Geoffrey smiled, enjoying the

inadvertent moment for humor.

"間以?"

"Never mind. Was just a joke."

Laskar mimed a gag through a lack of air, "No. *Choke.*"

"You mean oxygen supply?"

"Yes. Long thick pipe. For mouth."

Geoffrey sniggered as she pointed toward her esophagus. "Maybe once we've left Earth's orbit, eh?"

"間以?"

"If nothing else, it'll alleviate the boredom of space travel."

She pointed at the back of her throat once again, "No teeth, just throat."

"You've clearly done this before."

Laskar closed her mouth and squinted at the man, prepared to take offense.

"What is funny?"

Geoffrey burst out laughing and tried to allay her frustration. "I'm sorry, I'm sorry. I'm just being silly."

She poked him in the chest with anger.

"*YOU. Man.* Be silly," she said and ran her fingertip across her neck in a threatening manner. "I cut your balls down."

Geoffrey swallowed his laughter and cleared his throat. "*Off.*"

"Wot?"

"I cut your balls off."

"No, I cut *YOUR* balls off. Silly man."

Angered, and suspecting Geoffrey of making fun of her, she sliced across her neck with her fingers and scowled at him.

"Balls removed. Put in stir fry."

Geoffrey calmed down and cleared the amusement from his throat, "Uh, okay?"

"HA-TCHAH!"

She sliced her opened hand down through the air, enacting a sword-like chop.

"Whoa, steady on."

"Then. I cut your penis in half. Make Bonzai tree from shaft."

"Okay."

"Me. Perform *penicide.*"

It was at this precise moment that Geoffrey fell in love. Alas, his desire to communicate the fact to his intended would have to wait.

A race needed to be won.

"What you sayin', Jeffwey?"

"Okay, that's quite enough nonsense for now," Geoffrey said as he made for the door. "I guess I should get changed as well. There are spare suits in the locker room."

"必要があ?" Laskar asked, giving up the desire to translate.

"Please, if we're going to be traveling together, we need to speak in a common tongue."

"あ?"

"Speak English."

"*Speak-ah Engr-r-rish,*" she parroted, clearly unable to decipher what she'd just said. "Is me?"

Geoffrey pointed at his own chest. "Me. Spaceman."

"You. Space Man."

He pressed his finger to her chest. "You. Cargo."

"Me," she repeated blindly. "Cargo."

"Yes. Very good."

"Ah-so," Laskar took a brief bow, happy with the resolution. She pointed at the door to the changing room, "Please. Space suit acquisition. *Wearing.*"

Ten minutes later, Geoffrey activated the suit's self-adjusting feature and his baggy suit tightened up around his body. He appreciated the fact that he could move freely in the Stereotype Inc. spacesuits, but he was a little self-conscious at how his genitals protruded through the material.

"Please. You assist," Laskar said from the other side of the lockers. "So tight. I have need for you."

"God help me. Please be the suit. Please be the suit," he repeated like a mantra as he came to the next row where Laskar was changing.

"Please." she said, looking over her bare, left shoulder. The suit rode up over her ass, naked from there on up. She covered herself with one arm as she tried to pull the suit on with the other.

"So tight."

"I bet you are," he said, adjusting the crotch of his own suit.

"What you say?" she asked, blinking her eyes in what Geoffrey had to assume was a joke. No one blinked seductively by accident.

"Um, you have to release the suit before you put it on. Right here," he said, pointing to the controls on his wrist.

"Ah-so."

She found the same controls on the floppy wrist of her suit. "Which button?"

Geoffrey felt a chill run through him. Was his nose bleeding?

"This one."

Geoffrey, being a man of the world, knew what was going to happen next. In fact he had seen this very anime a dozen times. The only things missing were the huge, round eyes, and daft schoolgirl pigtails.

He had a choice.

Press the button, and watch as the suit became loose and fell off, exposing her to him, where she would then hit him over the head for being a pervert. Or he could press the button and walk away before the pants fell down.

She would think he was standing there, but when she would go to yell at him he would be walking around the corner. This sounded better, but then for the rest of the series she would be in love with him, and try her best to catch his eye.

The second option sounded better for a few reasons. First, he didn't get hit in the head. Second, he could pretend to ignore her advances, if any were forthcoming.

However, there was the problem that his suit would betray every semi he got and give him away.

He decided the second option was best.

Laskar slapped the shit out of him.

POW.

"Agh. What the fuck?" he yelped, looking down to see Laskar standing with arm over her breasts, and her suit around her ankles.

Her pink panties with a panda on the crotch seemed a little over the top. He had been thinking about what to do, and forgot that he had already released her suit. *Fuck, this was going to be one of those animes, eh?*

He turned his back to her.

"Sorry, Laskar. Uh, just put the suit on and press the button again. It'll tighten up on you automatically."

He heard the rustling of clothes behind him, then the click of the button, and a sound like cloth rubbing on cloth as the suit tightened.

"Oh, my. Is so tight," she moaned.

Geoffrey put his face in his hands. "Good grief."

"Okay. I finish."

He turned around and just as he thought, she was showing off her skin tight suit that left absolutely nothing to the imagination. *Why would they make suits this tight?*

"Great. Looks really good. Don't forget the, uh, *helmet,*" he said, indicating the sleek glass and metal helmet in her locker.

Were her breasts this big before the space suit? Shouldn't the compression make them smaller? This was no way to run a space program.

She turned and reached for the helmet. Geoffrey couldn't help but stare at her butt as she 'struggled' to reach the top of the locker.

Jesus, it looks like her suit is being actively sucked into her ass crack. Who designed these things? A sexually deprived blind man?

He looked to see if his suit was riding up his own ass, or if it was just a feature of for the women.

"Hoh-kay. I ready."

Laskar turned and posed with her fists on hips. Somehow she had grabbed the helmet and put it on, tucking her long hair in perfectly in a second.

"Where did your hair go?" Geoffrey asked. "How did you do that?"

There was a second click and she pulled the helmet off, flipping her head from side to side as she did it. Her long black hair slipped out in a fanning motion like she was in a shampoo commercial. "What?"

Geoffrey rolled his eyes, "Nothing. Nothing at all. Let's go."

***

Checks were done.

Tempura Four was ready to launch.

"はジェフリーとその," Laskar announced.

"Say that again?"

"Is correct?"

Geoffrey looked to the copilots seat. Laskar buckled up. Somehow, she had the shoulder straps in such a way that her breasts had been pressed together in a very seductive manner.

It took him a few seconds to see that she actually did have the straps on properly, they were just designed to press breasts together. The lower strap rode up between her thighs, suggesting all sorts of inappropriate visuals in Geoffrey's mind.

"Uh, yup. You got it right," he said, before blowing out a breath. "We're all checked out here. Mag rail launch system is a go," he reported over the radio.

The radio crackled then the game show host voice boomed out.

LADIES AND GENTLEMEN. *MUR'KROZNITCK... HAS... BEGUN!*

Tempura Four rocketed down the mag rail without anyone having hitting a button.

"What? Who launched us?"

The *G* force pressed him back into his chair. He grunted with the effort, flipping the switches to bring the reactor online and the new Ion thrusters burning. He hit the switch just in time as the launch sled hit the end of the mag rail and launched them into the air. The thrusters kicked in, pushing them even harder back in their chairs, and he jerked the stick back, pointing the nose of Tempura Four up to the sky.

"Oh, my. So powerful, your thrusts," Laskar moaned. "Experiencing strong G String."

"*G Force*, Laskar," he said. "G Force."

"May the force be with us," she added, loudly.

He glanced over and saw that she was wide eyed and smiling as her chair vibrated under her.

Was her seat vibrating extra hard? He didn't think his was shaking quite that much.

Laskar's eyes rolled in the back of her head, and her mouth fell open. *Oh, shit. She's passing out.*

UUUUGGGHHHNNNNNGGGGGG!

The long moan slipped out of her gaping mouth.

So, not passing out. Geoffrey thought turning a few shades of red.

He cleared his throat and focused on piloting. He turned them towards the horizon and they raced into the upper atmosphere. He checked his instruments, and double checked the heading they were on.

UHHH, UHHH, UUUUHHHHHGGGGNNNN!

Space flight was exciting, but he wasn't sure it was *that* exciting.

He checked the radar, then took a double take. There were multiple ships up here with them. One of which was close to half a mile long!

"Are you seeing this?" he asked Laskar, pointing at the radar display.

UUUUUUHHHHHHHH!

Nope - she was not seeing anything at this point in time.

Geoffrey's pants grew painfully tight in the crotch, but he couldn't adjust his junk due to the straps holding him in place.

The shaking and *G* forces finally evened out as they passed into space. The ship was calmer, and the noise levels were less of a pain in the ass than before.

They flew in silence for a few minutes. Geoffrey not wanting to speak first in case Laskar was not quite... *done.*

"Oh, my. Pleasurable ride," she said, finally.

"Yup."

"It was good for you?" she asked, innocently.

"Oh yes," he said, shifting his hips, trying to keep his space suit from bursting. "It was magic."

"Magic cock."

"Huh?"

She indicated the dashboard and flying controls, "Pit of cock."

"Cockpit, you mean?"

She held out her hands and mimed a giant ball shape. "Very big action fun."

"Why don't you speak properly?"

"はとその?"

"Fuck's sake, I give up."

"You feeling okay?" she asked.

The indicator flashed and buzzed, letting him know that they were in a stable orbit of Earth. He quickly hit the buckle release on his seat and pushed himself out of the pilots chair, keeping his throbbing erection out of sight of Laskar as best he could.

"Going to hit the head. Be right back," he said, in as cheery a voice as he could muster.

"Hit head?" she asked, full of confusion.

"Yeah, as in go to the toilet—"

"—How you say. English. *Hit head?*"

"Uh, no."

She enacted the motion of a man masturbating, "Head of cock. Like big *wank?*"

"Yeah. It's probably better you stop talking for a while."

Geoffrey slipped into the bathroom, closed the door, and proceeded to have a good cry.

Chapter 15

Low Earth Orbit

"Where is this thing taking us?" Andrei asked as he pressed his face to the window.

The Earth was becoming rounder the further they blasted away in the armored security vehicle. He was sure they were high enough that air should have been a problem.

An oxygen-based problem, at the very least.

"I do not know, darling," Yulia said. "But I do seem to have control of the vehicle."

The armored car veered in the direction she turned. She pushed down on the wheel and the front end dipped down as well.

"Oh, yes. You can get us back home."

The radio buzzed - **This is an official race vehicle. If you choose not to participate we will be forced to reassign the drone to a new team. Please make your choice now.**

The engine suddenly turned off and began to tumble towards the Earth.

"Agh," Andrei screamed, his vice hitting a new octave. "My sweet! Do something."

"Oh, shit," Yulia yelped as she became weightless in the free fall. "We accept. We Accept."

The truck revved back to life, and leveled out.

We accept your acceptance. Have a great race!

Yulia pulled the steering wheel back and stepped on the gas. The heavy armored truck shot back up into the air.

"What the fuck are you doing?" Andrei screamed.

"What the fuck does it look like? I am fucking joining the fucking race."

"Why? We can't fly this thing into space. It's an armored truck."

Yulia swiped her hand across the darkness in front of them.

"Darling, please. Look out the of window. You will see that we are already in space."

"But, but—"

"—Make yourself of use and go check on the diamond. Use the pass-through door."

"But it is dangerous, my sweet?"

"Nah. I do not think so."

Andrei backed away from the gun. "Okay. Okay, I will check."

He got up from his seat and faced the small door. He took a few quick breaths to psych himself up, then slid the door open.

He expected to be greeted by a pool of blue goop, but there wasn't any. He just stared at the empty cargo space.

"Well?" Yulia asked, scanning the windscreen for the Burj Khalifa. She had lost it when they had tried landing.

"The back. It is empty," he said.

"Empty?" she turned and looked over his shoulder. Sure enough, there was nothing back there. Even the diamond on a stick was gone.

"What is happening, my sweet?" he asked.

"I do not know, darling."

Yulia averted her gaze to the huge building racing through space ahead of them. "But I think I found someone who might."

She stomped on the gas and the truck rocketed forward. She steered towards the huge building, hoping that someone there would know what the hell was going on.

***

"Yonder" - Low Earth Orbit.

"Noooo," Bobby Jo screamed, reaching for the shit-covered Satchel, but it was too late. There was a sucking sound and Satchel was dragged out of the camper in a violent blast of air.

"We're fucked," Bucky shouted.

To everyone's surprise, they were not, technically speaking, *fucked*.

The sucking stopped almost immediately. A blue film covered the open camper door like a force field. The door swung back shut and the radio buzzed again.

Hull breach detected. Counter measures enacted. Try not to kill yourselves! it said, cheerily.

"Oh, my gawd. Did you see that?" Bobby Jo asked as she pressed her face against the small window in the door. She jerked her head back.

"Oh. That's just nasty."

"What? Is Satchel all right?" Bucky asked, looking out the side window.

Satchel, or at least what was left of him, floated beside them. He had suffered what was called explosive decompression.

In other words, ripped apart and turned inside out. The sight of gore hanging in space didn't put Skeez off his beer, however.

"Nope. He ain't all right."

"That's your brother. Aren't you at least a little upset he just died?" Bucky asked.

Skeez shrugged and burst out laughing, "Hell, naw. That guy was an asshole."

"What the fuck is so funny?" Bucky asked in horror.

"I always told him cigarettes would be the death of

him."

Skeez took another look out the window and observed the meat pulp that was once his brother.

"Fuckin' asshole."

Bucky squeezed the 'GO' trigger and they shot forward, leaving the red mist and meat chunks behind.

Skeez squinted at something approaching from behind the milkshake of flesh and organs that used to be his brother.

"Wait. Is that the *Popemobile*?"

Bucky looked around him, but didn't see what Skeez was talking about.

"Where?"

"Oh, I see it. What's the fuckin' Pope doin' out here?" Bobby Jo asked.

She knelt beside Skeez so they could share the small window without blocking Bucky's view.

"Space ain't no place for prayin'"

"I still don't see it. Wait. Is that a sky scraper?"

"Yeah, I saw that thing like five minutes ago," Skeez said, looking at Bucky like he was an idiot.

"Well, why the fuck didn't you mention *that*?"

"Because I got distracted," he said, knowingly glancing down Bobby Jo's shirt.

Bobby Jo caught him leering and delivered a swift punch to his dick.

"Huurrrrrrr," Skeez growled, doubling over and falling to the floor.

"Fucking pervert," she growled.

"Speaking of perverts, why would the Pope be out here?" Bucky mused, ignoring Skeez's moans as he rolled back and forth on the ground.

Bobby Jo slapped Skeez's hand away when he reached out for help, "I don't know, but it looks like it's headed this way."

The Popemobile grew bigger. Bucky got a little nervous

at how fast they seemed to be closing in. He put his finger on the 'UP' trigger just to be safe.

After a minute or two, Bucky was able to make out the adjacent racing vehicle a lot better as it pulled alongside them. It was definitely *not* the Popemobile, unless this was the suburban version of it.

The bump on top where the Pope would usually sit was made of metal like the rest of the car. It resembled a new Ford Taurus with cancer all up its back.

"Naw. I don't think that's the Pope," Bucky said, squinting to get a view of who was inside. "What the fuck is that?"

Skeez had recovered enough to pull himself up to the window again. He coughed, then took a deep breath. "That's a pressed ham."

"A what?" Bobby Jo asked, cocking her head to the side trying to make sense of what she was seeing.

"Pressed ham. There's a black kid in that car pressing their ass against the window," Skeez said.

Bucky suddenly made sense of what he was seeing. It was indeed a black ass pressed to the window.

"Oh, *fabtastic*," Bucky yelped with extreme sarcasm. "How do a bunch of idiots like that have a flying car?"

Skeez looked between Bobby Jo and Bucky. "Really, guys?"

The person removed their ass and sat back down. Now they could see there were actually three young people in the car. And all three of them flipped those inside the camper the bird.

"Motherfuckin' *delinquents*," Bucky exclaimed in shock.

Skeez flipped the three a casual bird himself while taking a drink of Rollneck.

"Fuck em."

The three kids seemed overly pissed at Skeez's finger and, in a sudden move that scared the two passengers, the driver jerked the wheel and the car shot towards the Yonder.

"Agh!" Bucky yelped, and pulled the 'UP' trigger.

The camper shot up, but the incoming car was moving too fast.

There was a crunching squeal, and the trailer began to do a barrel roll. Bobby Jo and Skeez were flung to the ceiling then fell to the couch. Bucky nearly fell out of the recliner but, fortunately, he had thought to strap himself in with a tow strap after the rough takeoff. He pulled the triggers till the camper stopped corkscrewing.

"Oh, fuck. My ass," Skeez groaned from the kitchen. He was rubbing where he had landed on one of the cans of Rollneck Kojack in his pocket.

"Everyone all right?" Bucky asked as he scanned the windows for the psychotic kids in the cancer Ford.

"I'm good," Bobby Jo sputtered. "A little bruised, but I'll make it."

"Go back into the bedroom," Bucky started, but was cut off by Skeez.

"Now ain't the time, you two."

"Shut the fuck up Skeez," they both yelled.

"Go back in the bedroom. The closet. You'll find my shotgun. Let's show these fuckers what West Virgina is all about," Bucky said with a shit-eating grin.

***

"What the fuck you doin', man? Are you off your rocker?" Barry shouted as Danny veered the car at the flying caravan with the poorly drawn stripper painted on it.

Danny smiled viciously as they closed in on the caravan.

"Nobody disrespects me like that. Did you see what that redneck prick did?"

The caravan shot up, but not fast enough. They slammed into its back wheels. The impact sent the caravan spinning on its axis.

"Ha! Look at those stupid fucks. Get blended you

fucking sister-fuckers."

"You're fuckin' mad, mate," Barry whined.

"Hit 'em again," Chelsea smirked.

"Really show 'em how we do."

He jerked the wheel to the other side, and they careened towards the unsuspecting silver monstrosity. At the last second, the caravan rotated to show them the steel undercarriage of its frame. They sideswiped it, ripping the side view mirror off the Mondeo.

"Yeah, yeah!" Chelsea beamed. "Do it again."

Holy shit, is she getting off on this? Danny thought. He was more than happy to help that along, so he lined up for another go.

The caravan rolled back around, and they were midway between its front and back. Perfect placement for a side swipe. Danny wrenched the wheel again, and dove in at the side.

The door to the caravan was kicked open, and Danny had to do a double take at what he saw - a beautiful blond woman in cutoff jeans that were so short the white pockets were visible below the hem. She had a black and red checkered flannel shirt tied up so that it only covered her arms and breasts. The most riveting thing about her was the pump action shotgun she held.

The woman racked a shell and aimed the barrel right at Danny's face.

"AAAAGGGGGGHHH," Danny, Barry, and Chelsea screamed all together.

Danny pulled the wheel up and they saw a flash of fire as the gun went off. The hood of the Mondeo let off a shower of sparks as dozens of steel pellets gouged into it.

Chelsea grabbed Danny's arm and shook him, "She's fuckin' mental, man. Get us outta here,"

"Get the fuck off me, man. I'm trying to drive."

He stomped on the gas and jerked the wheel up and spun it to the side. They swooped over and past the caravan, leaving it alone for now.

They all breathed heavily.

"Where now?" Barry asked after a few minutes.

"I dunno. Pass me a joint. That shit was too intense to be thinking right," Danny said.

He knew Barry always had a stick on him somewhere.

There was a sparking of a lighter then the car filled with a sticky blue haze and that familiar smell. After a puff or two, the joint was held out between Danny and Chelsea. The former snatched it and gave it a nice long pull.

They hot boxed the entire joint, not having the ability to roll down the windows. Now that they were out of the line of fire, high as a kite Danny got down to thinking.

"We should head for that flying skyscraper thing. Maybe we can get aboard and steal some shit. There's gotta be some guns or whatever in that thing. Then we can come back and fuck these fuckin' rednecks up proper."

"Cool," Chelsea said, with red bleary eyes.

"Cool," Barry agreed.

Cool. Cool, the radio said in a classic stoner voice.

"Cool?" Danny said, too high to realize that the car was just as high as its occupants.

He stomped on the gas, forcing them towards the huge, lumbering skyscraper-cum-spaceship.

***

Surface Base of Bunker - Unknown Location: USA

"Should we be worried about that?" Hacker asked, pointing at the hologram above the javelin floating in the large open research space.

The time to race start had come and gone. The once blue display was flashing red. It was very disconcerting.

"I guess it's fine," Dr. Gwen Furj said. "Nothing bad happened when the timer ran out. Besides, we still have a few more tests to run."

"A few more? Haven't you guys been running tests for

days?"

"Sure, but this is the discovery of the decade. There is so much we can learn from this," she said as she glanced at the numbers on her tablet.

Hacker felt the proceedings were of much stronger significance.

"Discovery of the decade? This has to be the discovery of, like, *ever*. It's an alien probe. And it's communicating with us."

"Oh. Right. Sure, discovery of all time," she said unconvinced.

Before Hacker could dive into that bit of cryptic word play, his phone rang. He looked at the caller ID and sighed. "Hello, Colonel."

"Hastur. What the fuck is going on in that yellow suited zoo? Why don't we have a ship in the air?"

His voice was loud enough that Gwen could hear every word clearly. She whispered, "Tell him the time to start hasn't come yet. He won't know the difference."

"Uh, sir?" Hacker said. "I'm being told that the start of the race hasn't come yet. They want to follow the rules laid out by the probe, sir."

His voice trembled. He was not a good liar.

"Bull fucking shit, Homer. NORAD has picked up at least four ships taking off and on their way to the Moon. One of them is the Goddamn *Burj Khalifa*. You mean to tell me that a bunch of tribesmen in the fucking Middle East are ahead of us in this race?"

"Sir, the UAE is hardly a bunch of tribesmen. Dubai is one of the most advanced cities on the planet."

"Don't you give me that line of bull crap. I want our ship out there now. Ya hear me? You are on a secret base. No one knows where you all are. I would hate to have to send some people to find you and put you on the right path. Am I going to have to do that?

"No, Sir."

"Am I getting through to you, boy?"

"Yes, Sir. We will have a ship up and in the race in no time, Sir. You can count on us."

"You better, Hooker. You better."

The line went dead.

Gwen smiled at him as he slipped the phone in his pocket.

"Trouble in paradise?"

"Your line didn't work. NORAD has multiple ships in the air all ready. If we don't get ours up soon, we'll be answering to some people we don't want to see."

Gwen threw Hacker a sigh. "Fine. We have samples. The tests are all running. I suppose we can get things going here. I guess we should bring in a ship."

"You have one already?" he asked, cocking his head. How had they had something just sitting around for just such an occasion. Though he did figure they probably had a space shuttle stowed away somewhere. Maybe an old rocket.

She handed her tablet off to a passing man in a yellow hazmat suit.

"Yeah. Follow me. Let's head down to the basement. You can pick something out."

The elevator hummed along, dropping into the Earth at what felt like a precipitous speed, but they had yet to come to what was labeled on the buttons as **Sub-basement 4**.

"How far down does this go?" Hacker asked.

Gwen smiled at his naivety. "A few hundred feet."

She had taken off her white hazmat suit, and now wore a pair of blue scrubs that somehow made her look incredible.

"How many hundred?"

"I'm not really sure. Ah, here we are."

The elevator dinged, and the doors slid open. Hacker's jaw dropped at the enormous room beyond the doors. It went on so far that there was a haze obscuring the far side.

They were about twenty feet up on a catwalk that overlooked thousands of metal shelves holding uncountable numbers of wooden crates.

"What the hell is all this?" Hacker asked, stepping off the elevator and leaning on the metal railing.

"This is where we keep the good stuff we don't really know what to do with."

She stepped off behind him and headed for a set of stairs.

"Come on, Hacker. We still need to go a ways."

He pushed off the rail and followed her down the steps. There was a small desk with an elderly man in a security uniform with his feet up and reading a newspaper at the bottom.

"Hey Gary," Gwen said, as she passed by.

The man didn't put the paper down as he spoke, "Hey Doc. You taking the cart?"

"Yup. Gotta show the rookie some stuff," she said as she slid into a golf cart beside the desk.

Gary turned his paper over.

"Be sure to bring it back. My old legs can't go hiking to find it anymore."

"You got it. Coming Hacker?" she asked, patting the seat beside her.

"Uh, yeah."

He jogged around the cart and sat down.

As soon as his ass hit the seat, she took off. They drove down one of the rows, crates flashing by as the cart picked up speed.

"What did you mean by the good stuff?" Hacker asked, trying to fill the silence.

"Oh, you know," she said with a straight face, "Tesla's safe contents. The Ark of the Covenant. Lilith's spear. All the good stuff."

His jaw dropped in amazement, "Oh. You're fucking with me, aren't you?"

"I'll let you decide when we get there."

After what seemed like an hour, they finally came to the end of the row and into an open space filled with… *things*.

"We're here. The ones on the left all work, but are out of fuel. The ones on the right either don't work, or we don't know how to use them. Which one do you like? From our analysis any of them should work with the blue goo."

A smirk stretched across her face. It was fun blowing Hacker's mind.

It took him a few more beats to fully comprehend the enormity of the show on display, "Oh, wow. These are alien space craft?"

"Yup. We've been collecting them since the thirties. Pretty sweet, huh?"

Hacker stepped out of the cart and approached something that looked suspiciously like an X-wing from Star Wars.

"This is incredible. Why are they here? Why haven't we told anybody about them?"

"We do. You notice how that one looks like an X-wing? Who do you think gave ol' George the idea? We slip the designs into popular media all the time. That way, when the inevitable invasion happens, the people won't freak out too much. They've sort of seen it before."

"What about the aliens that flew them?"

"Uh. We can talk about that at another time. Let's just say if they were still around we wouldn't be holding onto their ships."

Hacker decided he didn't really want to know what that meant. He went from the X-wing to another ship.

"Oh, my god. This is Buck Rodger's Thunderfighter."

"Yup."

Hacker pointed at another vessel.

"That one is Slave One."

"Look at you being all cultured," Gwen giggled as

hacker spotted a poppadum-shaped spacecraft. "Correct."

"*Holy shit.* That's the Millennium Falcon."

"Yeah, we really got a lot of mileage out of Star Wars. So, I say just pick one and we can use that. All of these are space worthy, but I have no idea how were going to get that goo to do its thing. But, we have to start somewhere."

Hacker disappeared around the Falcons landing gear. His voice echoed through the open space.

"Oh, man. This one. I want this one. It's perfect."

"Well, you can't have it I'm afraid," Gwen said.

"What?! Why not?"

"Because it's copyright infringement."

"Huh?"

"Look, if you go up into space and start pissing around with the controls and furry dice and stuff and people think you're in Star Wars, we could get sued."

Hacker hung his head like a petulant child and kicked his feet across the floor.

"Aww. S'not fair."

Gwen giggled and made her way over to a stupid pair of plastic curtains concealing a spaceship she deemed to be more than suitable for his mission.

"The ship behind these plastic curtains is something I certainly deem more suitable for your mission, Hacker."

With little-to-no interest, Hacker lifted his head and wiped the tear from his cheek. "What is it?"

"Look."

WHUP.

"Check this bad boy out."

Hacker's eyelids lifted to the roof of his eye pits and threatened to ride up his forehead, over his scalp, and unzip down his spine and let his organs flop out, he was that fucking impressed.

"Oh, wow!"

"Yeah. Pretty cool, huh?"

"You bet your chewy camel toe it's pretty cool," Hacker spat as he tiptoed toward the ultra-secret spacecraft. "What's it called?"

"An unused prototype NORAD has been keeping under wraps. George didn't want it. Something about him wanting to add an apple to it, or something."

"What's it called?"

Gwen licked her lips and giggled and hit a button on the wall, "It's called…"

— THE CENTURY SAMOSA—

"Created in 1975, the Century Samosa is a marvel of space exploration and technology. Measuring fifty feet in diameter, and with a stupid bulb-like pilot area at the front, the spacecraft resembles the shape of your typical Indian restaurant samosa."

Thousands of Indians in Saris are pictured running toward it and pressing their fingers to their bindis in awe.

"Blood 'ell, vould you look at dis?" one Indian woman said.

"It's velly, velly good," another man remarked.

It may look like a stupid spaceship that has been baked in a clay oven for three weeks, but make no mistake - The Century Samosa is the last word in badassery.

Unique due to its unusual fuel operation.

Unconvinced? Take, for example, the sixteen mega-ton hyperthruster at the ass-end of the ship. Capable of reaching speeds of up to 16 mph in less than a fortnight, it can be set to autopilot or manual at a flick of a—

"Yeah, whatever," Hacker said. "I guess I'll use this."

"Good. It's just been sitting here taking up space," Gwen said. "If you'll forgive the pun."

"What?"

"Nothing," Gwen muttered with disappointment.

A masked lab technician walked through the plastic covers and tugged on a carbon fiber rope.

"He's here, Dr. Furch."

"Ah, very good," Gwen said. "Bring him in."

Hacker punched the button on the airlock door. It flung up and nearly socked him on the jaw.

"Whoa."

"Be careful with that," Gwen said. "We've not used it in over thirty years—"

MOOOOO.

The lab technician struggled trying to wrench on the rope.

SCREEEEEEECH.

The bull's feet slid across the floor. It didn't seem too happy to be brought into the secret bay area.

"What's this?" Hacker said. "A cow?"

Gwen kicked a foot stool out from under the table and picked up a metal bucket.

CLANG.

It landed in front of the bull's hind quarters.

"What does it run on?" Hacker said.

TWO MINUTES LATER.

SQUIIIRRRTTT.

Gwen folded her arms and watched Hacker jerk the bull off into the bucket.

"Don't make that face with me, Hacker," she said. "You're the one who wants to fly the Century Samosa."

"Actually, I wanted the Falcon, but you said I couldn't—"

SQUIIRRTTT — MOOOOO.

A torrent of thick ejaculate spunked into the metal bucket with such force it nearly toppled the bastard over.

"—Ugh, if I had known I needed to masturbate a cow, I would've used the X-wing, or something."

"Hey, just be glad the jizz is used to power the spacecraft and not the script for some shitty, tenth-rate prequel trilogy."

"I guess."

"Are you done wanking off that thing?"

"I dunno," hacker said, wiping his gloves off on his pants leg. "Have I got enough?"

"The bucket carries ten gallons."

Gwen tried to lift it.

"Yep, seems you've managed to milk the fucker enough to power the spacecraft. Good work."

"Why in the fuck did you guys build a spacecraft that runs on bull spunk?" Hacker asked.

He moved away from the bull with the bucket in hand, not at all comfortable with how that bull was looking at him.

"It was the seventies," Gwen said.

No further explanation was necessary.

After a few coughing starts, the engines of the Century Samosa barked to life. Even in the tight confines of the bridge, the roar of the engines sounded like a 76 Cuda revving up.

"Why is it so loud?" Hacker shouted into his radio.

Gwen had backed away from the ship and took cover behind a row of crates, "It was the seventies," her voice crackled over the radio.

"Is that the answer for everything about this piece of junk?" Hacker asked.

"It was the seventies."

"I guess so," Hacker huffed above the roar of Century Samosa's engine. "Okay, its running. Now what?" Hacker shouted.

Gwen pointed to a shaft opening up in the roof.

"Take it up through there. It will come out in the hanger. I'll meet you up there." She waved and jumped onto the cart. The tires squealed and she shot off back the way they had come.

"Great. How do I fly this thing?"

There were buttons everywhere, along with

unrecognizable gages. The one thing he did recognize was the flight stick between his legs and the two pedals under his feet.

"Okay, it can't be that hard."

Hacker pulled the stick up. The Samosa leaned back, its front coming off the ground, in a barking cough of smoke form the exhaust. Hacker pressed the right pedal and there came a roaring from the engine before the ship lurched off the ground, making Hacker yelp in surprise. It was like he had hit the gas pedal in an over-powered muscle car.

He pressed the pedal again, and the ship shot forward.

Hacker felt his sphincter tighten as the roof came rushing forward. He jerked the stick and tried to line up with the opening in the ceiling. He almost made it, but still clipped the edge of the hole, sending sparks showering over the windscreen. Then the darkness of the shaft enveloped him completely.

Dr. Gwen came into the research tent, a smile on her face. There was a large hole in the floor of the room, now that the hatch to subbasement 4 was open.

Jeffries raced over to greet his boss, "Hey, Doctor."

"Hey."

"Did he select a ship?"

"He chose the Falcon, but I told him he couldn't use it for licensing reasons."

They both had a good laugh over that.

"So which one did you get him to choose?"

"The Century Samosa," she said with as straight a face as she could possibly muster.

Jeffries gave her a look of horror, "You made him jerk off a bull?"

"Ha. Yeah."

"That's messed up."

Gwen shrugged, "I'm not giving up any of the good ships for this fool's errand. The Colonel wanted a ship in the air, so we're putting a ship in the air.

"Okay."

"The Colonel also wanted to do anal on me, so this is my subtle way of telling him to go fuck himself."

"Good one."

"Yeah. I left Hacker in the cockpit and told him to bring it up."

"Ma'am, that ship is notoriously difficult to fly. Will he be all right?"

"He'll be fine. The Samosa is nearly indestructible. They so over-engineered that thing. It would be a miracle if he couldn't get it up here in one piece. Besides, I just wanted to scare him a little. We have trained pilots to actually take it into space."

The men running tests on the craft began to run away in haste. Gwen turned towards the commotion in time to see the diamond spinning up, the red flashing hologram spinning with it.

Castrations! Your ship and crew have been selected! You are starting the race with a handicap of ninety seven minutes. Please race responsoorribly.

"What the fuck does that mean?" Jeffries said.

"Oh, shit," Gwen said. "It's talking funny. Something's gone wrong."

The javelin and diamond suddenly liquefied. Instead of splashing to the ground, the liquid arched over the room and into the open hole to the subbasement. There was sound like a muscle car making a speed run coming from the hole before a splashing *GLOP* drowned it out.

Everyone stood stock still glancing around to see what would happen. After a few seconds, everyone began to calm.

BBBRRRRRRAAAAAWWWWWWWWW!

The Century Samosa shot from the hole in a roar of Hemi engine noise. It ripped through the tent roof, then with a squeal of metal on metal, it punched right through the hangar roof.

Gwen stared up at the sunlight streaming in through

the hole. "Oh, shit."

Chapter 16

Burj Khalifa - Outer Space - First Place Position

It has to be said that the skyscraper was only in first position because its sheer enormity.

The spire made all the difference. The blasted structure was over a damn mile long.

Close to twenty thousand civilians found themselves technically imprisoned in the Burj Khalifa when it took off a couple of hours ago.

It was well on its way to the big ball of cheese in the sky.

Needless to say, everyone in the building was utterly perplexed at the event that had occurred.

After the initial shock of realizing that their skyscraper was actually a spacecraft, they wondered why the gravity pull enabled them to stand upright on the floor.

A simple explanation, really.

A gravity generator, built in secret, was buried within the mall at the base of the ship. It also contained the compact thrusters that enabled it to propel through space.

Even the elevators continued to work as normal.

And - yes - it did look as stupid flying through the air as it surely sounds.

There was only one man in the entire skyscraper who wasn't alarmed at the news.

Sheikh Yur-Bhutay.

203

He'd used the confusion of the launch to swipe the briefcase containing *whatever it was* from under Micah and Goldie's curling sideburns and fuck off to the toilets on the seventy-fifth floor.

Less happy with the goings-on was his right-hand man, Akram, who ran after him.

"Sire, what is going on?"

"We've got the fucking diamonds is what's going on," Sheikh said.

He held up the briefcase and chuckled to himself.

"Do you know what's in here?"

"No, I do not."

"Only one hundred million dollars' worth of blood diamonds."

"South African?"

"Who cares," Sheikh said as he moved off down the corridor and headed for the franchised *Bean Flicker* coffee store. "They do not have them anymore. We do."

"Ah, most excellent, you excellency."

"Now I do not have to pay those pompous assholes a dime, even if it was a great discount."

"But, sire?"

"Yes?"

"There is a trifling matter of our beloved building flying through space?"

The Sheikh lowered his voice and leaned into the man's ear, "Ahmed, listen."

"My name is Akram, Sire."

"Whatever. It does not matter. I meant to tell you this. My cousin, he did not *only* build a magnificent skyscraper."

"He did not?"

"No," the Sheikh continued, wondering if he had made the right decision in spilling the beans, "Not content enough was he in constructing the biggest erection on the planet. He also installed rockets in the basement. Conditioned each and every window at great expense to keep the vacuum of space out."

"What?" Akram said. "That's absurd."

"Yes. We wanted to keep it a secret until that pot-smoking Tesla inventor infidel got into space, but—huh?"

A flurry of terrified patrons ran screaming into the corridor - next to the fountain of a statue of a little boy pissing fresh water out of his little willy into a stone jug.

"What in the name of Allah is going on around these here parts?" the Sheikh barked at the patrons.

"Sheikh Yur-Bhutay, Sire," a frightened man said. "What do we do?"

"What we what... *do*?" the Sheikh muttered, quizzically, as everyone turned to him for a solution to their crisis.

"Have you seen it out there?" the man bawled. "We are flying."

"Yes—"

"—In space!"

The Sheikh held out his robed arms and nearly dropped the briefcase.

"Yes, yes, yes, yes, yes, yes, yes, yes, yes, yes, yes, yes, yes, yes, yes, yes, yes, yes, yes, yes, yes," he screamed like an enraged child. "I have eyes, you know. I *can* see. Now, everybody, please. Calm down."

"We shall not calm down," the twenty-strong crowd of scared patrons said.

"Bloody well shut up or I'll kill you," the Sheikh roared. "There is *nothing* to be concerned about."

A young Arab man cradling a white, terrified poodle, dared ask what was going on.

"What's going on? Why are we flying in space? Where are we going?"

"Ohh, Allah in a fucking basket weave, shut your cake hole."

"Okay, your excellency. We trust you."

"Fuckin' A right, you do. Now, listen. You are all perfectly safe. There's no cause for concern at this time."

Yip-yip-yip.

The white poodle jumped out of the man's hands and

darted through everyone's legs, headed for the staircase.

"Aw, *shit.*"

"Listen to me," the Sheikh said. "There is nothing to be alarmed about. Follow me, and you shall see."

The Sheikh waved at the young, scantily-clad woman behind the Bean Flicker coffee counter.

"Madam."

"Sire?"

He reached the window and pointed at the moon.

"See that over there?"

"That big ball of cheese?"

"The very same," the Sheikh said. "It is my understanding that we are headed for the moon. Some kind of contest. Us versus Western scum."

"This is asinine," protested a young woman.

"Bollocks and bullshit," her friend recommended.

"It is neither genitals nor cow pie, "the Sheikh said. "Neither is it aniseed."

The two women turned to each other, confused, "Aniseed?"

The Sheikh took a deep breath and continued.

"We are en route to the moon. It is my belief, for it is based in fact, that there are infidels attempting to race with us. Furthermore, we intend to win."

The crowd didn't take to the news at all well.

"Booooooo."

"Okay, shut the fuck up and look at this," the Sheikh held up his briefcase and wiggled it around. "Somewhere in this building of magnificence are a pair of Jews looking for this blasted contraption. If you find them, kill them."

"Oooohhhhhhhh," the crowd said in awe of the expensive case.

A young man said, pointing out the window, "What the fuck's *that?*"

Everyone, including Akram and the Sheikh, turned to the giant glass window and saw a tiny white-and-green armored car whizzing towards them through space.

"The *fuck* is that?" they all said in unison, except for Akram, who widened his eyes and saw a white and green vehicular-based devil race towards them.

"Muhammed be damned," he squealed. "They are headed straight for us."

The Sheikh lowered his bag and barged past the crowd of onlookers.

"Everybody run away very, very quickly."

Armored Security Truck - Second Place Position

Yulia hit the gas and spun the steering wheel all the way to the right.

"I don't give a shit if that *is* the fucking Burj Khalifa," she screamed. "They are *not* going to win this race."

The security truck banked to the right and twisted onto its left wheels, tearing two strips of orange fire across the space/time continuum.

Andrei grasped the overhead barrier and clenched his buttocks.

"Ohhhhh, fuck my asshole. What are you doing?"

"They are cheating, *darling*," Yulia snapped with a steely determination to cause them harm. "Look at them. They are using a massive skyscraper to get to the moon. They barely will have to move much further than one inch to win because of the giant spire at the top. And what we have? A stupid security truck the size of your penis."

Sure enough, the Burj Khalifa looked incredibly impressive rocketing towards the moon like a giant fucking vibrator.

"What are you planning?" Andrei said.

"Let's see how they like *us* penetrating them."

WHOOOOSH.

The stars turned to milk and bled across the windshield of the security truck as the engine roared twice as loud, propelling them to the side of the skyscraper.

"Darling, hold onto something."

"Okay, my sweet. I hope you know what the fuck you are doing at this hour."

"Take this, you fuckers-of-mothers," Yulia squealed.

VROOOOOOOM — KRA-BA-BAAANNNGGGG,

The front of the security truck smashed through the giant *Bean Flicker's* window, wiping out dozens of the concerned patrons in one, fell swoop.

CHOMP — BOMP — SPLATCH.

Predictably, the vacuum of space entered through the glassless frame and sucked anything that wasn't bolted to the ground through the newly-formed hole.

SCHWIP — SCHWAAAP.

A young, recently-wedded couple were the first to go.

The bride's clothes whipped off her torso and waist, revealing her naked body - which subsequently bolted shoulders-first through the window, turning her organs and skeleton inside-out the moment she slid through the frame.

"My wife" the young man squealed as he gripped the window frame. His feet lifted into the air.

His shoes bulleted off his feet, followed by his feet, shins, knee-bones, and thighs - all torn away from the bottom-half of his body in a messy, gory rope.

"Gwaaarrrgghhhh!" his mouth screamed as it tore away from his face, taking his skin and scalp away from his skull (which exploded) forcing his brains to twist out the top of his skull like someone thumping a tube of toothpaste.

Dozens of civilians tried to outrun the force, but couldn't.

WHUP — FLING — FWIP.

One by one, they launched into the air and turned inside out - and inside their clothes - forming a pretty array of instant, sparkling death mere yards from the window.

PING — PANG — SLOOOO.

The individual coffee cups rocketed through the hole in

the wall, as well, adding a creamy, brown mixture to the fleshy gore collecting outside.

SCREEEECHHH.

The security truck battled the force of the vacuum pull. Despite its tires locked into position, they scraped over the dead bodies, crushing them to pieces, causing mini explosions of flesh and bone to cough up the tailpipe.

"Damn it, my sweet," Andrei screamed. "We're being sucked off."

"Sucked *out*, darling," Yulia yelled back. "We are not yet at our wedding night."

"I hope we survive long enough to enjoy it."

"Any other suggestions, my darling genius?"

Andrei pointed at the robed Sheikh running off towards the elevators with his briefcase.

The radio buzzed to life as Andrei lost his shit.

"We commandeer this ship and—"

Alert. Alert. Please can we have your attention. Violence and undue force will not be tolerated in this race.

"What the fucking goddamn fuckety fucking fuck-fuck?"

"*Fuck.*"

Andrei flung forward and knocked his head on the dashboard.

BOP.

"Owwww."

Yulia wound down the driver's side window and peered out. Blue goop slithered across the shattered window and immediately sealed the contents within the building.

"My God. That stuff really does work wonders."

She climbed out of the truck and looked around the room she was now in. A battered coffee shop that had seen better days, littered with the corpses of approximately one one-hundredth of the people aboard the Burj Khalifa.

"Andrei, get out."

WHAAAARRRRRK. WHAAAAAARK.

The bulbs in the Burj Khalifa shut off, replaced by emergency strip lighting.

A bizarre medley of Arabian muzak (the first being *The Girl From Ipanema*) played over the speakers.

"Praise be to Allah," the voice over the announcement said, "We regret to inform most esteemed cohabitants of our most magnificent building that the ship has been invaded by infidel scum. Please make your way to the really fucking expensive shopping mall in the basement."

Yulia squinted, "Huh?"

The announcement continued, "When you get there, please do not mind the loud roaring sounds like those of tigers. They are just the thrusters."

Andrei hopped out of the truck and stepped onto a squishy child's corpse. He tumbled onto his ass and banged the back of his head on the floor.

"Owww. My sweet, I doubt my head can take any more punishment."

BRRRRRRRRRROOOWWWWWW.

The back doors of the truck flew open and coughed out a deathly noise of God.

Yulia wasted no time.

She ran to the back and checked out what was going on, unaware that the back of the truck was on display for all - who remained alive, which weren't many - to see.

The diamond was back and now spun around so fast it became a blur.

"Darling! The diamond thing."

Yulia froze on the spot, hoping the stupid object wouldn't develop sentience and attack her or her intended.

"What of it?"

"It's fucking spinning, that's of it... *what.*"

Andrei picked himself off the floor and stumbled over to his bride-to-be, "Is Ivan there?"

"No, darling. It's just the—"

CLICK.

The barrel of a handgun jabbed into Yulia's temple. A

nasally Jewish voice followed the threat.

"We shall take it from here, young lady," the voice said.

She raised her arms, not wanting to have her pretty little head blown clean off her shoulders.

"Do not shoot."

"We shall not."

"We?" she asked, catching Andrei's puzzled and petrified look.

"My sweet. Do not argue with them."

The handgun belonged to Micah, whose index finger was wrapped around the trigger. His associate, Goldie, swung his inordinately huge machine gun at Andrei.

Micah shook his head, "Oy *vey*. My sweet? How very sweet."

"My sweet, is it?" Goldie chuckled. "Are you two an item?"

Yulia and Andrei acted as if they weren't.

The very last fucking thing they needed right now was the two bad guys to know they cared about each other ~~in some cheap expository character are to make the reader care about them. (Andrew Note: Charley, can we think of something subtler, here?)~~

"Raise your hands, Bismillah," Micah said as he lifted his weapon.

"Okay, okay."

Andrei raised his hands.

"What is this? In the back of your truck?" Micah asked. "It is a diamond?"

"Yes," Yulia whispered. "But we do not know how—"

"—Silence! Soviet pussy hair," Micah said. "It is beautiful. And now, it is ours."

"What?"

Micah turned to Goldie, "Please. Show our young lady friend here how we do things."

"Pleasure."

Goldie squeezed the trigger and shot Andrei in the

face.

SCHPLAAAATTTT.

Andrei's head exploded like a cantaloupe, sending chunks of skull and bone into the air as the rest of his body slumped to its knees.

It then fell to the side on top of the dead child.

Yulia screamed in really, really slow motion and dropped to her knees.

"NOOOOOOOOOOOOOOOOOOO!" her voice slowed into a long, long echo.

She slammed to her knees.

Her entire life flashed before her eyes.

A beautiful sunset where she and Andrei first met.

They shared a margarita together.

They made love on the hot, golden sand, with the ocean waves lapping at their bare feet.

Inaudible conversations in bed, discussing their future, and how, after getting married, they'd like to start a family.

Three beautiful sons, all with blue eyes and blond hair.

A life spent in luxury, with their extended families taken care of.

Sadness, and loss, played out on Yulia's face - all to the sombre tune of Barber's *Adagio for Strings* ~~(Charley note: Okay, Mackay. That's enough. Stop it.)~~

Yulia wept for Andrei, her life in tatters, now that the contents of his skull were racing along the floor and into the nearest metal grille.

"Darling," she gasped. "I'm sorry."

Micah turned to the astonished Yulia and took a step back, all the while aiming his gun at her head.

"Right. I know that was a bit harsh. But I hope you find us sufficiently hate-worthy, now, young lady?"

"Why you did this?" she screamed.

"Klutz. Because me and my associate are looking for the terrorist scumbag who stole our jewels. Now, we may have found remuneration with your diamond. Tell me.

Where you get it?"

"We found it. I do not know where it came from."

Micah lost his temper and thumbed the hammer back on his handgun.

"Confound it, woman. Tell us from where you derived this diamond, or else you will be joining your dead soviet friend in hell."

"We stole the truck. It was inside when we took it. It killed one of our friends."

The diamond made no attempt to correct the woman. It continued to revolve elegantly, sending bright, shiny sparks of beautiful light bouncing around the interior of the truck.

"It is our diamond now. Yes?" Micah threatened.

"Yes. I have lost everyone I love. I do not care any longer."

"Spare us your sob story soliloquy," Micah smiled. "You will not mind if my associate takes the truck?"

"Be my guest," Yulia said, secretly developing a desire for blood behind her sad-as-fuck face, "This godforsaken thing has been nothing but trouble for me."

Chapter 17

The Century Samosa - Outer Space - Fifth Place Position

BLAAAAAASSSSTTT.

The giant Samosa-shaped vessel rocketed through Earth's atmosphere carrying with it a very frightened Hacker at the controls.

"Waaaaaahhhh—" he screamed like a fucking girl as the skin on his face swept behind his skull. "Murrrrr."

SPA-TCHOOOOO.

The damned spacecraft just *wouldn't* let up. The tiny sparkling stars spread into long ropes as he blasted through Earth's atmosphere and into space proper.

WHUP.

Hacker flew forward and banged his manboobs on the flight deck.

Everything slowed to a halt, affording him a view of the solar system tucked behind the gray ball of light.

"Whoa."

Before he could get himself together, the radio on the dashboard flickered to life.

SRIISSHHH.

He unclipped the headset from under the console and clumsily placed it over his head. Like a twat.

"Hello?"

"Hackweed?" Colonel Dumas's voice came through the ear piece. "Are you in space, or what?"

"Ugh, yes, colonel."

"Good. Now, tell me what you see?"

"Umm. *Stars*, Sir."

"Don't get funny with me you little runt," Dumas' voice dipped into a frenzy of lost impatience. "Run coordinates on your panel and tell me what it thinks the destination is."

"Okay, sir," Hacker said, vying to speed up the instruction before his superior got intensely angry.

"Umm."

He punched a random button on the console. A screen twisted up from inside its enclosure and buzzed to life, accompanied by Indian restaurant music.

"Greetings," it said in a thick Indian accent. "How can I be assisting you today, thank-you-please?"

"Uh, yes," Hacker said. "Run coordinates, please."

"Certainly," the screen said. "Would you like fries with that?"

"Uh, no. Just the coordinates, thanks."

"Velly good. One momentum please, thank-you-please."

The screen tilted down and thought over its response. In actuality it was running some peculiar diagnostic on Hacker's request.

"Hatcher?" Colonel Dumas asked. "What's that weird curry music?"

"Hang on, Sir."

Brriippp — *bud-bud-bud.*

The computer beeped and whirred as it performed its coordinates.

"Excuse me?" Hacker asked the computer.

"What?"

"How long is this going to take?"

The screen bobbled its head from side to side and *really* accentuated its Indian accent, "Oh, deary me. You *vanna* do it yourself?"

"No, I can't do it myself. How long is it going to take

you?"

"It is nearly finished."

"Oh. Good."

The computer lifted its head, "Confirming coordinates. Are you ready?"

"Yes, I'm ready."

Hacker rolled his shoulders and prepared to record a series of inordinately lengthy coordinates on his screen.

Biddip-boop.

"The."

"The..." Hacker parroted.

"*Moon.*"

"Moon," he said, ready to continue writing. "Yep?"

"Yep, what?"

"Go on."

"I am afraid I cannot *go on.*"

"What do you mean? Are we finished?"

"That is very correct, oh-yes-indeed-thanking-you-very-much-please."

"*The moon?*" Hacker blurted with incredulity, "Is that it?"

"Why, yes, thank-you-very-much-please."

"Why didn't you just say that in the first place?"

"What?"

"I was all ready to write down a series of inordinately lengthy coordinates, like they do in those films and books they have, now."

"I am afraid I am not knowing what you you are meaning, Dave."

"My name's not Dave."

"Many apologies."

An exasperated Hacker slumped in his chair and tossed his screen on the floor, "Ah. Fuck this."

"Fuck vot?"

"You know what?"

"Vot?"

"Oh, *forget it,*" he muttered quietly. "Stupid *Korma-*

Puter."

"Oh, bloody hell. I am most sorry, madam," the computer piss-taked. "If you would like to make a complaint, you must speak to my master—"

"—Hacksaw?" Dumas interrupted. "Who's that curry-based nitwit speaking at me?"

"No one, Sir. It's the computer. It's just—"

"—I must say, I am *most* displeased with your attitude towards me," the computer droned.

Dumas jumped in, "Hacksaw?"

"Yes? What?"

"Don't *what* me, you little shit—"

"—Sorry, Sir."

"—Fucking let me speak, ass hat."

"Fuck's sake, Sir."

It all got too much for Hacker. He thumped the console and accidentally hit a red button.

WHARK—WHARK.

Fuckin' ejector seat initiated. Please keep your ass on the seat at all times.

"Oh, *shit.*"

Hacker slammed the button with his fist, hoping whatever alien force had spoken would change its mind.

"What in the name of Beelzebub's ass hair is going on, Hackman?"

VINDALOO - VINDALOOO — GAAAAAAGH.

"The ejector seat, Sir," he screamed. "It's been activated."

FIVE… FOUR… THREE…

"Eh? How'd that happen?"

"Peshwari nanbread," the computer added, unhelpfully.

"The ejector seat," Hacker continued. "Oh dear. I think I may be in some trouble."

TWO AND A HALF… TWO…

"Damn it, Hitler. Stop playing with yourself, boy, and deactivate the blasted thing."

Hacker smacked as many dashboard buttons as he

could reach. Each thump produced a bizarre Bangra-esque musical note.

"Ohhh, for fuck's sake."

BOING — TWANG — CURRY-PING.

"Hackford, cancel the fucking ejector seat thing."

"Umm. I'm trying, Sir."

TWO-POINT-EIGHT...   TWO-POINT-TWO-AND-THREE-QUARTERS...

Hacker reached for his safety belt and knocked his elbow on the wall.

"Yaow."

He double-took at the wall and noticed a picture of a six-armed elephant holding some text reading: "Ejector Seat Deactivation."

"Oh, thank God."

WHUMP — KRICK.

He elbowed the glass and reached for the handle. It wouldn't lift down. Instead, it delivered a small sheet of wrapped paper into his hand.

"Eh? What's this?"

TWO-to-the-power-of-THREE-Times-Six...

Hacker unfolded the paper and scanned the writing.

Thank you for purchasing the Ejaculator-9000. Please read instructions carefully before using.

NOTE: Under NO circumcisions must you push the red button before usage.

"Ah, *shit.*"

Hacker tossed the instruction sheet over his shoulder and jumped out of his seat.

"It's all written in Vindaloo."

ONE... ZERO... MINUS-ONE...

"Huckleberry, what's going on?" Dumas asked.

Hacker ran over to the other side of the cockpit and covered his ears with his hands.

BRRRR — SPRRROOIINNNGGGG.

The ejector seat whooshed into the air on a giant coiled spring like a daft Jack-in-a-Box and crashed through the roof.

"Waaaahhhh."

Hacker lifted his head up and watched the last of the seat disappear into vanishing point.

"Uh, S-Sir?"

"What is it now?"

"I think I've damaged the ship," Hacker said.

"I'll damage you, you fucking nitwit. What are you talking about?"

A giant undercarriage whizzed over the crack in the roof - only to be hit by the ejected chair.

KRA-BAAAAAAAMMM.

"Oh deary me," Hacker shouted. "Um, I'm sorry."

"Hack-ass?" Dumas billowed. "What is going on up there?"

"The ejector seat hit another ship, sir."

Tempura-Four - Thirty Seconds earlier...

Geoffrey, dressed in his superior space suit, stood in the cockpit looking all Captain-like and serious.

The moon loomed in the big, big space behind the windshield. It looked as if they were going to win the race. Traveling at speeds of six trillion light years per Pink Floyd album meant that they'd reach the moon sometime last month.

Which, in turn, meant that they'd win the race really easily.

"Laskar?" Geoffrey asked.

"Yah, sur?"

He said and pointed his gloved finger at the moon.

"Seems we're going to win whatever this race is, you know."

"Ah. So."

"So? Look at her. Isn't she beautiful?"

Laskar took a bow in agreement.

"Yah. It look vewwy nice, like big ball of cheeses."

"You know, some people think the moon is made out of cheese."

"Like big dick cheese," Laskar said. "Yum-yum."

Geoffrey pressed his face against the windshield and fogged up the glass with his breath.

SQUEAK — SQUEAAAKKKK.

He drew a heart shape in the fog and wrote Geoffrey on one side, and Laskar on the other.

He finished it off with a big fat arrow going through the heart.

The gesture wasn't lost on the woman at all. Dressed as she was in exceptionally tight, thigh-hugging leggings - black, of course - the man had fallen in love the moment he laid eyes on her ~~tits~~ beautiful face and ~~tight, bowling-ball buns~~ wonderful personality.

Geoffrey struggled to think of anything else since he fell in love with Tokyo's foremost translators. Indeed, shortly before they launched, he'd become so smitten with her that he forgot to take food with him.

And an oxygen mask.

And a couple of firearms just in case they found some aliens and stuff.

But, to him, it didn't matter.

The way Laskar looked at the stars made him fall for her even harder. The confines of his space suit proved to be a challenge. The poor man nursed a perpetual and unrelenting hard-on for over three hours now. He'd put the discombobulating sense of confusion down to a lack of blood flowing to his head.

"Look *atta* stars," she said with her bountiful lips. "They so *pweeeeeety.* Innit?"

Geoffrey ignored Laskar's regression into parrot English. She sounded more Japanese than ever - as if, somehow, she'd managed to *unlearn* the goddamn language.

"Yes, you are," Geoffrey hushed, failing to realize his faux pas. "I mean, *yes*. They are."

"Why? You no like me?"

"What?" Geoffrey spat in defiance. "God, no. I didn't—"

"—Ah. So. You no likely?"

"No, no, I didn't mean to say that. I do like you."

"Then why you lie, Mistah Jeffweeeeeey?"

"Wait, stop. I think we've got our wires crossed, here."

Laskar opened the side compartment where all the really important tubes and shit were and proceeded to tug on them.

"You want me uncross wire?"

"*FUCK NO.*"

Geoffrey bolted over to her and grabbed her forearms, "Don't touch those, you stupid woman."

"Unhand me, Mistah Jeffwey," she barked angrily and wrestled him away. "Me breaky wire."

"No! No *breaky wire*, you stupid pecker head. You'll get us killed."

"Me no peck head."

"Fuck's sake. Put the flippin' wires back or you'll get us—"

KERRRRRUUUNNNCCCHHH — CRACK.

A discarded ejector seat bulleted through the floor, narrowly avoiding Geoffrey's legs and genitals.

Laskar and Geoffrey's arms went limp as they slowly turned to inspect the commotion.

That fucking ejector seat waved around on its severed coil like a spare prick at a wedding.

"Why you do that?" Laskar asked.

"Why I do *what?*"

"Why you shit out big chair?"

"I did *not* shit out a big chair," Geoffrey protested at once.

He slammed the compartment wall shut, trapping the distended wires in all directions like pubic hair on an especially hirsute gorilla.

"Where it came?"

"I don't know."

Geoffrey raced over to the controls and yanked on the lever, sending Tempura-Four spinning around one-hundred-and-eighty-degrees.

The ship screamed around and pointed down, facing the Century Samosa.

"It's *them*."

Geoffrey pressed his finger into his ear.

"This'll show them," he said. "Slightly Antagonistic Computer? Do you read me?"

"Yes, Geoffrey?" the computer said in its quaint, upper-class English accent. "This is SAC, reading you."

"Oh, good. Look, Slightly Antagonistic Computer, can you establish some semblance of communication link-up with that Samosa-shaped spacecraft, please."

"Whatever," SAC huffed. "Not like I don't have a billion other things to do."

"Just shut the fuck up and do it or I'll kill you."

"You'd be doing me a favor," SAC complained. "Hold on, dickhead."

"What did you just call me?"

Boop-boop.

SAC sprang to life with good news.

"Right. The fucking connection is titting-well established, you overpaid cock head."

"Thanks," Geoffrey said, before realizing he'd been verbally attacked. "I beg your pardon?"

"What."

"Did you just call me a smarmy prick?"

"No. An overpaid cock head."

"Fuck outta here with that homo talk," Geoffrey spat.

He shrugged off the unusual jibe and launched into serious-about-space mode.

"That curry spaceship down there just tried to attack us

with its ejector seat. I want to know why."

"Well, you can ask them," the computer said. "I got shit to do, mate."

"Very well. Connection established?"

"*Duuhh*," the computer mocked. "I fucking told you already, didn't I? It's *on*, you deaf nonce."

"Good—What?"

"I said the connection is established, you secret alcoholic."

Laskar's head bounced left and right as the verbal slanging match between man and machine played out.

"I'm not an alcoholic," Geoffrey said.

"Then stop acting like a drunk cunt hair and leave me the fuck alone."

"Fine. Suits me."

"Fine."

"*Fine,* then."

"You want me to enable predictive speech?" SAC asked.

Geoffrey winced at the suggestion. He'd heard of predictive *text* before - but predictive speech was a new one on him.

"Um, what is that?"

"Call yourself a fucking scientist?" Sac spat. "Do you want it or not?"

"Umm. Yes. Okay. Why not."

BRRRIIIPPP.

"Predictive speech enabled," SAC advised. "Okay, the fucker's on."

"Right."

"Right. I'll leave you to it."

"Thanks."

Tempura-Four scorched across the nothingness of space and tilted down to face the top of Century Samosa.

Geoffrey's voice beamed out from the giant *Beetz By Dr. Trey* speakers attached to the front of his spacecraft.

This, of course, did nothing in the vacuum of space, but they looked good, according to the Stereotype Inc's Research & Development team. Luckily, the message was sent over the radio as well.

"This is Tempura-Four wishing to make contact. Please identify yourself."

Hacker grabbed the steering wheel of his spaceship and adjusted his helmet.

Please be advised. Predictive Speech enabled.

"This is Pvt. Hacker of the Clandestine and Unidentifiable NASA-like ~~Tits—Twats~~—*Team*, for fuck's sake" Hacker said, struggling with the predictive speech module. "I'm sorry I accidentally fucked your spaceship with my ~~ejaculate~~—ejector ~~shit—shitting~~—*seat*."

"What did you say?" Geoffrey's voice blasted through hacker's headgear.

"I'm ~~sari, soiree, swanky~~—*sorry*. Fuck's sake. Sorry. I'm sorry."

"You *will* be sorry, you little ~~park—prelude... placard?~~ Fucking *prick*. Fucking hell."

"If it's of any ~~constellation—Cumberbatch—Cabbage patch~~—consolation, I don't have a chair to sit on, now."

"No, it's not of any consol—" Geoffrey's voice stalled, arriving at something of an epiphany. "Hang on."

"What?"

"Your unit's name."

"Clandestine and Unidentifiable Nasa-like Team? Yes? What of it?"

"It spells C.U.N.T."

"Oh. Yeah, it does," Hacker said.

"You're not a ~~cock—cracker~~—*cunt*, are you?"

"You what?"

"Sorry, I mean to say *cunt*, not cracker. This fucking predictive speech thing is ~~antagonizing—antithesis~~—what the frig?"

"Eh?"

"Annoying. I mean to say annoying."

"I'm not a cunt, Sir. Not last time I checked, anyway."

"Well that was a very cunty thing to have done, you know," Geoffrey said. "You can't just go around firing ejector seats at other racers in this race."

"What race?"

Hacker chewed over the information in his mind. Then, as if on cue, he saw the Ford Mondeo and Yonder blast alongside him.

A light bulb appeared above his fringe.

"So *that's* what this is," Hacker muttered. "It *is* a race!"

"I'm afraid you've earned yourself a bit of an ass-punching, now, my friend," Geoffrey said into his microphone and snapped his fingers at Laskar.

"Hey, you."

"What it is?" she asked.

"Engage the fucking cannons. Fifteen through twenty-eight, and aim it at this, uh *cunt*. Please."

"You wan' me to fire big rockets up that cunt?"

"If you'd be so kind, yes."

"My pleh-zhur."

Laskar ran over to the big-ass seat with the periscope on it and sat inside it.

"Fiiiiyyaaaaahhhhhh," Laskar screamed as she gripped both penis-shaped joysticks in each hand, causing no end of turmoil in Geoffrey's pants.

"Oh, dear."

"Give it a good squeeze, I will."

"Now she's talking like Yoda," Geoffrey said. "I think I'm gonna cum—"

"—*Cum* to mommy," she said as she yanked on the trigger. "Hahahahaha."

SCHPEEWW — SCHPEEWW.

Tempura-Four opened fire on Century Samosa, firing

all sorts of pretty neon tracer bullets at it.

"Waaahhhh,"Hacker screamed as he yanked on his joystick, sending Century Samosa into a backwards nose tilt and blasting off towards the moon.

"He's getting away! Keep firing," Geoffrey screamed as he raced after Hacker's ship. "Go, go, go!"

"I trying, I trying," Laskar screamed from within the periscope visor. "It is velly difficult to cum on him."

BLASSSSSSSSTTT.

Tempura-Four shot towards the moon after Century Samosa.

Chapter 18

Ford Mondeo - Third Place Position

Danny grabbed the controls of the Ford Mondeo and pushed forward with all his might.

"Let's see how them redneck pricks like a shunting."

"Danny, man! What you doing?" Chelsea squealed.

He stomped on the gas, the engine revving, and pushing the Mondeo up Yonder's behind.

RAMMMMMMM.

The hood of the Mondeo daggered into Yonder's back which flipped the queen size bed against the wall.

Bucky climbed to his feet after the camper had jolted forward and shouted at Skeez, who was half asleep on the couch with a half-empty bottle of Rollneck Kojak in hands.

"Skeez, get up and see what that was."

"Uhhh, why me?"

"Because you're a good-for-nothing tool using up our oxygen."

"Oh."

"I need you to keep an eye out on anything trying to stop us getting to the moon."

"It's probably them kids," Skeez said.

Bobby Jo had just about enough of the two bickering boys and took charge.

"Fuck y'all prissy little bitches," she fumed as she

stormed into the bedroom. "If you want something assessed, you gotta assess it yourself."

"I'll *ass*-ess your, uh, *ass*," Skeez blurted, thinking he was the funniest man in space.

"Fuck you."

She deliberately shoved Bucky aside and kicked Skeez's ankle as she pushed past the pair.

"Owww, my foot," Skeez complained, sloshing the contents of his beer all over the place.

Bobby Jo glanced through the back bedroom window. She clapped eyes on the kids in the Mondeo. It was about to ram them once again.

"It *is* them fucking kids."

"What are they doing?"

"They're coming straight for us again," Bobby Jo said. "If they try to fuck us up the ass again the whole camper's gonna break."

She spotted the goo covered hole in the back of the camper.

"Shit."

Bucky ran back to the driver's seat and inspected the dashboard. "I don't get it. There must be some way of outrunning them—"

WHOOOOOOSSHHHH.

The entire camper rumbled, shaking the walls and the ground like a food mixer.

"The fuck was that?"

Bucky looked up to see the Burj Khalifa rocket above them. The endless series of windows, complete with terrified civilians, shot past him at an incredible speed.

Bobby Jo ran over to Bucky and pressed her fingers to her ears. The noise of the ship was so loud it nearly made her eyes bleed.

"What the hell is *that*?"

"Another... *ship*?"

"Fuck," Bobby Jo screamed over the commotion. "It's

overtaking us."

Please be advised. You are now in *third*.

"Third?" Bucky screamed. "How can we be third?"

"Step on the fuckin' gas, man."

That's exactly what Bucky did. He squeezed the taser trigger as hard as he could.

"Nggggggg," he yelped. "Hold tight."

KA-BOLT!

Yonder screamed forward, keeping level underneath the enormous Burj Khalifa, and right over the top of the Ford Mondeo.

The acceleration of the camper above the Mondeo astounded Danny. A blast of streaky white lights zipped over Yonder's roof and then appeared to shrink to a tiny dot in the distance.

VROOOM — VROOOOM.

"Fuck's sake, man," Danny slammed on the gas in a futile attempt to catch up to the silver bullet, "That's them rednecks, man. They're getting away."

Chelsea looked around the dashboard for a button that might help.

"Can't you make this useless piece of shit go faster?"

The dashboard lit up when it had heard Chelsea's last two words.

Go Faster? Asked the strange voice from the dashboard.

"Go faster."

Go Faster.

"Yeah, mate," Chelsea said. "Go faster—"

WHIRR—SPROING.

A chunky, green button shoved out from the dashboard with "Go Faster" written on it.

Thrusters enabled. Please use responsibly.

Barry leaned forward on Chelsea's seat and eyed the button, "Huh? It's as simple as that?"

"Shall I press it?" Chelsea asked. "What if—"

"—Fuckin' *do it*, mate," Danny roared and slammed the steering wheel. "Stop stalling and press it."

"Okay."

Chelsea clenched her fist and slammed it on the green piece of plastic.

WHUMP.

"The fuck you doing?" Danny blurted. "I said *press it*, not *wank it off*."

"It's a big-arse button man. I wanna make sure it works—"

Chelsea didn't get to finish her sentence.

The stars hanging in the black void of space stretched into a grid of white lines.

The ambient sound in the vehicle bleached into a whirlwind of nothingness as the three kids slammed into the back of their seats.

"Agggghhhhh," Danny's voice caught up to his screaming lips about four seconds after they opened. The noise turned into an white audio wave and flowed like a rumbling ocean around his shoulders.

The button worked. The Mondeo blasted towards the moon at an alarming rate.

"H-How do w-we m-make it stooooooooop?" Chelsea's wails appeared after her mouth asked the question.

"My b-balls feel like th-they're g-gonna ex-explooooode," Bucky yelped as he held onto the passenger door handle.

"Shiiiiiiiiiiit—"

Danny's scream flowed into Barry's ears, causing his nostrils to bleed.

***

The Sheikh and Akram had made their way to the square mile mall at the bottom of the building.

It only took them five minutes to get there.

PING.

The Sheikh and Akram ran out of the elevator and widened their eyes at the scene. Hundreds of terrified shoppers didn't know what to do, or where to turn.

It seemed the gravity generator did not work so well if you were too close to it.

People and things were clinging to all different surfaces, as if gravity was behaving in different directions over very short distances.

One such shopper stood on the wall of a clothing store named The Brand. He turned to the floor by his face and watched another patron's dog wag its tail and bark incessantly.

Dogs, of course, weren't especially clued up on the workings of scientific endeavors, but when it saw its owner scrambled across the ceiling to safety, it knew something was up.

WOOF. WOOF.

"Cleopatra," its owner said, trying to keep his balance beside the roof's upturned chandelier, "Calm down. It will be okay."

An interesting assessment, all told, as its owner felt the bottom of his robe lift into the air and promise to reveal his underwear.

"What in Allah's name is going on here?" Akram gasped. "Why is everyone on the walls?"

The Sheikh looked to his feet to find that he and his colleague were standing on the door.

"The thrusters," The Sheikh said. "I remember my cousin said that it adjusts once it is out of orbit."

WOOF — WOOF.

The dog wagged its tail once again, flicking specs of blue goo all over the place.

"Why it does not lift the animal?" Akram said.

The Sheikh clutched his robe and hulked the briefcase in his right arm, "I do not know nor care. Come, Akram, we must find ourselves to the basement and find what is powering the building."

The pair moved off towards the service door by the gold fountain hosing the ceiling (which acted as the floor) careful not to get their feet wet.

***

The Basement - Burj Khalifa

The Sheikh and Akram pushed through the service door and closed behind them.

A giant diamond measuring a foot across revolved on its javelin in the middle of a bank of computers.

BLLAASSSSSTTTTT — BLAAASSSTTT.

"What is that sound?"

"It is the thrusters at the arse-end of the ship, Akram. Pay no heed to it at this time."

The Sheikh set his briefcase on the ground and looked at the object hanging before him and his colleague.

"Aha, look," the Sheikh said. "I knew it. I bloody knew it."

Akram's eyes opened as much as his jaw dropped.

"My God. What is it?"

"It's beautiful, isn't it?"

"Yes, but what is it?"

"All my life I have waited for this moment," the Sheikh said. "A thing of beauty. Wondrous, unfettered brilliance. A mere three days ago, the gift arrived. Now, it has taken upon itself to ensconce itself in the most revered and magnificent of buildings."

Akram, dazed and in awe of the diamond, took a few small steps towards it and reached out with his hand.

"Can I touch it?"

"I do not know. I probably would not advise it."

The glint of brilliantine light shimmied in Akram's pupils the closer he got to the jewel.

"It is God?"

"Akram, do not touch."

Ignoring his master's advice, Akram's fingertips pressed against the smooth, cold surface.

"It is fine. It does not harm me."

The Sheikh stepped forward, jealous of Akram's bravery in touching the diamond.

"Come, sire. Join me. Absorb its beauty."

"I will."

WHUMP.

A strange knock came from behind the Sheik's foot as he stepped forward.

"Huh?"

He turned around to see the briefcase had fallen over.

"Huh."

The Sheik ignored it and stepped towards the diamond with his arm raised.

LATCH — KER-KLUTCH.

"What's that noise?"

The sheik looked over his shoulder to see the case had unlocked itself.

"Umm, sire?" Akram asked as he walked along with the diamond. "I, uh, cannot move my hand away—"

The briefcase vibrated up a storm and producing an holy white light.

"My God," the Sheikh said. "The case. It moves."

One by one, the diamonds in the case popped out of their foam housing and lifted into the air.

The Sheikh averted his gaze to the giant diamond to see it spinning faster - taking Akram around and around with it, who had to jog quickly to keep up.

"My hand, my hand, I can't remove my hand!" he screamed, fearing that he'd lost his arm.

"Akram? Let go."

"I cannot!"

Akram's jogs turned into a sprint as he tried to keep up with the giant diamond's revolutions.

BLUERRUUCCHH.

The surface of the diamond turned to a jelly-like substance and absorbed Akram's fist, then swallowed him up to his elbow.

"Arggghhhh."

Petrified, the Sheikh took a step back and watched his associate shunt into the diamond as he continued to run.

"Akram?"

"Ngggggg," the man grasped his upper forearm and tried to tear it away. The more he pulled, the worse it got.

Akram's feet lifted from the ground and sprung into the air.

"Sire, help me—"

GULP.

The diamond's bleach surface absorbed the man in one fell swoop.

"What the—?" the Sheikh said as each of the one hundred diamonds lifted into the air like a slow fireworks show.

"My God."

Please be advised. Interference with your Moronium receptacle is strictly prohibited.

"Strictly prohibited?" the Sheikh muttered. "Who said that?"

A movie trailer-esque voice escaped the diamond, even thought it had no visible mouth or vent to speak from.

I did, you imbecile.

"The diamond? It talks?"

Yup. Crazy-ass language you guys have got here. You wanna see how the other receptacles got on with their racers, mate.

The Sheikh lost his patience, but stopped short of launching into a tirade with the celestial beast.

"My friend, Akram. What did you do to him?"

Ah, yeah. Him. Yeah, he touched me so I ate him.

"But... *why?*"

The diamond spun so quickly it blurred onto a ball of gelatin blue gas.

Sorry about this, fella. I'm afraid we'll have to consider this as a disqualification.

"Disqualification? What the hell are you talking about?"

We'll be taking the diamonds as forfeit, too. But, look, thanks for taking part in the race. It was a pleasure having someone from the Middle East taking part.

That sentence was the last straw.

The Sheikh's precious diamonds danced around behind him, seeming to take the piss. The spinning diamond before his eyes revolved even faster as to render itself practically invisible to the naked eye.

The Sheikh's fortunes were about over. And it pissed him off to an unusual degree.

"Now, you listen to me," he said, ready to punch the shit out of the diamond. "Do you know who I am? I am Sheikh Yur-Bhutay. You will not talk to me like this. I will not accept insolence from a strange alien being like you."

The diamond didn't respond.

Instead, it spun faster and faster, emitting a bright white shell which ruptured violently.

"Return my associate at once, or you shall feel the wrath of my—"

KRAAAAA-BAAAAAAAAMMMM!

The diamond exploded in a shower of of exceptional bright sparks, taking the Sheikh with it.

The basement didn't survive the explosion.

Neither did the shopping mall.

The dog and its master were the first to detonate, followed by the hundreds of shoppers.

The glass frontages of each store exploded as the walls, floor and ceiling burst apart.

After the basement and the mall, each level of the Burj Khalifa joined in the destructive serenade, exploding floor by floor, taking out all the screaming patrons with it.

A cacophonous detonation taking place in space. Those on Pluto or at the end of the galaxy couldn't ignore it.

***

Micah and Goldie climbed into the front of the security truck and fastened their safety belts.

Yulia had little choice but to watch the armed men commandeer the vehicle. They seemed intent to drive right through the hole in the wall with the diamond tucked in the back of the truck.

"So long, *schmendrick*," Micah said to Yulia as he rolled the driver's window up. "Thanks for the jewel, and good luck with your dead friend."

"Bastards," Yulia scowled under her breath as the truck's engine roared to life. "I hope you fucking die."

VROOOOM. VROOOOOOM.

Micah roared the engine and stepped on the gas.

"What is going on?" Micah said, wondering why they weren't moving.

"You klutz," Goldie spat and pointed at the handle by Micah's left knee. "You have failed to lift the handbrake."

"Oh."

YANK.

Micah lifted it up, but the security van failed to move forward despite his force on the accelerator.

"We are not moving—"

ERROR.   ERROR.   ILLEGITIMATE OCCUPANCY. PLEASE DISEMBARK VEHICLE.

The dashboard complained and wailed its alarms.

Yulia moved forward and stealthily opened the back door of the security truck.

A flurry of panicked patrons rushed into the coffee store, not knowing where to run.

"There's been an explosion," one of them said.

"I beg your pardon?" Yulia screamed back as the store filled with hundreds of civilians. "What are you doing—"

"—The basement just exploded," the man said. "We need to take cover."

"What? In outer space?"

Yulia climbed into the back of the truck and tried to pull the door shut. The man bolted forward and begged her to make way.

"Please, don't leave us here," he yelped. "We will be killed."

"Fuck off."

Yulia kicked the man away and used the doors to swipe the oncoming horde of terrified Arabs.

"I said fuck off."

VROOOOOOM. VROOOOOOOM.

Micah and Goldie were more preoccupied with the fact the truck wouldn't move. The latter grabbed his seatbelt harness and went to unfasten it.

"Confound it, man. Make the damn truck go."

"I'm trying, damn it. I'm trying," Micah yelled over the roar of the engine.

Please be advised that due to a flagrant disregard for the rules a penalty must be issued. Please standby.

"Penalty?" Micah shrieked and caught the commotion in the store in his wing mirror, "What is heaven?"

"Help, let us out, we're all going to—"

BRAAAAZZZAAAAAPPPPPP!

A metal casing formed over Micah and Goldie's seatbelt and proceeded to electrocute the men in their seats.

FIZZZZ — SPARK — BURRRRNNNN.

"Gaaaaaaaah."

As Micah screamed, the flesh on his face sizzled and melted away from the flesh on his skull. A plume of fried human smoke billowed into the driver's compartment.

Goldie fared less well.

His clothes caught fire as his seatbelt pumped north of a million volts through his body.

"Gwwuuurggghhhh."

Micah lifted his right hand in an attempt to grab at his friend. The moment he did, his elbow dislocated and burst into flames.

"G-G-Golddiiieeeee—"

This'll teach you to snatch someone else's ride. It won't be tolerated.

The dashboard roared with alien laughter as Micah's heart exploded through his chest and splattered up the inside of the windshield.

Goldie managed to grab his thighs and remove his leg away from his hip joint. Ropes of thick, gloopy blood stringed out as he screamed blue murder.

"Gwwaaaarrrr—"

BOP!

He shoved his leg into the door and pushed it open. The crowd jumped back in astonishment as the messy amalgam of ex-human dropped from his seat and splattered across the floor.

His seatbelt remained fastened, acting as a slicer to dice Goldie's body in three.

"S-Someone h-help m-me—"

"—*Fuck that*," Yulia barked.

She slid past the spinning diamond in the back of the van and hopped over the driver's seat, only to land in a gory concoction of stinking Micah soup.

"Ugh, this is disgusting."

BOUND — BOUND — WOBBLE.

The back of the truck shimmied around under the intense weight of fifty civilians cramming themselves inside - the only safe haven left.

Yulia looked in the rear view mirror and scooped the melted remains of Micah's arms from the steering wheel.

"Goddamnit, what do you think you're doing?"

"Help us, please. Don't go without us."

"Get the fuck out of my fucking van—"

KRA-BA-BOOOOOOOOOOOOOOM.

The entire store and floor level ruptured around the truck. The blue goop on the giant window slithered away, offering the security truck a way out.

Correct participant has now been verified.

Welcome back.

"Thanks," Yulia yelped. "Now get me the hell out of here."

Simply hit the accelerator and you're back in business.

"You got it."

VROOOOOOOOOOOOOM.

The security truck blasted forward, screaming towards the blue goop that covered the broken window.

Hold on tight, racer. It's going to be a bumpy ride.

"Just get me out of heeeeerrrrreeee—"

KRA—SMAAAAAASSHHHHH.

The security truck crunched through the wall, forcing ropes of blue goop in all directions.

As it traversed through the glass on the floor, the civilians in the back of the truck tumbled backward and bounced through the flapping back doors.

WHUMP — KERRACCCKKK — CRUNCHHH.

The back tires trampled over the bodies of those who fell in the truck's path, shattering limbs and cracking skulls all over the once-pristine floor.

"Gaaaaaaaah!" Yulia roared as the security truck lifted up and through the side of the building.

WHOOOOOOOOSH.

Yulia caught her breath as the truck blasted into outerspace and headed for the moon. In the wing mirror, hundreds of civilians screamed and punched the air, deeply unhappy about their predicament.

Their displeasure would only last five more seconds.

For, as Yulia and her truck bolted into the vast vacuum of space and headed towards the moon, the Burj Khalifa exploded in earnest.

KRAAAAA-BOOOOOOOOOOM.

The bottom half exploded in all directions, pushing the force of the detonation level by level right the way to the top.

Those inside were incinerated in an instant.

The levels at the top proceeded to explode all the way to the summit, forcing the spire to catapult towards the moon.

"God rest you poor souls," she whispered as she crossed her head and chest. "This is for you, Andrei, my darling. May you rest in peace."

Amen.

"Right, let us get this fucking party back on track."

***Fucking* party back on track. Please be advised.**

"Do not talk your shit to me. Stupid computer."

I'm sorry. I am neither stupid, nor, strictly speaking, a computer.

"Could've fooled me."

Yulia spun the wheel to the right and zoomed alongside the exploding Burj Khalifa. It was only as she escaped the explosion she felt a number of small rocks hit the side of the truck.

CLUMP — CLIP-CLIP-CLUNK.

"What is that?" she muttered as she hit the gas. She'd soon find out.

"Oh, my God."

Hundreds of tiny, unmolested diamonds sparkled their way across her windshield, ejected from the bottom of the building.

"Diamonds?"

BOP.

Another dull thud hit the windshield. The open briefcase that once-upon-a-time contained the beautiful shimmying jewels.

VROOOOOOOOOOOOOM.

Yulia angled the gear stick to the right and pushed it forward, rocketing towards the moon.

Chapter 19

Century Samosa - Fourth Place Position

Pvt Hacker couldn't believe what he saw. A giant black hole formed in the distance in front of a superior silver-colored spacecraft.

The lasers shooting from the sleek spaceship formed a spectacular light show. Lucky for Hacker the Century Samosa was made of some pretty hard stuff, and shrugged off the blasts like they were nothing more than mosquito bites.

Dumas's voice came through his headset.

"Hackweed?"

"Uh. Yes, sir?"

"What the in the name of baboon pussy-fingering is going on up there? Why aren't you communicating with us?"

"Uh, sorry, Sir," Hacker said. "I just, uh—"

"—You had better report back to us with some damn answers or I'll visit your mother's house and have my way with her. You understand me?"

Hacker ignored the pithy remark and squinted in awe at the hole forming in the middle of space.

"Yes, Sir. Right away, Sir," he said.

"How are you on cow jizz, by the way?"

"Hang on a minute, Sir."

Hacker looked at the dial to the left of his joystick thing and squinted at a little window that showed the remaining percentage of cow cum left in the fuel tank.

Percentage of Cow Cum Left in Fuel Tank-o-Meter
= *11.8%*

"Quite low on *bull nut*, Sir."

"I thought as much," Dumas said. "That Century thing you're driving guzzles baby-making fluid like a nympho with low self-esteem—"

"—Yes, Sir—"

—At a Bukkake party."

Hacker hung his head and sighed. It wasn't an image he wanted to entertain, so he veered the conversation back to more pressing matter.

"I just hope I have enough to get to the moon, though, Sir."

"I'm sure you'll be fine, Whacker," Dumas continued. "Just go easy on the calf-maker as best you can. I have that pretty little filly helping out as we speak. She's gone down on me to see if—"

"*Gone down* on you, Sir?"

"No, uh, not *gone* down. What's the word? Oh! Yes, gone down *for* me. Not on me. She's gone down to the underground lair for me—"

"Phew. Thank God for that."

"—Yeah, to see if we have any more ships we can send up."

"Okay. Thank you for letting me know, Sir."

Dumas chuckled at his own faux pas, "I mean, heaven forfend. Could you imagine if she really had gone down on me while I was on satellite link-up with you?"

"Yes, Sir."

"I mean, that'd just be plain *weird*, wouldn't it?"

"Yes, Sir. It would."

A loud grumbling and swallowing ran through Hacker's headset, followed by a burp.

"Oh, that was rather a lot of semen, Colonel," Gwen's

voice could be heard before his hushed response.

"Good girl, good girl. Now, go wipe your chin off and head back to the secret underground place."

"Yes, Sir," she finished.

Hacker ignored that exchange and put it down to hallucination - which was weird because there was no hallucinatory drugs or stuff that would make him hallucinate.

Instead, his pupils dilated as he took in the wonderful event taking place a few miles away in space.

The newly-formed black hole lightened in texture and tone. A giant swirling *thing* resembling milk being poured into a cup of black coffee.

A giant spoked wheel made ostensibly of toothpaste, centered around a brown sliver of spinning light.

"Is that a... *brown hole?*"

A spiderweb of cracks blasted out from the brilliant white center like a set of wrinkles.

"My God. What do they think they're doing?"

BLAAAAAAAMMMMM.

Hacker reached for his headset and moved the mouthpiece to his lips.

"Uh, sir? Can you hear me?"

"What is it now, Hockley?"

"I think you may want to inform NORAD and everyone else that there's a hole in the galaxy."

"What kind of hole?"

"I'm not sure, Sir," Hacker gasped. "Kind of like... an *ass hole.*"

***

Yonder zoomed forward. He, Skeez, and Bobby Jo watched the remains of the Burj Khalifa streak its fiery way across the blanket of space.

"Looks like they've been disqualified," Bucky said. "Skeez?"

"What?"

"Stop jerking off your tiny pecker and look at this."

Skeez let go of his withered penis and stood up from the couch. Bucky pointed to the moon and indicated a metal circle with little red flags all around it.

"That must be the finish line."

RAAMMMMMMMM.

The camper shunted forward, throwing Bucky and Skeez into their seat. The latter landed penis-first on Bobby Jo's chest.

"Ugh, gross. Gerrof me."

"Sorry."

"That's okay, just get your filthy jerk-hands off my tits."

Bucky ran to the back of Yonder and looked out the back window.

"Ah. Fuck."

"What?" Bobby Jo asked.

"It's them again."

"The kids?"

Bucky ran to the front of the van and punched his fists together, "I'mma keep Yonder on the straight and narrow. Do something about those assholes."

"But, what?"

"I dunno. You're the brains in the family. Think of something."

Bobby Jo bit her lip proceeded to think of an answer. As she did, she saw Skeez rubbing his private parts and licking his lips at her cleavage.

"Huh?" Skeez double-took and blinked at her. "I never saw nuthin'"

"Aha," Bobby Jo snapped her fingers, "I got it."

"Yeah, I think I got it, too."

"No, you dummy," she said as she pressed her hands on the back window. "I'll put them off. Go join Bucky at the front."

"Okay."

Skeez trundled off - tail between his legs - and left Bobby Jo to do what she thought was right. She untied the front of her shirt and waved at the Ford Mondeo.

"Hey, boys."

Danny peered through the windshield of the Ford Mondeo and pointed at the redneck girl in the window of the back of the camper they were chasing.

"There's one of them. Look."

"Huh?" Chelsea said. "That skank-arse whore?"

"Yeah. She's doing something, man," Barry said from the back seat. "What she doing?"

Chelsea clocked the action - one that was all-too familiar to her.

"Uh, oh fuck's sake, mate. She's taking her *shirt* off."

"Saaaaafe," Danny and Barry beamed, together.

The former licked his lips and watched as the left breast on Bobby Jo's chest popped out of its bra. To aid the distraction, she licked her lips in return and fondled her breasts with her fingers.

"Nice, nice," Barry giggled. "Dem some big titties she got, though."

Danny chuckled in agreement. "Yeah, you know. Nice and firm."

Bewildered, Chelsea stared at the two boys, "Are you two serious, right now?"

No response from the red-blooded boys - just major tit-*oglage*.

"You're not gonna fall for her shit, are you?"

"Mate," Danny said as he licked his lips at the second breast plopping out on display. "I'll crawl through five miles of broken glass just to suck her shit through a sock."

Chelsea clipped Danny around the back of the head.

"Fuckin' disgusting prick."

"Wait till you see what I do with her when she's bent over my dashboard."

"Danny!" Chelsea screamed, full of incredulity. "I *am*

here, you know."

Danny licked his lips at the vision of beauty coming from the back of the van, "You can join in if you want."

"Prick."

Chelsea hit him and folded her arms in a huff.

VROOOOOOM.

Danny stepped on the gas and rode the front of the Ford Mondeo up Yonder's ass.

"Wanna get a closer look, mate."

Chelsea finally lost her shit. She pulled the front of her shirt apart. The buttons pinged off one by one revealing her not-quite-as-a-well-endowed-cleavage-as-Bobby-Jo's.

"What. Am I not good enough for you, is it?" Chelsea asked. "You prefer *her* to me?"

"Mate, you're flatter than a five-year-old boy."

"Mate, fuck you."

Chelsea slumped in her chair and looked for something to hit.

Meanwhile, inside Tempura-Four...

Geoffrey clapped his hands together and observed the giant ASS-HOLE that had formed several miles ahead of the ship.

"This is it. This is how we win."

Laskar put the finishing touches on her Bonzai tree and looked up from the table.

"Ah-so?"

"How so?" Geoffrey smirked. "It's quite easy, really. I've engaged the secret brown hole tech and opened up a back door for us."

"Back door?"

"Before you start, please don't make any funny jokes about *going up the back door*, or whatever. It's unbecoming of you."

Laskar didn't have the first friggin' clue what Geoffrey had said, and returned to catching flies with her of chopsticks.

"Unbecoming on you."

"I thought you might say that. Here, look at this."

Geoffrey grabbed the back of her hair and lifted her to her feet.

"Owww, you hurt me."

"Yeah, whatever," he muttered and released her hair. "See that big brown circle thing out there?"

"It look like coffee."

SNIP-SNIP.

She clipped the ends of her chopsticks together, which irritated Geoffrey rather a lot.

"Can you please stop doing that? I'm trying to show you how we're going to win."

"We win."

"Put the fucking chopsticks down, Mrs. Miyagi."

"Solly. I put down."

In a frankly ridiculously-timed moment, she bent over and placed the chopsticks side by side on the table.

Geoffrey ogled her ass and licked his lips. His inner conscience complained in his right ear as he looked. For some strange reason, it spoke in a Glaswegian (Scottish) accent, sounding like Mel Gibson in Braveheart.

Aye, Geoffrey? Y'there, pal? This is your fuckin' conscience speaking, by the way.

"What?" he blurted out loud, wondering who'd spoken. "What did you say?"

Laskar remained bent over the table, perfectly aligning the sticks side by side which seemed to take an age.

I see you looking at that lassie's ass, pal. You dirty fucking pervert, ye. You know whuv' gorra race tae win, ken?

"I'm n-not looking. I'm just waiting."

Aye, reet. Waiting my urse. Get back tae work, y'numpty.

"No, waiting for her ass, if anything," Geoffrey mumbled as Laskar straightened her back, allowing her long, brunette locks to fall down her shoulders.

"Listen, pal. See you? Yuzza're gonnae fuck up the race an' that if y'keep gawpin' at her behind. Concentrate the noo on the urse-hurl and win the race, then y'can fill yer boots wi' nip's urse cheeks.

"Okay, fine."

Geoffrey blinked hard and managed to silence the stupid voice in his head. He smiled as Laskar as she shook her hair all around like she was in some fucking shampoo commercial.

"Why you look at me?"

"Laskar, there's something I need to tell you."

"What it is?"

Geoffrey held his fist to his mouth and cleared his throat.

"Se, the thing is, my wife and I aren't really sexually active anymore, and—"

"—You *marry*?"

"Uh, yes. I am. I'm sorry, I forgot to mention it."

Laskar put two and two together and arrived a five-hundred-and-twelve.

"Ah, you are marry."

"Yes, I'm afraid so. But we're going to get a divorce—"

"—What his name?"

"His?" Geoffrey fake-laughed. "Oh no, no, it's not a he. It's a *she*."

"Is not a she, is a he?"

"Yes," Geoffrey said. "No, that's not right—"

"—Aaaaaah-so. *He-she*?" Laskar took a bow. "Ah! Like, how you say, a *ladyboy*?"

"Yes," Geoffrey said before realizing he'd made a fatal error, "God, *FUCK NO*. No, not a ladyboy. I'm not gay.

My wife is woman—"

"—Ahhh, why you not say?" Laskar giggled. "Why you say you like ladyboy?"

"But I don't."

"I unnerstan'."

"Besides, aren't ladyboys from Bangkok and stuff?"

"Is okay Meestah Jeffwey," she said as she walked towards him seductively. "You like me, huh? That is what you sayin'?"

Geoffrey felt his heart climb into his throat and his penis try to escape his pants.

"Well, in not so many words. Yes."

"Ah fought you liked me?"

She smiled at him with her eyes and licked her lips. Her fingers brushed the side of his face. If an outsider was watching, they'd swear blind they were about to kiss - culminating in a most unfortunately-timed explosion in Geoffrey's pants.

"I like you, too, Jeffwee. I *love* you, yeah?"

She pursed her lips and moved her head to his. At last, the moment he'd been waiting for.

And with the serenade of the brown hole hanging in space, everything was perfect.

Their lips met in the celestial light produced by the brown hole, and they kissed for an eternity. Not a deep French kiss, but a prolonged peck.

The skin on their lips pinged apart, softly, as they looked into each other's eyes.

"Laskar?"

"Yeah?"

"I, uh," he fumbled for the words, but found the courage, "I love you."

"Me love you *looooong* time Mistah Jeffwey."

A smile of ecstasy formed across his face at what she'd said.

"I'm so glad."

A teardrop rolled down his cheek as he held her

delicate shoulders. "Oh. Laskar. What a perfect time to fall in love, huh?"

"Yeah."

He took a moment to look down at her cleavage, and then her midriff. Finally, he landed on the marvelous bulge protruding through the front of her space suit.

"I'd have it no other way—" he said, before looking back at her face in alarm. "I, just, uh—"

Geoffrey double-took when he saw the shit-eating grin on Laskar's face.

"The fuck?"

Geoffrey grabbed the bulge in his hand - yeah, it was *definitely* a cock.

"Eww. You're a *dude*?"

"Nah," Laskar said softly. "I am only woman. We go in brown holes now."

"God dammit. How many times am I going to fall for the secret dick thing?"

Four-and-a-half seconds later.

Geoffrey ran over to the flight deck and punched a command on the keyboard. Q-BRICK, the on board navigator *thing*, lit up, showing off its tiny red dot.

"Q-BRICK. This is Geoffrey Chaucer, pilot of Tempura-Four. Proceed with instruction."

"Hello Geoffrey," the computer said. "Would you like to proceed?"

"Uh, yes. That's what I said."

"Very good."

Biddip-boop. Boop.

The computer blinked and flashed. The red bulb dulled inside and twisted around.

"Commencing brown hole penetration."

"Very good. Get us in that hole and fire us out the ass-end, please. We'd like to win the race and all those fabulous prizes."

"I am detecting an irregularity, Geoffrey," Q-BRICK said.

"No, that's just Laskar."

"No, not that kind of irregu—"

"—Turns out she has a cock and balls and not a vagina as originally anticipated."

"No, Geoffrey," Q-BRICK interrupted. "Nothing to do with transsexualism. The irregularity is occurring outside the ship. One moment please."

"What is it now, you useless bag of nano-spunk?"

BLIP… BLIP… BLIP.

Q-BRICK dimmed, then went off line.

Geoffrey thumped the side of the console.

"Hello? What are you doing?"

Q-BRICK's red eye snapped back to life. It looked at Geoffrey strangely, and spoke in a movie trailer-esque alien voice.

Cheating is not allowed. This includes - but is not limited to - hyper-jumps, time-warps, and any other scientific advantage. Failure to observe the rules will result in penalty.

"Q-BRICK?" Geoffrey asked, puzzled.

This is not Q-BRICK.

"With whom am I speaking?"

Mur'kroznitck. Official.

"McWhatsit?" Geoffrey asked. "Who the hell are you?"

Be advised. Failure to adhere to the rules will result in penalty. Thank you.

"Rules? What rules?"

Geoffrey eyed the yellow thruster lever with "ass hole" written above it.

"Are you quite sure you want to do this, Geoffrey?" Q-BRICK asked.

The man licked his lips and just for good measure looked over his shoulder. Laskar shook ~~his~~ her head, sat up straight and puckered her lips.

"You want round two?"

"Fuck."

Geoffrey found himself in a dilemma. He could push the thruster and win the race. Or, he could *not* push the thruster, and get another frisking by Laskar. Either way something was going into a brown hole.

"Ah, fuck it."

WHUMP.

He rammed the thruster forwards and lifted his head to the brown hole hovering from the other side of the windshield.

"Let's win this fucker."

***

WHOOOOOSH.

Yulia yanked on her steering wheel and made a beeline for the side of Tempura-Four. She bit her lip and squinted at the perfect ramming position - where the airlock met the side wing.

"Okay, you bastard," Yulia said. "I've already gatecrashed one party. Let's see how you fuckers hold up against ten tons of metal."

SLAMMMMM.

As Yulia applied her weight to her right foot, a fantastic light show erupted to the side of her vehicle.

The brown, swirling ass hole spun around like a twisted lava lamp and threw several thunderbolts around its central ring piece.

"What in the name of beelzebub's bollocks?" she muttered as Tempura-Four sparked up a storm and began to elongate towards the swirling sphincter in the sky.

KRRRROOOOOOOOMMM.

Tempura-Four's front stretched towards the brown hole like a stringy piece of thoroughly-used chewing gum, headed right for the nucleus of the hole.

"Wah, wah," Yulia yelped, feeling the force of the hole suck her van towards it. She flung the stick shift into reverse and tried to back up and get away from its force.

"Noooooo. No."

VROOOOOO-SCREEEEECH.

Be advised. Cheating is not permitted during the race. Thank you for your understanding.

"What?" Yulia yelped. "It is not me. It is *them*!"

You are entering into a hole that will affect the outcome of the race.

"No," she protested and continued to ram the accelerator. "It is not meeeeeeeee—"

SCHEEEERRRIPPPPPPP!

Tempura Four blasted into the brown hole, swallowed through its central ring - never to be seen again.

Penalty initiated.

"What penalty?"

Bip-bip-bip-bip.

The diamond on the javelin in the back of the van began to bleep angrily.

Cheating in progress. Self-destruct initiated.

"What self-destruct?" Yulia screamed. "Goddamn it, you useless prick. I am not cheating—"

The security truck tires rolled around to useless effect. All it did was create a giant noise which reverberated through the truck.

The hood peeled forward and made for the center point of the brown hole.

SCHWAP!

Detonation in... five... four... three... two...

"Oh, God. Noooooo—"

GLUMPH.

The brown hole swallowed the security truck whole and burped.

The entire event was caught by Pvt. Hacker as he watched from within the Century Samosa.

"Christ, did you see that?" he asked no one in particular. "That thing just ate those two vehicles."

He turned around to find that no one had heard him. Of course, he was all alone on Century Samosa. He had been since his departure in the race.

"What the fuck happened to them?"

Disqualification.

Hacker eyed the dashboard and shrugged his shoulders, "What disqualification?"

In the race to the moon, they attempted to cheat.

Hacker pointed at the camper and Ford Mondeo hurtling towards the finish line.

"What about them?"

They did not cheat. Ergo, no penalty.

"Okay. I'm starting to get the picture."

Hacker turned the joystick to the right and fired up the thrusters.

The Century Samosa blasted ever-closer to Bucky's Yonder van.

"There's no way I can win."

SPRRIIISSSHHHHH.

"Hocker?" Dumas's voice came through his headset. "What was all that gay talk? Something about *not* winning?"

"Sir, it's me. It seems I'm so far back I don't think I can win."

"Bullshit, Hocker," he yelled. "You do whatever it takes to get ahead and win, you hear?"

"Yes, Sir. But—"

"—No buts, either, private. Buts are for smokers and faggots, you understand?"

"Yes, Sir."

"I don't care if you have to fucking *cheat*, you just make sure you—"

Cheating is not permitted in this race.

Silence.

"Who the fuck said that?" Dumas asked.

"Uh, I think that's the organizers of the race, Sir?"

"What, are they on board the Samosa with you?"

258

"No, Sir. I think they are communicating via our control bank."

We repeat. Cheating will not be tolerated and met with extreme penalty.

"Who the fuck asked you, numb nuts?" Dumas shouted at the voice he couldn't see.

"Sir, please. Don't make it angry."

Biddip-beeeeeeeep.

Observe this, *motherfucker*. What happens when you flagrantly disregard the rules.

"Huh?" Hacker gasped.

"Huh?" Dumas added.

"Sir, I—"

RUUMMMBBLLLLLEEEE.

The ass hole hanging amongst the stars seemed to clench inwards. The surrounding twinkling spots of white shimmied, indicating some kind of airless vortex drifting out from the middle.

"Uh, sir?"

"What is it now, Hacky?"

"Umm, something is happening in space," he said. "I don't think I want to be an astronaut anymore, Sir."

"The fuck you talking about—"

BOOOM - BOOOOM - BOOOOOOOOM.

"Uggghhhhh," Hacker closed one eye, not truly wanting to see what was about to happen.

KA-BLOOOEEEEYYYYY—SCHPLATTT-TAT-A-TAT.

The ass hole vomiting a torrent of liquid brown shit out from its middle. The puke fountained out like a tidal wave escaping a blocked pipe.

FAARRRTTTT — RAASSSSPPPPP!

The hole in the middle moved around like a boxer's mouth being hit in slow-motion, as the contents of a regurgitated Tempura-Four and Security Truck (notable by the white and green colors) twisted into a straight line and headed for the edge of the solar system.

The rest of the bowel movement screamed towards the Centurion Samosa.

"Hackwood, what are you doing—"

"*—OOHHHHH, SHHIIIIIIIIIIIIITTT!*"

Hacker closed his eyes and braced himself for impact. *KER-SPLAAAAAAAAAAATCH.*

A torrent of regurgitated vehicular slurry splattered up the front of Century Samosa.

A Russian woman's melted face slithered up the glass, followed by the severed penis and black pubic hair wrapped around a scorched pair of jeans.

Geoffrey, Laskar, and Yulia had been killed and spat out in the worst way imaginable.

"J-Jesus Christ," hacker stammered with fear.

We trust this message has been understood. This message brought to you by *SHLOOM* - The Official Beverage of Mur'kroznitck.

"Oh, shit. Oh, shit."

"Hackwood, you better tell me what the fuck—"

Hacker slipped his headgear down his neck and cut the call off, presumably sealing his fate into the process.

Alone and without direction in the void of space, he cared little for his own well-being, now. He needed to find out what was going on.

Why were they racing?

What the fuck was going on, generally-speaking?

He focused on the last two racing vehicles and hit the gas. *BIDDUM-FLIP. BIDDUM-FLIP.*

He flicked on the windshield wipers, which swayed left and right, and cleared the gore from his view.

"Right," Hacker huffed, determined for answers. "Let's figure this shit out."

Danny was practically stood on the accelerator. Everything the Mondeo had was being poured into the engine. With a cry of victory he saw that it was going to be enough. They were gaining on that Goddamn camper.

The Moon filled their view as they drew close. Its black and gray surface becoming clearer as the miles slipped past.

"You gonna pass 'em?" Barry said, leaning through the front seats to be closer to the action.

"Fuck that, mate. I'm gonna knock ten bells of shit outta that scrap heap."

As they closed in, they could see through the film of blue goo covering the hole in the back of Bucky's camper - the result of their last ram job.

Bobby Jo watched through the back window as the Mondeo closed the gap.

"Boys, I think those fellers might pitch for the other team. They're coming in hard for a rammin'."

Skeez opened the door to the bathroom, and smiled, enacting a forward-thrust with his hips, "Another thing me and them have in common."

"Shut up, Skeez," Bucky and Bobby Jo said together.

"Can you get a shot off?" Bucky yelled from the front.

He could see the ring of the finish line now, but it was still a ways off.

"They're too far out, and by the time they get close enough it'll be too late."

"Do it anyway. We need to keep them off us," Bucky said.

CHICK—CHACK.

Bobby Jo racked another shell into the shotgun, and sat on her butt to get a good line of sight through the hole. "You better think of something else in case this don't work."

Hacker stomped on the accelerator, revving the loud engine, and lurched forward.

"What the hell. How can I catch up?" he yelled, desperately.

You want the boost?

"You what?" he asked the dashboard.

You want the boost?

"Uh. Yes?"

You got it.

A large green button formed on the console in front of him. It read *'Go Fast'*.

With hesitation he reached out, but stopped.

"This is crazy. I'm not risking my life for a stupid race."

The head set buzzed around his neck as Colonel Dumas screamed into the radio. "YOU WIN THIS RACE OR I WILL REMOVE THE FLESH FROM YOUR BUTTOCKS AND WEAR THEM AS EAR MUFFS, HOOKER!"

Hacker smacked the button out of sheer reaction to that voice.

The Century Samosa shuddered then shot forward. The force threw Hacker across the bridge and against the wall.

"YEEEEEAAAAAAHHHHH."

The Samosa smeared across the sky in ungodly acceleration, leaving a streak of brown as the shit was ripped from its hull.

Bucky squeezed the 'GO' taser with everything he had. He had hoped they might get past the finish line before those asshole kids rammed the shit out of the Yonder. Then the clicking noise that went along with the taser began to slow.

"Oh, shit. Oh, shit," he said.

"What's happening? Why are we slowing down?" Bobby Jo asked from the back.

"The taser," he panicked. "It's running out of juice!"

The sound of Skeez taking a long leak in the bathroom gave him an idea.

"Skeez. Get your dumb ass out here, now."

The stream dried up as the bathroom door opened, "Yeah? What's up?" Skeez said, zipping up.

"I need you to piss out the hole," Bucky blurted over his shoulder as he attempted to coax every volt he could from the taser.

"I already did. The doc fixed me up so it don't leak inside no more."

"Naw, not your *dick* hole, dumbass. The hole in the back of the ship."

Skeez thumbed the door and pulled out a fresh tin of Rollneck Kojak.

"Sorry, man. All pissed out. You should have said something before I went in."

"Bobby Jo," Bucky yelled.

"I'm on it," she yelled from the back. "Just don't nobody peak, I gots a shy bladder."

Danny smiled like a maniac as the front of the Mondeo flew towards the back of Bucky's camper. They were about to blast the honky wagon to pieces.

"That fucking bitch," Chelsea huffed. "Her boobs weren't enough, now she's displaying her hummin' *twat* for the entire universe to see?"

Danny squinted at the view. Sure enough, the blond redneck girl was on her hands and knees with her vagina on full display through the hole they had punched in the camper's rear. "*Fuuuuck*," Danny marveled. "That bitch had a nice piece."

Chelsea slapped his arm, "Shut up, Danny."

The sound of Barry's fly zipping down told them that he had gotten a good look at Bobby Jo's hillbilly snatch.

He was going to *do* something about it.

Danny eyed the rear view mirror to tell Barry that now was not the fucking time to have a wank, but the words caught in his mouth.

Danny averted his eyes an inch above Barry's head to find a huge Samosa lifting into view through the back window.

"The fu—" was all he got out before the giant

appetizer slammed into the back of them.

The back of the car flew up, destroying anything behind the two front seats, including the masturbating Barry.

"Yaaooowwww—"

KER-SPLATTCHHH.

A spray of red mist and organs splattered onto the inside of the windscreen, blinding them to what was happening on the Yonder.

"Come on, Bobby Jo. It's just a little water play. You've done this a thousand times." Bobby Jo whispered to herself, trying to psyche herself up. "Just pee, already."

She felt her bladder holding on stubbornly, as she squeezed her stomach muscles while on her hands and knees.

She glanced at her arms and legs to see how close the Danny and his team were. A huge Samosa slammed into the back of the Mondeo and pushed them both directly at her.

"YEEEEAAAAAAA," she screamed, the terrifying sight of the two ships barreling down on her made everything let loose.

Her bowels turned to water, encouraging her bladder to join in on the fun. Both her ass and piss hole sprayed liquid at high velocity out the opening in the camper. Instead of passing through though it, her liquid effluence spattered across the blue film.

There was a terrifying second where the goo did nothing, and a little more piss and shit squirted out of her along with a lady like squeak of a fart. The two now-entangled ships closed the gap. It looked like they were going to slam into the Yonder at a million miles an hour.

Then the goo vibrated and spasmed.

Suddenly, Bobby Jo found herself plastered to the back window as the Yonder took off like a squirrel with its tail on fire. She watched out of the one eye smashed into the glass as they slowly pulled away from the oncoming ships, just barely.

"Woohoo," Bucky screeched from the front. "You did it."

The ring of the finish line flashed past the back window.

The other two ships passed through right on their heels.

"Ow ee onna sthap?" Bobby Jo slobbered into the window.

"Oh, shiiiii—"

SCCCRRREEEEEEE—BOOOOOOOMMMMMM!

Everything snapped into darkness as they blasted through the finish line in first position and crashed into the Sea of Tranquility.

Chapter 20

Mare Tranquillitatis (a.k.a Sea of Tranquility) - The Moon

Biddip-bweeeeeep. Bonk-bonk-bonk.

An unconscious Bucky groaned at the deafening beeps whirling around his head.

"Ughhh."

Biddip-bwip-bwip.

He opened his eyes carefully. The vision of something shiny and metallic in nature focused into view.

Perfectly clean and without any blemishes whatsoever. He felt the blood rush to his forehead and blink the crap away from his eyeballs. He was bent over a railing, his hands on a warm metal bar.

"Owww, my head—"

Biddip-bwaaaarp.

A strange sensation pushed against his stomach, like that of a particularly muscled arm wrestler.

"The fuck?"

He couldn't move. The rush of blood to his head wouldn't abate, aided none by a deathly snorting coming from over his left shoulder.

"Cramma-bin," screeched whoever - or whatever - stood behind him, "Alla'krab."

"What the fuck?"

Bucky squeezed the metal bar and tried to push himself upright.

"CRAMMA BIN," the alien advised.

"Cramma bin?"

"Larden," added the voice.

"Okay, y'all are crazy—"

Nggggggg.

Bucky applied his full body weight to the metal bar, but was stuck. Restraints held his shoulders in place. The shiny silver surface hanging in front of his face was a floor.

It was definitely a floor.

How did he know?

The shadow of a multi-limbed *thing* crept along it, indicating its position from behind.

"Cramma. Bin."

WHUMP-SLAP-WHUMP.

A series of fluorescent lights snapped on, each one serving as a colossal punch across the eyes, producing a God-almighty dagger of headache-inducing nastiness.

"Ugh, ugh," Bucky groaned. "What happened? Did we win?"

Bucky blinked and shook the fatigue from his forehead. When he opened his eyes, he saw someone he recognized, strapped in the same type of restraint.

"*You,*" Bucky spat at the black lad bent slumped over the metal bar.

Danny *fucking* Hook. An unconscious Danny Hook who was about to come-to.

His feet were fastened to metal moorings on the floor.

Like Bucky, he was bent over at the waist across a metal bar.

Worse, his jeans had been removed, his bare buttocks exposed for all to see (provided they were behind him.).

"Oh J-Jaysus," Bucky yelped, seeing once and for all the exact same position he was trapped in. "N-No, no—"

The stupid alien voice interrupted his interminable cry for help.

"Cramma Bin."

SCHTOMP — SCHTOMP.

The shadow on the floor slid towards Danny's and met the owner.

"H-Help m-me, I'm stuck," Danny complained, coming around and looking to Bucky. "What the fuck, man?"

"I d-dunno what's going on," Bucky said. "I swear to you."

"Get me outta here," Danny squealed as he laid eyes on the beast making its approach to him.

"Oh, *f-fuck me.*"

The giant alien stepped behind Danny and into Bucky's view.

"My God, you're one *ugly motherfucker.*"

The alien stood ten foot tall. It resembled a complicated amalgam of flesh, ribcage and more than twenty limbs. It tilted its "head" at Bucky and slapped Danny's left butt cheek.

"Yaaooowwww," the poor lad said. "P-Please, n-no—"

"—Cramma."

SCHLOOOOOOO.

Its tongue vacuumed the ropes of thick, white saliva drooling from its vagina-esque mouth. It ignored Bucky and turned its attention to Danny's behind.

It's twelfth tentacle whipped out from its body. The cuticles at the very end opened up like a flower and turned upwards like a palm.

A bizarre red ball hovered above its skin and gyrated on its axis.

"What's it doing?" Danny screamed at Bucky. "I can't see."

"Ummm. I think it's better you don't ask—"

SWIZZ-SCHWUNT.

The metal housing produced a giant robotic arm, which extended out and snapped its vice-like digits back and forth.

SNIP-SWIP.

Bucky prayed the unusual device wasn't intended for all

those weird things he'd heard about when people got abducted.

"Oh my God, I can't watch—"

"—"What, what?" Danny gasped and shifted around in his trappings. "What's happening?"

The end of the arm twisted around and stabbed Danny in the asshole.

"Yaaaoooowww."

WHIIIRRRRRRR — SNATCH.

The pronged-ends jutted out, yanking Danny's butt hole open.

"Ah, f-fuck."

The alien being moved its mouth towards the lad's bottom and held the glowing red orb in its "hand".

"Maaarrrsss," the alien said. "*F-Fabbolos... p-prize.*"

"Huh? *That's* the fabulous prize?"

Bucky couldn't bare to watch, but was acutely aware that something - some being - was approaching him from behind.

"Aww, *hell no.*"

"You've got an alien thing, now, mate," Danny screamed at Bucky.

Danny had no choice but to take whatever was coming to him - and Bucky. He watched the giant alien creep up behind his redneck opponent and produced a glowing red ball.

"Mur'kroznitck," the alien said as he watched a robotic arm extend out from Bucky's restraint.

"Mur-what-nick?" Bucky said as a cold, tingly sensation slid inside his butt hole. "What in the fuck—"

SCHWUP.

"—Oww. My *poor ring.*"

"Oh, shit," Danny offered as he watched Bucky's alien yank its "elbow" back and prepare to deliver a fatal blow to Bucky's ass.

"Mate, I'd bite down on something if I were you—"

"—What?"

PUNCH — SCHWOMP.

The alien socked Bucky in the asshole, delivering the red orb deep within his bowels.

"YaaoowwmyfugggggiinChrist—" Bucky screamed at the top of his lungs.

BWWOOOOAARRGGHHH.

Danny threw up at the sight unfurling before him, splattering the nice, shiny floor with the maize-based snacks he'd eaten during the race.

"Gwwwuuurrrrr."

FWOMP — SCHLAP.

"GAAOOOOWWWWW!"

Danny yelled as he, too, felt the vicious punch blast through his ring piece.

Inside Bucky's Bowels

The red orb traveled through the shit-smeared tunnel, avoiding small clumps of turd that had been resting there for years. Fragments of decade-old food stuck to the mass as it lasered through a pink wall and entered...

Inside Bucky's Digestive Tract

A long series of pink tunnels led the way through Bucky's body. The orb grew to twice the size it was when it entered his asshole. Now, it was clear to see - the orb resembled the planet Mars.

It continued its way through the labyrinthine tunnels of flesh and made its way towards Bucky's stomach.

Back in the peculiar room, Bucky clenched his buttocks together. The initial pain of having a right-hook delivered to his ass ring had abated and, in a peculiar turn of events, felt quite pleasurable now that the worst was over.

The alien stomped in front of Bucky's face and held

one its many goo-covered arms up at the bright, white wall.

"Shontcha-clip."

"Huh?" Bucky whined as he felt the planet wade through his body, causing all sorts of horrid complications. "Schontcha clip?"

BWIZZZZZZ.

A fifty-foot hologram appeared in front of the wall. The solar system, with each of its planets, hung in the middle of the room. Mercury, Venus, Earth...

Mars.

"Holy fucking shitting Christ on a pogo stick," Bucky said as the last identified planet glowed on screen. "Did y'all shove *Mars* up my ass?"

The beast turned to its colleague and nodded its head.

"Fredda-West."

"Fredda-West," Danny's alien confirmed.

Bucky's alien's vagina-face twitched and spat out a rope of clear fluid to the floor.

The pain subsided in both Bucky and Danny's body as the ball settled somewhere inside them.

Bucky felt his ears burn in time to the hologram of Mars growing at an incredible rate. A tinnitus-like feeling tingled through his ears as he felt his face warm up like a duvet shoved into a microwave.

"Fredda-West," Bucky's alien continued to speak, its bizarre language creeping into English mid-sentence, "Shwon-tip—understand what I am saying?"

"Huh?"

"You have probe," Bucky's alien's voice rumbled through his ear holes, "We learn language. You understand me what I say?"

"Yes?" Bucky said with confusion and made eyes at Danny. "What the fuck? What's going on?"

"I think they're tryna chat shit to us, mate," Danny yelped.

Bucky's alien turned to Danny's alien, "It appears they

understand us."

Danny's alien slapped the lad's left ass cheek in celebration.

"Hey, stop doing that," the lad complained.

"Good. It appears to have worked."

The two aliens approached the hologram of the solar system and folded all twenty-something of their tentacles together, waiting for the two men's attention.

"Please, let us go," Bucky blurted. "I swear, we won't tell no one—"

"—*NOT TALKING*," the alien yelled through its vagina-based mouth hole. He lifted his shoulder tentacle and pointed at Bucky. "You. Winner."

The alien's twenty-fifth tentacle extended its cuticle and prodded its own mouth.

"We. Mur'kroznitck. *Race*."

"Murcros-stich?"

The alien moved its tentacle and pointed at Danny, "Hooman?"

"Yeah, mate."

"*You*," the alien said, attempting to understand the black man chained before him. "*Man*."

"We're, uh, human," Danny huffed. "Who are you?"

The alien shook its pussy-lip-based visage in anger. He leaned into his colleague and whispered in its sort-of-ear, which looked more like a slab of penis dripping in fish batter.

"The fuck are they doing now?" Danny yelped.

"Telling us what's going on, I hope," Bucky mused and turned to the aliens. "Hey!"

The two aliens shot Bucky a look.

"What you desire?" the first alien said.

DIDDLE-OO-DOO-DIDDLE-OO-DOOO.

Danny's cell phone rang in his pants pocket. The ring tone startled the aliens, first into a fit of shock and then into a state of curiosity.

"Aww, fuck," Danny said. "My phone, my phone—"

Danny's alien lifted twelve of its tentacles and, instead of taking the boy's head off, it reached into his pants pocket and pulled out the ringing phone.

"What... *is*?"

"It's my phone, man."

"Fuuuuuurn."

The alien held the flashing screen to its face. The name **Stupid Bitch** flashed back. Beneath it, a bouncing green circle encouraged the user to swipe up.

Which is what the alien did.

"Danny, where the hell are you?" Deondra's voice blasted from the mouthpiece.

"Aww, shit."

"Hunh?" the alien sniffed the screen and jolted its head back. "Dee—ondruh."

"Who's dis?"

"Me. Bar-Fys."

"Bar-what?"

Danny closed his eyes as he witnessed the alien try to converse with his mother.

"Daniel Hook, you get your ass back home this instant or I'll—"

The alien couldn't bare the wailing voice any longer. He dropped the phone to the floor and stomped on it, cutting the call dead.

"Thanks, mate," Danny sighed. "Looks like I'm sleepin' on my dad's couch again, now—"

"—WHAT... YOU... DESIRE?" The alien yelled in its best impression of an English accent.

"We, uh, *desire*—" Bucky gasped. "To know what's going on."

Bucky's alien slid forward and seemed to smile with its ax wound for a mouth. "My name. Arg-Ned."

"Arg-Ned?"

"You. Bucky," the alien said as he pointed to his colleague. "Him. Bar-Fys."

"Arg-Ned and Bar-Fys, huh?"

"*Si*. It is, uh, very pleasure to make your acquittal."

"Yeah. Nice to meet you to," Bucky quipped with sarcasm. "Can you do me a favor?"

"*Fay-vor*?"

"Yeah, can you let me out of here and let me pull my pants back up?"

"Puhnts?"

"Yeah, and take Mars out of my ass, too."

The aliens turned to each other for a reaction. Then, both burst out laughing - at least, that's what it looked like.

A gentle slap on one of twenty-five shoulders as they laughed confirmed that they found the entire event *hilarious*.

"*Whugga-prack,*" the first alien said. "Bucky. Release."

"Aww, c'mon, man," Bucky complained and shifted around his restraints. "This ain't cool. You can't just chain us up and shove things in our asses."

"Yeah, mate," Danny added. "This sum gay shit, you know."

"Gay... *shit*?" the second alien asked, confused. "You. *Gay shit*."

"Allow me man, get me outta here—."

"—Allow?" the alien asked, scratching his head. "Allow."

Arg-Ned shooed Bar-Fys back to the hologram and turned to the two gentlemen shackled before it.

"What's it doing now?"

Arg-Ned's twenty-first tentacled whipped up and reached behind its head. He grabbed something in his cuticles and swung it in front of his body.

A microphone.

BWAM-BWAM-BWAM-BWAM-BWAM.

The beef-like curtain pulled apart like a theater stage as Holst's *Mars* played around the room.

A row of bare bottoms shackled in similar restraints lined the stage belonging to Chelsea, Skeez, Bobby Jo, and Hacker.

"Help, help," they all squealed in time to the music.

It took Bucky a few seconds to realize there was anyone else beyond the curtain, he was so enraptured in the spread ass of Bobby Jo.

Before them, rows and rows of aliens in stage seating clapped and cheered with all their tentacles.

Gala music sprang to life in the walls, followed by a spotlight on each of the shackled contestants.

"Ladies and gentlemen," Arg-Ned said into the microphone, suddenly able to speak with perfect clarity. "It's a real pleasurable experience to be here this evening. Standing, sort of, are the star players in our SPACE RACE! Bucky and Danny."

"That's right, Arg-Ned," Bar Fys said as he slathered his tentacles over to a brightly-lit scoreboard. "Let's see how they performed!"

1st Place:
"YONDER"
(West Virginia, United States)

2nd Place:
"NEXT GAY SHIT"
(Chrome Valley, United Kingdom)

3rd Place:
"CENTURY SAMOSA"
(Classified, United States)

4th Place:
"TEMPURA-FOUR"
(Harajuku, Japan)

Joint 5th and 5th Place:
BURJ KHALIFA / YULIA & ANDREI
(UAE and Russia)

Bar-Fys lifted his tentacles and produced a blinking, neon sign that read: "Applause"

The alien audience members cheered and hollered as two spotlights shone down on the two men.

"With them, their respective co-racers."

Arg-Ned waved the audience to calm down.

"Oh, please. You're too kind. Thank you, thank you."

Danny turned to Bucky in befuddlement.

"Man, what's going on?"

"I have a feeling we're about to find out."

BWAM—BWAM—BWAM.

A series of super-powered vehicles appeared on a second stage.

Each one rotated on its platform.

Equipped with weapons and futuristic shit.

They were all similar in design, all being long shafts with a slightly bulbous cockpit on the front. At the ends of the shafts were two large spherical engines. Along the shafts were armatures and weapon pods that laid against the hull, looking not unlike large veins.

"Oh my Gawd," Bobby Jo said, somehow making her restraints look sexy, "Are those giant cocks?"

Despite being chained up, with his pants around his ankles, Skeez couldn't help himself, "Little small if you ask me."

"You know I can see your junk, right?" Bobby Jo said, rolling her eyes.

Skeez's eyes went wide. "It's really cold in here."

"SILENCE!" Arg-Neg yelled into the microphone.

"Sorry. Please continue, squid man," Bobby Jo said.

"We have the cream of the crap among us," Arg-Ned said. "Now that the preliminary race is over, let's see how you Earthlings hold up against the *real* hard-asses of Murkroznitck."

As the music grew to a crescendo, the platform slid away and produced an elevating podium with five alien beings.

"Huh?" Bucky muttered.

"Ladies and gentlemen," Arg-Ned said. "Introducing, the very best of the universe's racers."

The audience cheered once again as five alien beings of all different shapes and sizes waved to the audience and enjoyed their adulation.

Arg-Ned continued into the microphone, "First the moon. Now, we're ready."

Bar-Fys elbowed a giant button the wall, which forced the dome to retract and offer a paralyzingly beautiful view of the stars and planets above.

"Place your bets, my friends," Arg-Ned said. "The Destination is Mars."

"Woohoooo!" the audience cheered.

"Mars?" Bucky yelped.

"We're racing to Mars now?" Danny added. "Man, these guy's be *bare* trippin', mate."

Arg-Ned's pussy lipped mouth shimmied as it giggled at Danny and Bucky.

"Gentlemen. Get ready... to start... your... *WEAPONS*."

(To be continued...)

Author Notes – Charles R Case

First and foremost, Thank you!

If you're reading this then I will assume you made it all the way through the book. And the fact that you're still reading says that you at least didn't hate what you read. That means the world to me.

So, on to answer the question of why I decided to co-write a comedy science fiction book with my good friend Andrew Mackay… Well, because it sounded like fun. And to be honest, it was exactly what I needed.

This book is so different from what I normally write. I'm sure those of you that found this because of my Space Fantasy series, War Mage Chronicles, are scratching your heads a little. But that was kind of the point.

Let me explain.

As a full time writer my job consists of sitting alone in my office and dreaming up a fictional world. The world I chose (War Mage Chronicles) is that of magic in space. There are politics, and space battles, and love, and a badass little black cat that changed the fate of humanity. And while the War Mage Chronicles are not literature by any means, it still takes a lot of thinking and 'being' in that world. There are some heavy thoughts I need to reconcile to get the next book to you all. I needed to recharge.

Let me put it another way.

I **LOVE** Mexican food.

It doesn't matter if it's Taco Bell, Del Taco, a fancy place downtown, or a local food truck. If someone suggests we eat there, I'm down like (insert famous sports figure) is for (insert their sport of choice). I will never say no to Mexican food. (let's just say my wife has looked on in horror as I ate the rest of the salsa with a spoon because we ran out of chips)

But. Sometimes I get over saturated, and Mexican food just becomes another meal. When that happens it loses its special status in my heart, and just becomes food.

Then I remember there is a whole world of delicious things to eat. Italian, German, heck, even a good old American hamburger is delicious. So, I have to switch it up. And you know what the best part of eating other things is? It makes Mexican food amazing all over again! (I just realized I may have an unhealthy obsession with food. I think my doctor (Doc Holliday (yes, that is their real name (I may have squealed like a little girl when my wife pointed that out))) would agree)

The point is, War Mage Chronicles is my Mexican food. I will always go back for more. But I want to be sure it's something special, and not just the next book I'm writing. So you're going to see a lot more things like Space Race from me in the future.

Space Race was a pleasure to write. It made me look at writing in a whole different light. Andrew's comedic chops taught me so much about humor in the written word. I think I will be able to take those lessons with me, and hopefully elicit a laugh or two from you in future projects, even if they are not in the comedy genres.

If you liked this book, and want to see more, please leave us a review and let us know what you thought. We have a million ideas for this series, but only if there is interest from you, our reader. If nothing else I hope you had a good laugh.

I will leave how me and Andrew came to write this book together for his author notes. He does a much better, and funnier, job than I could explaining the interaction.

Before I leave you to Andrew's tale of a multi-continental trip, bacon, and too much smoking, I have a few people to thank.

First of all, none of this would be possible without my wife. She has done more to make me a writer than anyone else on the planet. She pushed me to do something I only dreamed of, and I will forever be thankful.

Second, I would be remiss if I didn't thank the folks over at 20Booksto50K. Specifically Craig Martelle for setting up the 20Books London writers conference, where I had the pleasure of meeting so many great authors who showed me that writing is not just a dream, but possible.

And finally, Andrew Mackay himself. I'm so glad we were forced to step outside for a smoke at the conference. Who would have thought a bad habit could do so much good for two people.

If you want to read more from me, please consider following me on amazon by clicking here. There you will find my War Mage Chronicles series.

Thanks for reading,
Charles R Case
(February 7th, 2019 - Boise, ID, USA)

PS. Martha, sorry there was no raccoon in daisy dukes possessed by an evil god… that book is still in the works.

Author Notes – Andrew Mackay

Hello, dear reader.

Congratulations on completing the first SPACE RACE book!

Did you enjoy it?

Well, I'm guessing if you've made it this far… chances are good that you did. If so, I'm thrilled about that. I'm thrilled, also, to reveal that Charley and I are planning more books in the series. We actually just this second got off a video call about the second book. We've decided to call it 2Drunk 2Drive, after those silly Fast and Furious movies.

Fun times.

In fact, we have lots of ideas about where to go next.

Before I get into the behind-the-scenes of the making of this book from my perspective. My wife, obviously. I was a depressed teacher for most of my adult life. I jacked it all in and took a risk doing this writing thing. I've never looked back. I love it more than anything.
All I've ever wanted to do is tell stories, and if I'd have married the wrong woman, I'd still be teaching. Seriously, she's awesome. I can't begin to write about how lucky I am, so I won't. I don't want to write it any more than you want to read it.

You're welcome.

Outside of tedious sycophancy and nepotism, I'd like to thank two friends and fellow authors in the publishing game. Without them, this wouldn't have happened. Their names may be familiar to you - Michael Anderle and Craig Martelle. See, they run this group online called 20Booksto50K. Both have been instrumental in my success to this date. Apart from my groveling gratitude to these two wonderful guys it's necessary to point out that said group enabled Charley and I - two authors with a dream - to actually meet.

Back in February 2018 (to the very day, as of this writing) 20Books held a conference in London which Charley and I attended. Don't get me wrong, we weren't the *only* ones who went. There were about one hundred other authors. Anyway, because Charley and I both smoke, our paths inevitably intertwined outside the building and we hit it off immediately.

Fast forward to September 2018, and I found myself traveling from Jane Austen's own Hampshire, where I live, to Los Angeles, where Charley used to live.

I spent a few days with him and his charming wife. Why did I go? Because I could. See, this is what happens when you take risks (see paragraph on leaving the teaching profession). Now, writing is my livelihood - and to think, it could so easily have not happened. With free time and a bit of money thanks mostly to a character called Jelly Anderson in another sci-fi series of mine, I was able to take the trip and Charley was kind enough to put me up and show me the sights.

I'd visited most of the locations I had only dreamed of seeing with my own eyes. And we went to Vegas and met with other mutual friends.

I know, I know, this all sounds a bit wishy-washy. What's the point of me telling you this? Well, without this trip, you wouldn't be reading this. More than likely there wouldn't have been a SPACE RACE book for you to read.

Let me explain.

I remember it like it was five months ago at time of writing. I was standing on Charley's porch (no, that's not a euphemism - and before you get any ideas, *no, we are not.* We're both married, for one thing!) (mind you, that didn't stop Elton John, did it?) smoking a fag (not shooting homosexuals, incidentally. In the UK we call cigarettes fags, and unlike the US we can't shoot anything because we don't have guns).

Hang on, I've confused myself. Where was I?

Oh yeah.

Not much doing on the porch. Nothing to look at. A black railing and a couple of steps. The white wall of the building opposite reflected the sun in my eyes. An otherwise ordinary smoke, by all accounts. Then, for some *daft* reason, an idea spring into my mind. Wacky Races, to be exact. Dastardly and Mutley. That silly, spiky space vehicle of theirs.

So what? Stupid idea. I stubbed out my cigarette and sparked up another. I don't chain smoke as a matter of course (that's a lie) - it was just one of those mornings (not a lie.)

Next, a title appeared in my brain. Can you guess what it was? Yup, first time - correct. It was SPACE RACE. A smattering of lung damage later, and I had this vision of a bunch of rednecks in a trailer racing with others through space. They were going somewhere. It's all I had in my head as I walked back in and found Charley in the kitchen. I think he was making bacon rolls. Allow me to turn the conversation we had into prose.

***

Andrew sauntered like a handsome young man back into the kitchen, instantly illuminating the place just by his very presence.

He found it difficult to walk because he was so well-endowed, and well-respected within the community.

The whiff of the next cup of coffee drifted through his nostrils, adding to the taste of nicotine in his mouth.

He was keen to talk to his author buddy, Charley, about an idea he had. Before he opened his mouth, he wondered if the idea was shit. There was a distinct possibility that, due to his British heritage, the idea he was about to let out of the bag might seem offensive to your typical American.

Charley was your typical American, of course. At least to any common or garden Brit.

Hang on. Might it seem offensive? That's an interesting thought, Andrew thunk, and so decided to just come out with it.

"Charley, do you remember Wacky Races?"

Charley took the serrated blade and sliced through the pig flesh.

"Sure."

"I had this idea," Andrew chanced, hoping that if he sounded like a moron, that Charley would put it down to British eccentricity, "It's only just popped into my head."

"Oh, yeah?"

"Yeah. It's *Wacky Races*, but in space."

Charley thought the prospect over for a moment and raised his eyebrows.

"What do you think?"

"Pretty neat," Charley said. "Is that all?"

"Well, I was thinking it could be, like, a bunch of Rednecks flying a Winnebago. A bit like Bill Pullman and john Candy in Spaceballs. But it's all R-Rated and stuff, and really gross and stupid. And funny."

"Rednecks, you say?"

A light bulb appeared above Charley's head. As it happens there was an actual light bulb above his head on the kitchen ceiling, but this one was more metaphorical.

"Yeah, I like that."

"Yeah, and they're racing other stereotypes," Andrew continued. "So, like, you have the British, and the Japanese, and stuff. But the rednecks win."

"I like that."

"Yeah, but they have to win by mistake."

Charley's mind went into overdrive, thinking about the possibilities, "It'd be cool if one of them sort of stepped out of the vehicle and forgot he was in space, and exploded."

Andrew giggled at the idea.

"That's awesome."

Charley launched into a Redneck accent, "Oh, sheeet. I've done gon' and explodificated myself."

"Ooooh, I like that."

Before long, the pair had devised a lot of material for the rednecks. It continued throughout the afternoon, and popped up regularly in various chats they had.

"But how would we write it?" Charley inquired.

"I dunno. Lots of other authors write together but I think what might be fun is if we write it in sections."

"Sections?"

"Yeah, like, you know how at school you used to draw a head, and fold the paper and pass it to your friend so they could draw the body, and then they fold what they drew and give it to someone else to draw the legs?"

"Yeah, I did that at school. Got some funny-ass results."

"Why can't we do that with a book?"

Etc

I suppose there was a chance that the idea was just a conversation-starter and little else. I remember flying back to London and thinking about the possibilities of an idea like Space Race.

I needed to get back and finish my STAR CAT series before Christmas. I just about managed it. As is typical when you're a full-time author, other ideas come into your brain and demand attention while you're trying to finish the damned current work-in-progress.

Finally, the time came to talk Space Race.

Charley and I video called a lot about the idea. I'm not sure if Charley felt the same way, but I was getting to a point where I just wanted to get started.

Getting started meant plotting the whole thing out. For some reason, I wasn't too keen on it.

See, I usually start writing once I have the beginning, middle, and end. Some of the best material I've written as come about because sections were unplanned. It forces you to be creative and write your way out of problems.

So, going into Space Race - blind, as it were - was both a terrifying and exciting prospect.

Charley, being the easy-going fella he is agreed when I suggested we just write. See where our imaginations would take us.

We agreed on the beginning, middle and end (that is to say, introduce Bucky / Blast off / Arrive at the moon.) That was about as much detail as we had.

We agreed to write the book in the same way as you'd play that drawing game.

Charley would write the first quarter (5 chapters), then give it to me and I'd write the second quarter. Then he'd write the third, and I'd finish it with the fourth.

What a *stupid* idea.

But you know what? It worked - at least to our satisfaction.

Charley would set things up, and I'd knock them down - and vice versa. I think the word I'd use for the process would be *liberating*. Writing under zero pressure.

The only thing from my end was that we write these "quarters" to a strict deadline, or else it'd never get done.

We hit our deadlines.

And that was because there was no pressure.

I've written many satires and comedic books - you only need to check out my Chrome Junction Academy, In Their Shoes, and pure Dark series to know that.

Charley hadn't. But, now was the time to put the idea to the test.

There'd be times where Charley felt a little intimidated about having to be funny. I'm not sure he'd ever planned to write a comedy before we agreed to embark on this crazy idea. I told him not to give a shit and just write what he thought was funny.

And you know what? It turns out he can write comedy - and well.

Whenever there was a moment of self-doubt, I reasserted my own philosophy on the matter - *the first draft of anything is shit*.

"If it's funny, do it. If it makes you laugh, put it in. I'll tweak it if necessary. And I'm relying on you to do the same with me," I said.

We ended up with a perfectly acceptable - yet messy - first draft. We agreed each of us would take turns on the final manuscript with a specific focus.

We now refer to these passes as "cooks" --

A: Charley would go through the whole thing and kick it around to suit a Western flavor. And by Western, of course, I mean *American*.

He'd also yank on my reigns, as I have a habit of going much too far with my own comedy. Those of you who've read my previous works know I cross the boundaries very easily.

B: For my "cook" I'd go through the manuscript with two areas of focus.

- Make sure the prose, register and syntax of the whole thing was consistent. Fixing boring stuff like em-dashes, commas, and the way it all reads.
- Take out all the shit stuff. Things that weren't funny. Or, in some cases, make passably funny stuff funnier. Brevity is the name of the game when it comes to comedy, and the addition of one misplaced adjective can kill it dead.

You've just read close to 60k words- the result.

I'm sure it's not perfect. I'm *very* certain some of the gags didn't land for you. A mixture of satire, word-play, miscommunication, slapstick and general crude humor is never going to please all the people all the time, as they say.

It's a risk you take when you write humor.

But if more than, say, 60% of it raised a chuckle out of you, then I consider that to be a success.

We're not stopping here, of course. We left Space Race 1 on something of a cliffhanger.

Amazing, isn't it? From a silly little idea and an attempt to write a book from almost nothing, we now have zillions of ideas on where to take the series.

For you, dear reader, the ball is now well and truly in your half of the court. Just about the only way we know if we should continue the series is from the feedback we get.

If no one leaves a review at Amazon, we have no choice but to think that not enough people care. And you know, if that's genuinely true, then fair enough.

No big deal.

Charley and I will write something else, and/or carry on with our own individual projects.

BUT…

If you like/love the series and leave a review, it'll give Charley and me a good indication that we should continue. Individually, we're both in the market for creating *better* books than the last. I'm a firm believer in upping the stakes and improving the quality as books in a series go on.

So, please leave a review.

If we get enough positive feedback, you can bet all the space bucks in the world that Charley and I will drop everything and produce SPACE RACE 2 quicker than you can say *SHLOOM*! (The official beverage of Mur'kroznitck)

While you're waiting for our next masterpiece, why not follow both of us at Amazon right this very nanosecond?

You'll find the Chrome Junction Academy series, Star Cat, and a whole host of other masterworks you can chow down on with your Kindle Unlimited subscription.

Go on, you know you want to.

Follow me at Amazon!

I hope to see you at the end of the next book soon!

Andrew Mackay
(February 7th, 2019 - Hampshire, UK.)

Acknowledgments

Our immediate families, and *K*.

<u>Our JIT Team:</u>

Jennifer Long
Adele Embrey
Ali Quinn

All the CVB Gang Members / ARC Street Team
The members and admins of 20BooksTo50K

Up next: The SEQUEL!

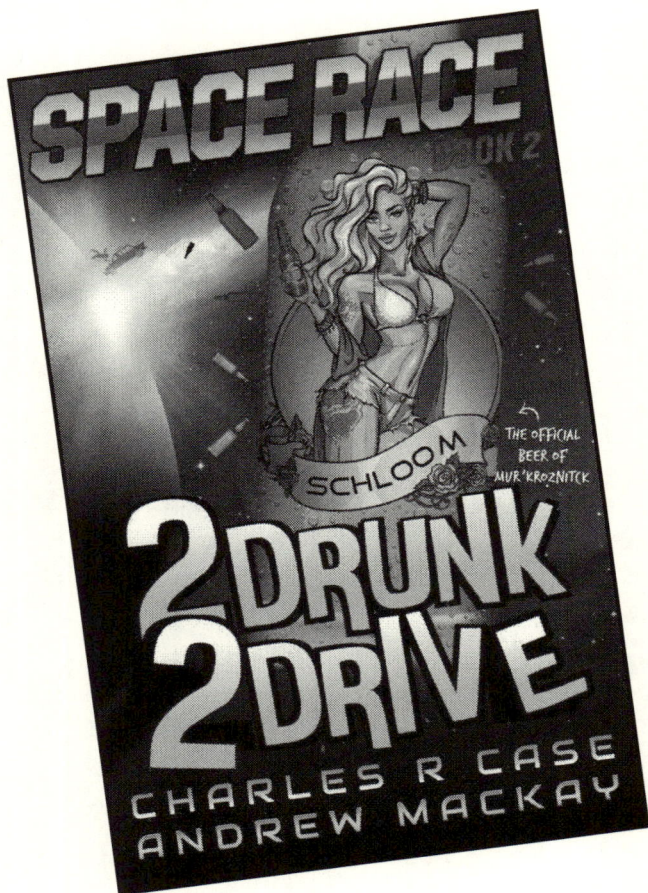

Manufactured by Amazon.ca
Bolton, ON